DEAD STRAIGHT

THE CURLY FAN CLUB

K T BOWES

DEAD STRAIGHT

Copyright © 2019 K T BOWES

ISBN-978-0-9951190-6-2

Give feedback on the book at:

www.ktbowes.com
admin@ktbowes.com
Twitter: @ktboweswrites

K T BOWES
HAKARIMATA PRESS

Published by Hakarimata Press

Dedication

I'd like to dedicate this novel to Lorraine Massey, the
genius founder of The Curly Girl Movement.
Her work with curly hair has revolutionised how we
view ourselves and how we cope with our curls.
She's the crusader who freed us from a world of frizz.

She took the heat, so our curls no longer had to.

"Naturally curly hair is a curse, and don't ever let anyone tell you different."

Mary Ann Shaffer

"Curly girl: It's more than just hair, it's an attitude."

Lorraine Massey

-1-

The Danger of Curls

A deafening crash shook the upper level of the house, making Kit Maguire drop her hairdryer onto her left foot. She let out a string of inappropriate curses and waited for the pain to subside. It took an effort to quell the overwhelming temptation to kick the hairdryer across the room. The price tag still emblazoned on the box helped. It gobbled up the last of her savings and changed her life. Not the hairdryer actually. The diffuser. The diffuser had changed her life.

"Ouch!" she hissed. Sinking onto the bed, she peered at the welt starting on her instep. Accompanied by a blue bruise, it sent out pain in an arcing radius of throbbing.

A yell accompanied the next crash and Kit frowned. "What are you doing in there?" she shouted.

A hail of complaint issued through the wall from the bathroom next door. Then a grunt and another. "I'm trying to get up!" a male voice shouted. "What did you use in this shower?"

Kit stood with a sigh and limped to the bedroom door. She bent to retrieve the precious diffuser which had popped off the nozzle of the hairdryer on impact. She set it on the dressing table with loving care. "Just conditioner," she lied. And sugar. And hemp oil.

"It's lube! You used lube in the shower!"

Kit's eyes widened and she limp-scurried into the wide hallway, colour flushing her cheeks a healthy, mottled pink. "On my hair!" she shouted through the door. "It helps my curls to clump. Then, when I Scrunch Out The Crunch, I get great body."

"Well, my body doesn't appreciate it!" The bathroom door flew open and Kit gasped and took a step backward. Her flat-mate stood in the doorway with a fluffy towel wound around his waist. Blond hair stuck up on his head like a row of antennae and a leaf of toilet roll soaked up a cut beneath his eye.

"Oh." Kit pressed an index finger over her lip as guilt seeped through her body like an oil slick. The blood made it real. "I'm sorry, Langdon," she gasped. Her usual sass abandoned her in the face of his injury.

"It's as bad as a skating rink," he grumbled. The toilet paper soaked up more of his blood and compounded Kit's sense of delinquency. A dusting of light hair feathered the impressive pectoral muscles which tapered to a trim waist. The towel clung to Langdon's hips with a valiant effort as he ran a shaking hand through his hair and dispersed the antennae into a series of messy spikes. Kit noticed a blue bruise spreading from a point on his elbow.

"How much longer do we have to share a bathroom?"

Kit swallowed. "I'm not sure. The landlord promised he'd get the plumber to look at mine last week." She nodded her head up and down like a nervous tick had taken over her neck. "I'll call him today. I know he wants to get it fixed before the house sells."

Langdon grunted and his gaze strayed to Kit's hair. A tumble of auburn ringlets cascaded from the top of her head and covered her shoulders in elegant curls. She'd been in the process of drying her hair upside down and she'd missed the optimum moment for making sense of the top layers. Langdon frowned. "You use sex lube on your hair. For real?"

Kit swallowed and the flush spread from her cheeks to her forehead, increasing in intensity as a mottled pink on her neck. Nodding, she drew back her shoulders for battle. "Yes." She usually took the time to squeeze the contents of the purple-willy-shaped container into a nondescript pot which she could pass off as hair gel. She'd made herself late laying out her new hairdryer for action before her shower and made the mistake of leaving her products on view. The frown burrowed deeper into the lines on her forehead as she reminded herself, she needed to retrieve her flaxseed gel and put it back in the fridge. "The chemical ingredient of certain lubes is the same as the expensive gels. It's my Curly Routine."

Langdon's brow furrowed and he waved away her explanation, stealing a glance at the sports watch on his left wrist. "Maybe invest in a bathmat," he suggested. "Or a handrail for the rest of us."

Kit nodded and watched red blood consume the toilet roll beneath his eye. She lifted a finger and pointed to it. "I'm sorry about that. Would you like me to get you a plaster?"

"No, thanks." Langdon shook his head and edged around her in the doorway. "I need to go to work. I'll fix it there if it doesn't stop." His intimidating muscular bulk stoppered the gap like a cork and gave Kit a heart stopping view of the Saint Christopher nestled over his chest.

"Excuse me." Langdon paused and his words nudged Kit out of the way. She slithered sideways with reluctance and they swapped places.

Langdon fixed strong fingers around his towel as it made a bid for escape and he padded along the hallway and into his bedroom. Kit's hand strayed towards a perfect ringlet nestled against her collarbone. She didn't notice Langdon reappear. "Kit," he said, his voice sounding tender.

His gaze moved from the curl she twirled between finger and thumb and then up to her face. His lips parted in the kind of smile that made middle-aged women flock to hear him speak. "Yeah." Chastened, her voice sounded subdued.

"Nice hair," Langdon said. "But perhaps while we're sharing a bathroom, you could work out a less hazardous Curly Routine."

"Okay." Kit nodded.

"And don't worry about the house. Maybe when it sells, the new landlord will let us continue renting it."

Kit stopped the groan escaping and fixed a fake smile on her lips. "I'm not worried," she lied.

=2=

The Wonder of Curls

"Langdon slipped on my lube." Kit let out an exaggerated sigh and leaned back on the sofa. "Now he thinks I'm a sex maniac."

Steph snorted and blew surf across the top of her mug. "He doesn't think that." Her brow furrowed. "Okay, he probably will think that. How did he know it was lube?"

"I didn't get time to change it out of the purple-willy-shaped container. Some splashed in my eye and I went blind for a second. I must have dropped a splodge on the floor of the shower. He went down with a hell of a bang. Twice."

Steph held her delicate nose to stop herself giving another unladylike snort. Tears leaked from her eyes instead. "Oh, gosh! I can just imagine it."

Kit shook her head. "He's gone to work with a cut under his eye and a bruise on his elbow. I feel terrible."

Steph's belly laugh didn't help. "What will he say when they ask how he did it?" Holding her nose made her voice sound nasal and high as she did a poor impression of Langdon. "Well, Mrs Peters, it's like this; I was washing this hot body in the shower and slipped on some aloe vera pleasure gel." She keeled over sideways, slopping coffee over her jeans and onto the wooden floor.

Kit made a stellar effort not to laugh, but it proved difficult, especially as the imaginary Mrs Peters' part of the conversation bubbled up from her darker side. "Ooh Vicar!" she squeaked in a fake old-lady voice. "Ooh Vicar!"

Steph gripped her stomach and slammed the coffee mug on the table before collapsing onto her knees in front of the sofa. Tears ran with abandon and her eyes made slits in her rounded cheeks. Kit bit her lip and glanced at the clock, noticing the way the little hand sped towards the one o'clock mark. "Stop, stop!" She flapped her hands at Steph. "He'll be home soon. It's not funny. It's criminal injury."

"Criminal injury!" Steph hooted again and bent double. Her ponytail flipped forward and dipped the purple ends into the coffee mug. She seemed surprised when she lifted her head and a brown drip slid down her nose. Her wide face curved into a grin. "Assault with a deadly weapon." She sniggered and Kit imagined the purple-willy-shaped container perched on the shelf next to the shower gel. Some of the humour left, replaced by embarrassment.

"I use it on my hair," she muttered. "Nobody will believe me."

Steph wiped her eyes on the sleeve of her shirt and squeezed coffee from the ends of her ponytail. "You're taking this Curly Bible thing way too far," she commented. "What happened to Kit the Ponytail Queen from all your mum's old photos?"

"I stopped shampooing my hair." Kit pulled a ringlet forward and inspected the perfect coil. "And I got rid of her bird's nest by avoiding silicone and sulfates."

Steph reached for her coffee and Kit saw her shoot a sideways glance at the fluffy wire wool making a break from her hair tie. Wincing, Steph ignored the mug and her fingers shot up to push her escapees back behind her ear. "Tell me about this group you belong to," she pressed.

Kit's eyes sparkled. "I'd love you to come."

Steph's expression soured and her fingers fluttered back up to touch the matted ponytail. "I'm fine," she growled. "I like my hair this way. It's a cult isn't it? You're in a cult." The conversation degenerated faster than usual this time and Kit felt the familiar tightness across her chest.

"Yep." She forced herself to sound dismissive. "A hair-religion cult. It's a Curly Takeover." Rising, she checked her watch and allowed fifteen minutes for the drive into Hamilton. Then she added another fifteen required for edging Steph onto the driveway. If things turned awkward, she might need longer. The Curlies were meeting at Pam's house for a demonstration on how to make flaxseed gel to the right consistency. She had no intention of missing it.

Her step-sister pushed herself off the floor and abandoned the mug and its dribbly mess on the coffee table. "You're obsessed." Steph frowned and the atmosphere plunged into one of resentment. The air crackled. Kit held her breath and counted to ten in her head. She refused to bite at the usual argument trigger and fixed a polite smile on her lips.

"All you talk about is your hair." Steph's face took on a crimson flush and creased into an ugly sneer. All camaraderie evaporated as her own inadequacies rose to the fore and she projected them onto Kit. They'd both spent their lives hair-challenged, but the Curly Bible had helped Kit remove a major factor in her lack of confidence. It left Steph and her frizz to heckle from the side-lines.

Or sabotage her. Like at Christmas when she bought Kit conditioner as a gift, knowing it contained the kinds of ingredients she needed to avoid. She'd pushed Kit until she had to admit she couldn't use it and then called her ungrateful. Or the time she told everyone at a family gathering that Kit hadn't shampooed her hair for over five years.

"I should leave." Kit rose and collected her handbag from the floor beside the front door. "I'll give you a ride home."

"Dad's picking me up from here after the game. He didn't expect you to throw me out." Steph bridled and stuck her chin in the air. Her blonde hair tumbled around her oval face, creating a softening halo edged by purple streaks. "He's not finished for another hour."

"I need to go." Kit stood her ground with a determined smile. "I'll drop you at the soccer ground. It's on my way."

Steph snarled and all sense of sisterhood vanished. She regressed into a snarky seventeen-year-old and Kit struggled to keep her temper. She channelled her sweet-natured mother instead and exhibited the kind of patience which would make Marian proud. Kit's poor mother had shot herself in the foot by marrying the fast-talking Kenny and ended up with Steph to raise when he couldn't be bothered.

"I hate your stupid car," Steph growled as she slammed the door without care. "Nobody drives bright yellow cars like this anymore. It's embarrassing."

Kit drew in a breath of good Yoga attitude and exhaled a firestorm of irritation. Steph spat bile all the way to the soccer ground and as she slammed the car door much harder than she needed to and left without a goodbye, Kit remembered she still hadn't removed the purple-willy-shaped evidence from the communal shower.

-3-

Curly Secrets

Kit arrived at Pam's house with her mood tainted and her lips turned down into a pout. The wide front door stood open and she stepped over the threshold without knocking and kicked her shoes off on the mat.

"Hey, what kept you?" Piper Davenport rose from a kitchen stool and wrapped her spindly arms around Kit, drawing her into an embrace which smelled of baby sick and talcum powder.

"Steph." Kit dumped her handbag and car keys on the floor and settled onto a spare stool. "Hey everyone." She gave a feckless wave at the women squeezed into Pam's small, modern kitchen. Some sipped mugs of coffee and others measured ingredients over a long bench near the sink. "Kenny dropped her at my place so he could watch the women's soccer game, but then he took advantage like he always does. I gave her breakfast, morning tea and then lunch. He still didn't come back for her, so I dropped her at the soccer club and she wasn't happy."

Piper wrinkled her nose. When she moved her head, a soft haze of perfect dark coils shifted around her face. "You could have brought her here. She's a Curly."

Kit's eyes widened in horror. "I offered, but she refused and I'm glad. She'd mock everything we're trying to do. She started calling us the Curly Cult on the way here."

"Curly Cult?" Pam looked up from the kitchen counter with a wooden spoon held aloft. "I like that. Curly Cult. What do you think ladies?"

A general hum of approval went around the room and the other eight women nodded in agreement. Pam beamed. "We can put it forward as a motion at the next full meeting when everyone's there. Curly Cult. I like it better than WWC, Women With Curls. It sounds more like a bathroom showroom."

Kit groaned. "It's bad enough at work. Jason already calls it Curly Central because of me and Piper."

Piper giggled. "I don't mind. He's sweet and he's had a monster crush on you for years."

Kit pursed her lips. "I don't need a man to complete me." She stated the familiar mantra to the roll of Piper's eyeballs.

"You two work together?" Pam sifted a handful of flaxseeds through her fingers, the rich brown colours catching the light from the kitchen window.

Piper nodded. "Yep. The car dealership on Te Rapa Straight. Kit works in the service department and I manage the accounts." She glanced down at a yellow spot on her tee shirt. "Well, I'll go back to it when my maternity leave ends."

"Right Curlies." Pam raised her wooden spoon in the air and waved it with all the elegance of a primary school teacher taking class. "Let's get this flaxseed gel made."

The women crowded round the hob to watch Pam add five tablespoons of flaxseeds to the already boiling water.

"Three cups of water," she announced, digging straight in with the spoon and swirling the little brown seeds into a jolly dance. "Medium to high heat for as long as it takes. Don't leave it too long, girls. We want snot, not putty."

"Snot?" One of the newer Curlies leaned forward to peer in the pan. Her short blonde curls looked defined, but she still battled a haze of frizz around her crown. "I don't know if I'll be able to do this. I've got a really weak stomach."

"Call it something else then, Cindy." Pam dismissed the woman's anxiety with a flick of her wrist. "It doesn't smell of anything, so you can add essential oils once it cools. The important thing to remember is that it only lasts two weeks in the fridge. After that it goes rancid and stinks to high heaven."

"Rancid snot." Cindy took a step back and jostled her way butt first through the eager crowd. "Yeah, not for me." She made a sound at the back of her throat like a fake retch.

"It's fine, really." Gabby stretched out her olive fingers and clasped Cindy's wrist. Afro ringlets danced around her face in a neat bob. "We're all just learning here. I've never made it before, but the shop bought gels are giving me FA."

"FA?" Cindy gulped.

Gabby pointed to her forehead, but her fingers didn't contact the carefully coiffed curls. "Frizz Alert," she said. "It happens to all of us, especially in humidity. And heaps of conditioners and gels contain glycerin. That sets it off really bad."

"Frizz Alert. Glycerin." Cindy parroted the words and her cheeks paled. "I'll never remember all this."

"I'll help you. We live near each other. Maybe we can share the cost of ingredients and do it together."

Cindy nodded with enthusiasm and moved closer to Pam and her wooden spoon. Kit leaned forward and watched the seeds bouncing around in the boiling water. A white foam had begun on the surface and swirled around like a rip tide. She felt Piper pressing against her shoulder so she could see. Pam jabbed at the wispy foam with the edge of her spoon. "This is what we want," she said. Her red lips curved upwards into a satisfied smile. "We put the snot on our hair."

"Berk!" Cindy made a sound in the back of her throat and clapped a hand over her mouth. "Berk!"

The women parted like a wave to leave Pam's back exposed. Some wore designer clothes and others jeans and tee shirts. Nobody wanted puke down their back.

"Oh dear," Piper breathed in Kit's ear. "We've got us a vommer."

"Berk!" Cindy's eyes watered and her gaze strayed to the growing white foam on top of the saucepan. Unconcerned, Pam jabbed at the mixture with her spoon and grinned like a serial killer.

"The consistency of snot is best," she said. "Like a decent bout of flu but not too runny. Avoid lumps." Entering a one-woman competition to say the word *snot* as many times in a sentence as possible, she added the descriptive noun *ectoplasm* followed by the adjective *viscous*. Then she raised her wooden spoon and a globule of mixture dangled from it. The bulbous end swelled in size as the long thread of gel thinned and gravity tempted it back towards the hot saucepan. "Perfect!" Pam announced. She waggled her eyebrows and her grey curls bounced across her shoulders. "Just like being with the first years during flu season. We want snot, not bogeys."

"Berk, berk, berk!" Cindy exited the kitchen at speed and tripped over the threshold on her way out the front door. A clatter sounded as she picked a fight with the terracotta plant pots nestling beside the porch. "Berk, berk!" She sounded like a small, frightened duck as her curls bobbed past the kitchen window towards the back garden.

"Can someone check on her?" Debbie wore a cooking apron and wielded a Kmart plastic pump bottle in her hand. Her eyes glimmered with a peculiar sheen at the prospect of funnelling Pam's perfect snot into the container. The apron stretched across her wide frame, a naked woman on the front. It created a strange illusion of a skinny woman trapped inside a fat one and Kit fought down the uncharitable thought that Debbie might have eaten her.

"I'll go." Kit pushed her way through the women's bodies with a sigh. She'd become an expert at making flaxseed gel in the past few years and didn't need to see Pam's legendary snot making. She reached the front door as Pam delivered her next set of instructions.

"Drop it into the coffee plunger and wait for the seeds to settle to the bottom. Then plunge the life out of the little buggers and pour the mixture into small pots. This stuff will freeze for months and you can defrost it when you need it."

Kit rounded the side of the brick house and stepped into Pam's immaculate garden. She followed the sound of Cindy's sniffles and found her sitting on a wooden garden bench with her head between her knees. A weeping ash wavered overhead as though primed to waft fresh air over the stricken woman. "How are you feeling?" Kit asked. She slumped down beside her.

"I'm okay as long as you don't say snot. Berk!"

"Then stop saying it yourself." Kit smiled. "It actually makes great gel. When it dries, it forms an amazing cast and holds the curl long enough for it to set. And it's cheaper than a gel. I bought a kilogramme of seeds at the start of last year and I'm still only halfway through them."

Cindy nodded. "It's just the thought of it. Berk! I can't imagine having that snotty stuff running through my fingers. Berk, berk, berk!"

"Just stop!" Kit squeezed Cindy's forearm. She felt the bones beneath, as fragile as a baby bird's. "Let's talk about something else. I use lube as well. It'll probably make a reasonable cast on its own. I haven't tried using it by itself."

Cindy sat up and ran the back of her hand across her nose. "Cast. That's the crunchiness, isn't it? Then you scrunch that out."

"Yep." Kit nodded, relieved to see the wateriness disappear from Cindy's eyes. "I use the purple-willy-shaped-lube just before I finger curl. It's water based." Her face fell. "But I forgot to transfer it from the purple-willy-shaped container and my flat-mate saw it. And then he slipped on some and cut his eye." She leaned forward and mirrored Cindy's defeated stance. "He thinks I'm a sex maniac and doesn't want to share the shower with me anymore. And he's a vicar."

Cindy gulped and the faintest hint of a smile lit her lips. "I thought my life was complicated enough with my husband's mid-life crisis."

Kit winced. "I'm single. Can't help you with that one, sorry. Do you work?" She steered the conversation away from husbands, lube and flaxseed gel.

Cindy nodded. "Yeah. My father owns Blackhawk Security."

Kit shook her head. "I haven't heard of it."

"It's a software company. We create websites, coding for appliances and do quite a bit of cyber security."

A scream pierced the gentle silence of the garden and birds flapped overhead in fright. A passing bumblebee changed direction and soared back over the perimeter fence in a wide arc. "No! No! No!" The wail sounded agonized and fraught with pure misery.

"What the hell?" Cindy gasped.

But Kit was already off the bench and disappearing along the crazy paving in her bare feet. She made it through the front door despite the shards of grit which dug into her toes.

A wall of shocked faces greeted her and the unmistakable sound of sobbing.

-4-

Curly MU

Kit ran into the kitchen at speed and collided with Piper. Her friend clasped her around the waist as she pivoted backwards. "What's happened?" Kit gasped as Cindy ran into her spine with a muffled grunt.

Piper released her and took a step back, her eyes flashing a warning and her head jerking towards a curious Cindy. "Gabby MU'd," she whispered.

"Oh." Kit winced and darted a look around the kitchen. Forgotten flaxseeds bubbled on the hob and welded themselves into a rubbery brown mass as the women gathered around a hysterical Afro in their midst.

"What's going on?" Cindy's blue eyes widened to the size of saucers and a delicate hand fluttered to her throat. "I can't cope with all this drama. It's time I went home and used my straighteners. I've made a terrible mistake."

Like Moby Dick rising from the deep, Debbie's head and shoulders appeared above the gaggle. "We don't talk about shampoo, brushes or straighteners!" she bellowed across the room. "Never. They're forbidden!"

Cindy took a series of steps backwards and her fingers searched for the front door handle. With her other hand, she made the sign of the cross and an expensive Pandora bracelet hooked itself around her cardigan button. Piper stopped hopping on the spot and reached to help her.

"Everything's okay," Kit reassured. She patted Cindy's shoulder without looking and accidentally prodded her left boob. "I just need to turn off the flaxseed gel before it explodes."

"Explodes?" Cindy sounded hoarse. She flapped at Piper's efforts to extricate her bracelet from the button and searched the room for her handbag with frantic head movements. "I need to get out," she chanted. "I need to get out."

"False alarm everyone!" Pam's reassuring voice rang out across the room and a hum of relief went around the women. They peeled outward like water from a broken paddling pool and surged back.

"False alarm everyone!" Piper picked up the cry and whirled around on the spot. Her dark eyes took on a crazed appearance. "False alarm. Nothing to see here."

Kit carved a route through the bodies and made it to the hob just as the congealed blob in the bottom of the saucepan began sending a blue haze into the atmosphere. She removed the whole pan from the ring and whirled around looking for somewhere to dump it. Handbags and car keys covered every available surface and she settled on running the cold tap and holding the saucepan under the stream until the sizzling stopped. The room smelled like baked silage and a black circle stained the bottom of the pan. Kit swallowed as the brown blob floated to the surface of the water and bobbed around in a raucous happy dance. She turned off the tap and removed herself from the scene of the crime.

"What was that about?" She edged closer to the

remaining bodies in the centre of the room and found Gabby perched on a stool sobbing. Pam and Debbie kept their heads bowed and made sounds as though praying for deliverance. Gabby gave an occasional nod and a sniff. When Pam popped upright, Debbie took full ownership of the sobbing Curly and sucked her into her copious naked-woman-apron. Kit pursed her lips and resisted the urge to wave Gabby goodbye. Debbie's hugs were genuine but bone-crushingly terminal.

"She thought she MU'd." Pam leaned sideways to whisper in Kit's ear. "But it's a false alarm."

Piper appeared next to Kit's elbow. She towed a reluctant Cindy in her wake. "Cindy wants to quit," she announced, ignoring the wriggle of protest from her captive. "She wants to go back to straightening."

"We don't mention straightening here!" Debbie bellowed. Gabby gave a squeal of horror and covered her ears with her hands as though Debbie's breasts weren't adequate enough mufflers.

"Okay, okay!" Pam sounded tired. She held both hands over her head and the room silenced like she'd flicked a switch. A phone beeped from inside a handbag and went unanswered. "Let's deal with what just happened, but first I need to check the flaxseed gel."

Kit held her breath as Pam moved towards the hob and then changed direction to peer in the sink at her ruined pan. She gave a sigh and turned to face the women. Like cows at a milking station, they edged forward and stopped as a collective. Piper kept a tight grip on Cindy's wrist.

"So, Gabby thought she'd MU'd," Pam began. "That means she thought she'd Messed Up and would need to start again. Things which cause us to Mess Up include using products with silicone, sulfates and certain oils."

A buzz went around the room. An older woman who'd been in the group since its inception tutted and put her hands on her hips. "And it doesn't help when certain manufacturers make products we can use and some we can't. They sit on the shelf next to each other and it's easy to make a mistake." A hum of agreement followed and several product names were mentioned.

Pam nodded. "Gabby overheard us discussing a product we can't use and recognised the manufacturer."

"And panicked." Debbie's voice rang out like a klaxon. "Curlies never panic."

Kit snorted and Piper pursed her lips. Curlies panicked all the time. Over everything. Too much frizz. Which hairdresser to use. To use protein or not use protein. The pros and cons of moisturising. Whether using a brush without Debbie finding out counted as using a brush at all. The list went on in an endless spiral of confusion. And then one day the curls just formed like dancing ballerinas and the world became a wonderful place. Compliments got given, the routine formed like a well-rehearsed play and the sun shone every day. Then came the inevitable trip to the supermarket to discover the product responsible for the life changing curls had been discontinued. Cue nervous breakdown.

"Curlies never panic." Debbie spun her head like something from The Exorcist and eyeballed each of the women in turn. "That's what our Facebook group is for."

"We panic on Facebook?" Gabby pushed her face free of Debbie's breasts, wiping her nose on the apron as she gasped for air.

"No. We don't panic at all. We post in the group and someone will help us." Pam rolled her eyes.

"Not always." A woman with grey roots and darker ends shook her head. "I stood in the supermarket for over an hour taking photos of products last week. I waited so long for someone to answer that my ice cream melted."

Pam sighed. "Then we need to do better. Curlies must stick together. Set your Facebook notifications to alert you to requests for help. We'll set goals at the next meeting and discuss what everyone wants from the group."

"What about the flaxseed gel?" someone asked. "It's ruined."

"I'll start again." Pam's shoulders slumped. She waved a hand at Gabby. "Then we'll discuss what happens with a genuine MU and how to rectify it. I've got some handouts around here somewhere."

Piper managed to stop Cindy leaving and Pam rustled up enough decent flaxseed gel to hand out a container to each woman. Nerves were soothed and fears allayed. It turned out there were different levels of Messing Up and none were life threatening. "Use the dish washing liquid and then just start again," Pam reassured them. "It's an MB which is the code for a Minor Blip."

"Minor Blip," Cindy whispered. Her hand shook and she looked like a woman on the edge. "Minor Blip." Her Pandora bracelet remained wrapped around her button and it pulled her cardigan up like a mangled wing. "Minor Blip."

Kit rolled her eyes at Piper and released a sigh. "These women are as crazy as blind pukekos," she whispered.

"Yep. We're in good company," Piper mouthed back.

The meeting ended early with the appearance of Pam's husband. While the Curlies acknowledged the existence of Male Curlies, they didn't encourage direct fraternisation within the group. The Curly Facebook page often featured women in various stages of undress on BCD's (Bad Curl Days) whilst standing in the shower and streaming naked, tearful videos begging for help. Pam and Debbie felt the presence of men might hinder the honest exchanges.

Pam's husband sported an incredible head of grey curls which hung in clumps of ringlets down his back. They presented a strange paradox against his biker leather jacket, but he fluffed out his helmet hair like a true professional.

"Rockin' those curls, Mr D!" Piper squealed and high-fived him on her way out the door. Kit gave him a polite nod and tried not to stare. Pam's handiwork oozed from every stunning curl bouncing against his broad back but alas, she could affect no miraculous cure for the front of his head. Everything below his crown was a testament to her skill with conditioner and flaxseed gel, but from there forward he sported a freckled dome of crinkly bald head. It looked like a wig that someone had slid back too far to the point where gravity might snatch it off.

Kit fitted her feet back into her heels and headed for the safety of her car.

"Ladies!" Debbie's voice boomed out across the heads of women still shuffling their feet around in the shoe collection on the door mat. "Don't forget that next time, we're meeting at Kit's house. She's demonstrating the various uses for sex lube."

Silence.

Pam's husband tripped over the doorstep and mashed his face against the wall opposite. Next door's children stopped bouncing on a trampoline with such suddenness, their father almost missed catching the toddler as it sailed past his left ear. A man doing a leaflet drop paused in the process of pushing junk mail into Pam's box and Kit forced herself not to react. Like a catwalk model she clattered across the pavement and kept walking, fumbling with her car keys and refusing to look back.

She stowed her handbag on the passenger seat and fired up the engine of her little yellow Volkswagen Beetle. A red flush gobbled up the porcelain skin on her neck and worked its way through her face to include her eyelids. "Well," she muttered. "Thanks for the advanced warning, Debbie."

-5-

Curly Scrounging

Kit slammed the front door and barrelled into the lounge. "Langdon you have to help me," she babbled. "It's an emergency."

Langdon's head lolled back against the arm of the sofa. He released a groan before sitting up again. "Does this involve lube?" he demanded. "Because I don't think I can take any more today." He leaned forward and slapped his forehead with his palm. "Oh, that sounds so wrong." The cut under his eye had gained bloodstained butterfly stitches and a bruise spread across the bridge of his nose. Kit experienced a moment of shame before launching back into her urgent request.

"I'm sorry about your face, Langdon, but yes it involves lube. I've just learned the group is coming here for our next meeting and they're expecting me to explain how to use it on curls. To make matters worse, they expect hosts to provide a sample of their chosen product for everyone else to take away and try." Kit lifted her tiny pump bottle filled with dubious brown goop. She waggled it from side to side and it shifted in a lazy arc around the base.

Langdon ran a hand over his face and covered his grinning lips with a wide palm. His quick brain made the giant leap to Kit's pressing problem. "So, you need to visit the supermarket and buy tubes of lube to give away? That's hilarious."

Kit shifted from foot to foot. "I figured if I asked friends to buy two each, then I should have enough for the next meeting. Every tube of lube should fill three tiny pump bottles without looking skimpy, I'll need..." Kit paused to count on her fingers and stare at the ceiling.

Langdon scratched his head and left his hair sticking up on one side. "A lot of lube." He finished her sentence. "By friends I take it you mean me and Raki? And you want us to go into our local supermarket and buy sex lube?"

Kit squirmed. "It's not sex lube. I told you it's hair lube. Please, Langdon. I can refund you in cash from our WWC fund."

Langdon blinked. "You have a lube fund?"

"No. A product fund. I'll give you back whatever you pay. I'll sort it out with Debbie."

"No. No way, no how and in the name of all that is holy, no. I'm a vicar. I'm not walking into our local supermarket and buying two tubes of lube."

"Please, Langdon. I'll lend you my credit card." Kit tried to shut off all his possible exits and excuses in her mind. "You have to help me Langdon. You're a Christian."

"And I'm still not doing it." Langdon stood and stretched his arms above his head. His fingers almost touched the ceiling. The black shirt covering his torso rode up to reveal defined abs and an outie belly button.

"Please Langdon, I'm begging you." Kit set off across the floorboards still in her high heels. The left one snagged against the lounge rug and she tripped. Falling forward onto her knees with a thud, she reached out to save herself. Halfway down, her clawed fingers found the sides of Langdon's smart black pants and she down-trousered him with a horrible tearing noise. Langdon gave a shriek which sounded almost feral and in the shocked silence that followed, someone cleared their throat.

Kit flipped over onto her back like a tortoise and released the fabric of Langdon's pants. "Hi, Raki," she said, trying to make her voice sound normal.

Their flat-mate stood in the doorway to the lounge, a pot with a wilting gerbera clutched in his hands. His slanting eyes crossed over each other. "I just drove for ten hours," he announced. "Am I hallucinating?"

"I tripped." Kit pushed herself up onto her hands. She heard Langdon behind her rustling his pants in an effort to sit them back on his narrow hips. Raki nodded and shook his head at the same time, creating a strange circular movement.

Langdon gave an irritated gasp and Kit turned to look at him. His fingers fluttered over his ripped zipper and tugged at the loose thread where the button used to be.

"My mum sent stuff from Blenheim for the flat." Raki clutched his shell-shocked plant and looked from one to the other. "Please can you help me unload the car?"

Kit nodded and scrambled upright using the furniture. Her attention fixed on Raki with unnatural interest. Her eyes saw a skinny Chemistry student, the son of hard-working Chinese immigrants. But her mind identified an impressionable young victim who could possibly be coerced into buying enough purple-willy-shaped lube to keep the WWC going for quite some time.

-6-

Curly Devastation

"I can't drive another metre." Raki flagged, his eyes bleary and his responses delayed. "I'm knackered. I'll crash."

Langdon snorted. "We're not taking my car. Three of my parishioners work at the supermarket and the other half live in this suburb. I refuse to drive a getaway car before Evensong."

"We can do it afterwards." Kit gnawed on her lower lip and tasted strawberry lipstick. "Or maybe do it every night for a week."

"I don't want to do it at all!" Langdon straightened his pristine white dog-collar and pursed his lips. He snatched up Kit's car keys. "Let's get this over with. It's a one-time only offer as well. And if anyone recognises me in your ridiculous car, I'll sell both of you down the river to save myself."

"Charming!" Kit frowned and pushed both men through the front door, locking it after them.

They arrived at the supermarket to find the usual Sunday crowd filtering out through its sliding doors. Langdon parked on the other side of the car park, nearest the gas station. Raki fell asleep on the five-minute drive there and Kit leaned over the passenger seat and shook him awake. He looked groggy and one eye seemed permanently shut. "Wake up!" she shouted, squashing herself between the head rest and the ceiling to chase him across the seat. Her backside mooned the whole of Rototuna through the windscreen from under her short skirt. "Get back here!" she squeaked, her hands flailing as Raki tried to dodge her and snuggle into the seat. "You promised."

A sharp rap sounded on the driver's side window and Kit screwed her body around to peer past Langdon's head. His face took on a sickly, pale appearance. He wound the window down and gave a watery smile. "Uh, hello Mrs Rogerson."

"Hello Vicar." She poked her head through the window and ogled Kit's bottom. "Busy I see?" Langdon's reply sounded like a croak. "Any news on who's buying your house yet? You're welcome to use my spare room any time you need it. Just say the word."

"The landlord seems to have taken it off the market. The board is still outside, but he hasn't done any viewings for the last few weeks. Hopefully he's sold to someone who wants the place as an investment. I'm rather happy where I am."

Mrs Rogerson poked her head further through the window. She eyed Kit's rounded bottom with interest. "So, I see," she retorted.

"Raki won't wake up," Kit whined. "I've got some scissors in the glove box. I'll jab him. Please can you pass them to me?"

"Just a little joke," Langdon croaked. "See you at Evensong." He depressed the gas pedal and the car lurched forward leaving its Volkswagen logo on the floor behind it with a clang. He almost decapitated Mrs Rogerson from the ears up. Kit gasped as her chest slammed against the seat and wedged her tighter into the gap. Raki disappeared into the foot well. The car roared out onto the main road leaving tyre marks in the car park exit. When Langdon slammed on the brakes for the roundabout, Kit shot backwards and cracked the back of her head on the dashboard. She yelped and heard Langdon battling with the gear stick before kangarooing onto the roundabout.

"Careful!" Kit pushed herself into her seat and scrabbled for the seat belt. She reached out to stroke the gear stick. Her lips parted in disgust at Langdon's misuse of her prized possession. "It might look like an old heap, but it's mine." Her other hand felt for the bump on her head which would have been worse but for the curly cushioning.

"I should never have agreed to this!" Langdon spat. "I'm driving to Evensong and you can do what you like. One of the deacons can drop me at home."

"Noooo!" Kit wailed. "This is a flat outing. We're bonding."

"We are not!" Langdon growled.

"One more. Just one more!" Kit begged. She cut her losses and figured if she could get Raki to do a single haul, she might salvage the disaster. "Drive to the Te Rapa store and I'll buy you a mochaccino from their cafe."

Langdon stayed silent on the five-minute journey into the city and Raki snored from the foot well behind Kit's seat. She struggled to do the maths in her head to work out how many tubes of lube she could manage with as a minimum. Only the newbies and a few die-hards had turned up to the flaxseed gel demonstration because most of the older members could make it in their sleep. Gmail showed her that Debbie had already sent out the minutes from the afternoon's disaster. She'd included the invitation to Kit's house for the next meeting and her phone began beeping with excited texts from the other group members. Lube was a new ingredient in their complicated Curly lives. Kit started it after Raki pointed out the chemical components in her expensive hair gel were the same as those in sex lube. Trust a chemistry student to notice. Kit opened a text from Sally.

'Oh my gosh! You are totes the LQ. Count me in for the next meet.'

Kit made a sound in her throat like a mewl. "They're calling me the LQ," she whimpered.

"What's that?" Despite himself, Langdon allowed the curiosity bug to bite him on the ass.

"The Lube Queen." Kit squeezed the bridge of her nose between finger and thumb. "Damn you, Debbie. Just damn you."

"Don't curse on people," Langdon snapped. "If you won't pray on them, you shouldn't curse on them either."

"Do you pray for me?" Kit's soft blue eyes appealed to him for divine assistance and Langdon kept his gaze fixed on the view through the windscreen. She suspected he cursed her. Often.

"Vicariously," he grumbled. "I'm usually praying for my own safety at the time. You seem to crop up an awful lot."

Langdon parked in the furthest possible car parking space that could still claim allegiance to the Te Rapa supermarket. Any further and they would have been out on the main road. He hunkered down in his seat with a towel he found in the glove box pulled over his face. Kit frowned. "I use that cloth for cleaning my windows," she growled. "You look ridiculous."

"I don't care." Langdon tweaked the towel, so it covered his whole head.

"Coward." Kit clambered from the car and hauled Raki from the foot well behind her seat. She kept pulling until he slithered out onto the car park floor. "You look like a robber," she puffed, jerking her head at Langdon's head gear. "I bet they're watching you on the security camera's already."

Langdon gulped and hid the lower half of his face with his hand. "It doesn't matter because I'm not coming in," he informed her. "I'll wait here."

Kit let go of Raki's tee shirt sleeve and heard his head hit the floor. "You're bottling it?" Her voice rose and Langdon flapped his hands in distress. His fingers curled around the steering wheel.

"If you draw attention to me, I'm driving off," he threatened. He lifted a corner of the towel and his gaze slid to his watch. "You've got ten minutes and then I'm leaving. Evensong starts in half an hour and I need to unlock the church."

With her mood edging closer to frantic, Kit got Raki standing and herded him towards the front doors of the supermarket. They weaved across the pedestrian crossing like a couple of drunks. Kit propped Raki up outside the entrance and slapped both his cheeks until he appeared able to listen to her instructions. "Look for this product," she said, pushing her phone screen right in front of his face to show him the picture. His eyes crossed over with the effort. "Aloe Vera lube. It's purple and willy-shaped. If they don't have nine, I want everything they've got." She pushed her credit card into his hand and pleaded with Langdon's God not to let the shop decline it. Then just in case, she pulled his front jeans pocket apart and upended a tin piggy bank into the gap. Raki shifted his leg and ten cents bounced away. Kit went after it and just stopped a small boy claiming it for himself. The boy's lower lip gained a life of its own and started to wobble off his face. Kit edged away in horror. "Sorry," she muttered. "I don't do kids." His eyes widened as she dumped the faded metal piggy in the dustbin.

Raki leaned against the brick wall and seemed a little more focused.

"I've given you my credit card and some cash," Kit instructed. "If the credit card gets declined, use the cash. Can you remember the pin number for the card from when you got me the conditioner last week?" She took his awkward head jerk as affirmation. When his legs moved, the coins in his pocket made him sound like a slot machine. She wagged a finger at the end of his nose. "Do. Not. Substitute. You need to get the purple one. My hair hates the others. Besides, some of them are oil based and that's not Curly Approved."

"Purple. Approved." Raki gave a wavering nod and stood upright. The weight of the coins in his front pocket meant he needed to hold on to his waistband. He set off towards the doors and waited for Kit. She followed him in and then shook her head as she pressed a red shopping basket into his spare hand.

"I'm going to the veggie aisle," she hissed. "I can't let anyone see me with nine tubes of purple-willy-shaped lube. People know me. You're a student. You can get away with murder."

"Right. Yep. Murder." Raki wandered away on unsteady feet and Kit hit the vegetable aisle.

Her dwindling reserves permitted her the purchase of a single cucumber and she held onto it as she tracked her tired flat-mate around the store. If Raki only bought eight tubes of lube, she could mug him for the last of the cash and buy the cucumber. If not, she intended to abandon it somewhere, certain the cashier would confiscate her current account card if she dared try to use it. The hairdryer and diffuser emptied her account until pay day. She'd begun to regret the ludicrously large purchase she'd made at the start of the month. Still unable to tell anyone the magnitude of her stupidity, Kit swallowed the familiar sickness induced by the thought of handing over all her money to a smiling man in a suit. They'd know soon enough. Everyone would.

Five minutes and forty-three seconds ticked by as

Raki searched for the right aisle, having forgotten all her careful instructions. Kit hid when he stopped to ask a shop assistant for help. Hand gestures accompanied his alarming inquiry and her heart sent a flush of embarrassment that started at her knees and ended at her hairline. The shop assistant took him to the paper goods' aisle and involved another staff member. Two more minutes ticked by and added a grand total of four other people complicit in her nightmare.

The X-rated hand gestures continued as Raki described the purple-willy-shaped tube to the first shop assistant again and repeated it for the second. Then thankfully a woman appeared and she led Raki straight to the toiletries, jabbing a finger at the empty shelf. Kit followed at a discreet distance, her fingernails digging into the cucumber. Wait. Empty shelf...

"What the hell?" All dignity forgotten, she powered up the aisle behind Raki, squealing to a halt on her stilettos. "Where's the lube?" Her auburn ringlets bounced as she shook her head from side to side.

"It's the boat," Raki said. His speech sounded slurred. "The one that wrecked off Tauranga. It was carrying toiletries when it got stuck on the Astrolabe Reef. There's no deodorant either."

Kit paused as the female shop assistants stared at her. Two male shelf stackers hung nearby like rubber neckers watching a road traffic accident unfold. Raki winced and slipped an arm around her shoulders as a strange blockage began in her chest. No lube. No curls. The thought occupied the forefront of Kit's mind and left no room for anything else, not even breathing. No lube. Frizz Alert! Her hair would go back to looking like a toilet brush. No lube. No curls. PP. Permanent Ponytail.

Kit's body shook as Raki tried to make the best of a bad job. A fizzing took over her lips as she started to hyperventilate. Raki jingled like a kid's money box and patted her back. "It's okay, Kit," he promised. He yawned and swayed on his feet. "She's got people coming over," he explained to the shop assistants. "She needed nine tubes."

The women backed away at speed with disgusted looks on their faces. The males edged closer.

"What will I do?" Kit wailed. "If everyone comes, that's thirty people all wanting it. I don't know what to do."

Raki abandoned the shopping basket but kept Kit and the cucumber. He steered them towards the cashier and used some of the coins in his pocket to pay for the single, limp green vegetable. Juice oozed from beneath Kit's fingernails and she refused to release it onto the conveyor belt. They'd exited the store before she decided whether she wanted to eat it or bash someone to death with it.

"Nearly there," Raki soothed as he edged Kit towards her yellow Beetle parked at the furthest edge of the car park. His clothes smelled of soy sauce with a hint of Bunsen burner. The car headlights flashed on, wasted in the bright afternoon sunshine. Langdon removed another layer of tyre tread as he revved the engine and screeched towards them at speed like a heist driver. Raki pushed Kit into the rear seat and followed her in, but the door slammed on the cucumber and left a perfect half on the asphalt behind them as Langdon tore away.

Kit's confidence ebbed to nothing, slithering from the seat to the foot well as Raki fought to belt her in. Stripped of her curls she'd become that fat schoolkid with the frizzy hair who everyone made fun of. All rational thought left her. She reached for her phone to text her mum. Her fingers battled the keypad until she managed to formulate her jumbled thoughts.

'I'm coming over,' she wrote. *'I need a skinhead.'*

.

-7-

Les Mères sans Des Boucles
Mothers without Curls

"That's ridiculous, Kit. I'm not giving you a skinhead. Anyway, Kenny broke the clippers trimming his beard. And I wouldn't even if he hadn't." Kit's mother sank into a dining chair with a sigh. Langdon screeched out of the driveway in Kit's yellow car. Marian glanced through the window and frowned. "Your vicar drives like a maniac, dear." Her fingers reached for a strand of poker straight blonde hair framing her almond-shaped face.

"He's late for Evensong and blaming me." Kit pouted. "Is Raki okay on the sofa? He just drove up from the South Island."

Marian gave a tired smile. "Hopefully he'll stop snoring soon." She winced. "Now, tell me why you want a skinhead. I thought all the hair drama was behind you, sweetheart. You hit twenty-something and joined the other

Curlies in your little gang and you seemed happy. I love how you don't hide your ginger behind hair dye and boy cuts anymore. And you've lost so much of your puppy fat in the last few years. I can see your ankles."

Kit waited for Marian to pause for breath. "It's not a little gang. Well, it kinda is. Hair dye isn't Curly Approved. And that wasn't puppy fat. That flab was pure unhappiness right there. I hated myself. Sorting out my hair seemed to make everything else better."

"So, what's gone wrong? Steph said you were fine yesterday." Marian's slender features clouded and her lips pursed into a line. "Although she didn't talk much when Kenny dropped her home."

"Dropped her home?" Kit rolled her eyes. "So, he dumped her on me and then palmed her off on you. No wonder she has issues."

"He's busy." Marian defended her husband as always. "She's at a friend's house now."

Kit let her forehead rest against the table. "Why Kenny, Mum? Just why? You had Dad's pension. It would've been okay."

Marian dodged the issue before Kit stepped into the familiar rant about Kenny's shortcomings. She rose to continue folding a pile of clean washing. She laid it on the arm of a nearby sofa and Raki snuffled and turned over. A line of dribble left a wet line on the fabric. Marian fussed, shifting the pile onto the table before covering Raki with a soft knitted blanket. "He's a nice boy," she murmured. "You should snap him up, Kit. Scientists make clever babies."

"Yeah, in test tubes." Kit scowled, crinkling her lips into a snarl. "I don't need a man, Mum. I'm happy as I am. Most of the time."

"And yet here we are." Marian slid her needlework basket to the side. A clever sleight of hand hid the sharp scissors under a tiny tapestry with a half-finished kitty on it. Kit twisted her lips into a knot and contemplated lurching for them and holding them against a curl just to see Marian's reaction. As though reading her mind, Marian rose and shifted the basket onto the sideboard out of reach.

"I am happy." Kit sounded petulant even to herself.

Marian cocked her head and reached for her mug of cooling coffee. "Perhaps notify your face," she suggested. "It doesn't look like it got the memo."

"Mum, can I ask you a personal question?" Kit lowered her voice and saw a wave of discomfort leave Marian writhing in her seat.

"If you must," she replied. "I might not answer it."

Kit asked her question, but it's possible Marian didn't see that particular ball coming from left field. She changed colour a number of times before settling into a diluted shade of puce. Her legs struggled to a standing position and then gave out beneath her, sending her back into the seat with a thud. "Well, do you?" Kit demanded. Desperation made her pushy.

"I might have." Marian flapped a hand in front of her face. "But maybe not."

"Oh, please, Mum," Kit begged. "Just tell me. And is it the stuff in the purple-willy-shaped container? I really hope it is."

The bottom of Marian's mug scraped across the table as she collected it and rose. Sweat beaded on her forehead. "Let's talk about you," she suggested. Her fingers shook as she ran water into the sink. "Marry the nice Chinese boy on the sofa. Or the vicar. Definitely the vicar. He's very handsome and he'll make you happy. He needs to drive with more care though."

Kit scoffed, a sound like a snort leaving her lips and nose simultaneously. "They're not interested, Mum! Stop trying to palm me off on someone else."

"Oh." Marian turned from the sink with disappointment in her eyes. Soap suds dripped down the front of the cupboard door below. "Gay ones. I should've guessed. Are they together or separate?"

"Neither!" Kit felt her temperature hike and a sideways glance at her fringe saw a tell-tale tendril of frizz escaping from a coil. Calm, she told herself. Calm, calm, calm. Kit lifted her right hand and began her Yoga breathing, covering alternate nostrils and taking deep breaths. It didn't work. Her right nose hole felt blocked and she endured long seconds of heart stopping suffocation followed by hyperventilation. Two more wispy tendrils of hair joined the first. "They aren't gay," she puffed. "Single and happy. Single with no interest in mingling. Like me. We like who we are alone."

"But the vicar's taken your car, dear," Marian persisted. "And the scientist is here on the sofa. They must feel some attachment."

"Lube, Mum," Kit groaned. "Please can I have it?"

A tour of both ensuites and the family bathroom garnered nothing. Kit pulled everything from the cupboards and Marian tidied it and put it all back. Between them they filled the recycling bin with empty product bottles and a stash of discarded gel containers from Steph's tiny bathroom. Kit peered at the ingredients and frowned. Silicone and sulfate heaven filled the labels. They were the smiling assassins of the ringlet world, promising to ease frizz while sabotaging unsuspecting Curlies.

"Are you sure you had some lube?" Kit's voice wobbled with the effort of keeping her cool. She sounded like an addict and Marian cocked her head.

"Certain. I'm quite partial to the purple-willy-shaped one too. I'll get some more at the supermarket."

Kit groaned. "You can't. There's a national shortage. The boat sank on the Astrolabe Reef and the whole shipment went down with it."

"Oh." Marian nodded with enthusiasm. "I saw that on

the news. The crates have washed ashore and people are collecting the contents as salvage."

"Salvage?" Kit's voice rose an octave. She reached out and gripped her mother's wrist. "Mum, please will you drive me to Tauranga? I need to check the beach."

"No!" Marian withdrew her arm and kept her hands behind her back. "The police have cordoned it off. Besides, I saw people grabbing bottles of wine and furniture. One man swam ashore with a double bed on his back. He looked like a turtle. I saw nobody with purple-willy-shaped tubes."

"The media wouldn't show them!" Kit squeaked. "I bet that's where the shipment is. All over the beach on the east coast. Please drive me, Mum. It's important."

"No." Marian stepped forward and took Kit's cheeks between her cool palms. Gentle blue eyes observed her daughter. "I'm concerned about you, sweetheart. Are you in some kind of sex cult? Are the scientist and the vicar involved? We can get help. Maybe the vicar can exorcise the lube demons."

Kit's chest tightened with every passing second as her mother's gaze bored into her soul, seeing none of the deep and relevant stuff buried there. It's as though she sifted through a rubbish pile looking for flower petals and missed the ugly, festering decay. "I'm fine." Kit forced out the shuddering breath. "Why don't I help you sort through your wardrobe until Langdon comes back with my car?"

Marian hid her relief badly. The smile wavered on her rosebud lips, but she'd been asking Kit for help with sorting out her old clothes for months. Laying aside her anxiety, she allowed Kit to toss the contents of her wardrobe onto the bed and bag most of it for donating to charity. When the doorbell rang an hour later, she owned only a pair of jeggings and a boob tube of Steph's which got mixed up in the wash.

Raki opened the front door while scratching the back

of his head. He swayed on his feet and sighed as Langdon strode across the threshold. "Where am I?" he whispered. "Did someone kidnap me?"

Langdon snapped the white collar from around his neck with a shrug and stuffed it into his jacket pocket. He released the top button of his black shirt. "Where's Kit?" he demanded. "I want to go home. Mrs Baker murdered The *Lamb of God* and my eye is killing me."

Raki gasped. "She murdered the lamb of God? That's sick!"

Langdon gave a long blink and whirled on his feet. "That's old news, Raki. And it's a hymn. Mrs Baker plays the organ. Where's Kit?"

"I'm here." Kit struggled down the stairs tugging two giant black sacks of clothing behind her. "Mum's donating all this for your garage sale next month."

Langdon gave Marian an appreciative smile as she tottered behind Kit. She'd left the other two bags upstairs, doubts creeping in about her brave new tween wardrobe. "I'll drop everything off at the church tomorrow," she promised with a convincing toss of her head. Her eyelids flickered and she developed a deviant twitch.

Kit pushed her feet into her stilettos and pressed a kiss to her mother's cheek. "Thanks, Mum," she whispered. "You've really cheered me up."

"Oh." Marian clasped her hands over her heart and beamed. "Sweetheart, I'm so glad. Take care on the road, won't you?"

"Yep." Kit beamed with inner assurance as she snatched the keys from Langdon's hand. "Everything's gonna be just fine." She clattered through the front door and the boys followed.

"Where am I?" Raki persisted. He towed behind them like an obedient puppy and climbed onto the back seat. "I don't remember anything after the supermarket."

Langdon slammed Raki's door as Kit fired up the

engine. He ran to push himself into the passenger seat before she released the hand brake. "Where's the fire?" he demanded.

Kit waggled her eyebrows and gave a wicked smile. "The beach," she replied.

-8-

Wet Curls

"I'm not swimming out there!" Langdon shoved his hands into his trouser pockets and glared out to sea. "My head hurts and I want to go home."

"I'll do it for an ice cream." Raki shaded his eyes with his hand and peered at the wrecked container ship stranded on the horizon. He'd woken up on the outskirts of Tauranga and demanded food from the moment his eyes opened.

"Are you a strong swimmer?" Kit's brow furrowed as she watched the tell-tale signs of a rip tide sneaking between two patches of surf.

"I don't know." Raki shrugged. "I've never tried."

Langdon shook his head and gnawed his lower lip. "I can say your last rites before you dive in," he offered. "Save a bit of time." He sighed and turned to face Kit. "Why does this matter to you so much?"

"It just does." One of her shoes dropped from her fingers and she left it where it fell, hanging her head and digging her toes into the warm sand. "Learning to manage my hair changed everything for me. I feel less out of control somehow. Frazzled hair summed up how I felt on the inside. A big fat mess. I lost weight, changed my attitude and started helping other people do the same. Finding the lube matters because it's part of my routine, but also because I'm explaining how to use it to a group of other Curlies struggling with the same issues."

Langdon heaved out a sigh. His arm wrapped around Kit's shoulders and gave her a side-hug. "Fine," he grumbled. "Let's do this. But if I get arrested and lose my job, you're posting bail, paying for lawyers and taking responsibility."

"Promise." Kit crossed her fingers behind her back. "Do you want to pray or something first?"

Langdon shook his head. "I've got it covered," he sighed. He jerked his head back towards the car. "I'll strip down to my boxer shorts on the back seat."

"Thanks for doing this." Kit held the car keys out for him to take. His palm felt warm as her fingers brushed against it. "You're not planning to do a runner, are you?"

Langdon's lips twisted into a smirk. "Contemplated it," he admitted. His long legs took him back across the beach to the car and Kit released a held breath as he opened the rear door and climbed inside.

"It's a disaster," Raki said, kicking at an abandoned mussel shell.

"It is," Kit agreed. Her fingers strayed to a windswept curl as it drifted around her face. Five years earlier, she would've worn a hat over ninety million bobby pins to stop her head turning into a cotton ball. "I could probably do it with eight, but nine is better."

"Just think of all that diesel," Raki continued. "I've seen underwater photos of the Astrolabe Reef and it's stunning. It won't be after this."

Kit cleared her throat and a flush of shame crept up

her neck. Steph's accusation returned to taunt her. Hair obsessed. Kit turned her attention to the other disaster, the one with the ability to wreck more than just heads. She shielded her eyes with her hand and nodded. "How long do you think it'll take to refloat it?"

Raki shrugged. "Not sure if they can. And these big ships use bunker fuel. The impact of spilling that is heaps worse than the marine grade stuff."

Kit shivered. "Let's hope it doesn't leak then." She frowned as Raki took a step towards the tide. The police had cordoned off the beach with tape. Several people ignored it as they waded into the water in search of anything they could claim.

Raki pointed at the shore where a man strode up and down with a frantic spring in his step. "What's he doing?"

Kit squinted against the glare off the water and shook her head. "Salvaging?"

"No." Raki took another step forward. "I think he's lost something."

A streak flew past them at speed. Kit jerked back as a set of keys landed on her bare foot. "Ouch!" she cried. She bent to pick them up amid a hail of curses aimed at Langdon's retreating back. "Why is he sprinting?" she demanded.

"He's in his undies," Raki whispered. "And he's a vicar. And you sent him into an environmental disaster to look for sex lube."

"It's not sex lube!" Kit shouted. She gulped and her head jerked to take in the various bystanders who turned to stare. "It's hair lube," she whispered and gave Raki's skinny shoulder a shove.

Raki lifted an index finger and pointed as Langdon reached the lapping tide and kept running. His striped boxer shorts flapped around a pair of ample thighs and the muscles either side of his spine rippled with the pumping of his arms. "He's keen," Raki remarked. "Looks like he's enjoying himself."

A shout reached them from the shoreline as Langdon disappeared beneath the foaming white surf. At first, Kit saw his arms spinning like human windmills and then nothing. The dancing waves created shadows in glittering troughs and Kit thought she'd spotted several sightings that became nothing. Her heart started pounding and guilt flooded her mind. She'd killed the vicar. And she'd end up on the national news with fluffy hair.

An arm flew into the air about five hundred metres from the shore. It appeared and disappeared in the blink of an eye. A muted gasp sounded to her right and Kit noticed a growing crowd gathering around them. The man at the edge of the water shouted something and jumped up and down on the spot. A woman pushing a pram turned to face Kit, excitement in her eyes. "It's a kid," she announced. "That man ran in to save a drowning kid."

As though she'd announced a half-price sale on laptops, the crowd surged towards the shore with sudden enthusiasm. The woman shifted the blanket covering her pram and Kit's eyes widened at the sight of several brown wine bottles with stained labels nestled inside. "Where did you find those?" Kit demanded.

The woman's features clouded and she turned her back on her. "Mind yer own damn business," she snarled. Her fingers twitched the blanket to cover her haul and she bumped the pram through the reeds and onto the pavement.

"I don't suppose you saw any lube?" Kit called after her. "Purple bottle shaped like a willy."

Many of the crowd turned from the watery scene to stare at Kit and her cheeks flamed bright red. "Not for me!" she shouted. She jabbed an index finger towards an unsuspecting Raki. "I'm asking for a friend."

"He's got him! He's got him!" Several voices rose as Langdon emerged from the water with a limp teenager clutched in his arms. Like Neptune emerging from the depths, he shook his head to clear his fringe from his eyes and sank to his knees in the sand. His chest heaved and his shorts clung to his buttocks like a second skin. Willing hands rolled the teenage boy onto his side and within seconds, he'd coughed up enough seawater to make a small puddle.

Raki ran forward, edging his way through the throng of curious beach goers. "Well done, mate!" He slapped Langdon on the back. "You're a bloody hero. You saved his life."

Langdon remained on his knees, folding in half as he swapped water for oxygen. His back grew pink with hearty slaps of congratulations. Kit hung at the fringes of the crowd, moving aside as an ambulance arrived and stretcher bearing paramedics carted the sorry teenager away. Langdon received a reflective silver blanket and a can of fizzy drink for his efforts. Raki sat next to him on the back step of the ambulance as the teenager's father sobbed over never learning to swim.

When the crowd dispersed enough to create a gap, Kit edged closer and pointed at Langdon's shin. "What's that?" she asked.

Black grime clung to the hairs on Langdon's muscular legs, making them look like seals in a shiny oil slick. Kit gulped and glanced out at the Nicola as she listed with drunken abandon. Shipping crates leaned in graceful arcs and as Kit watched, the uppermost one gave up the battle and plunged into the swollen tide with a splash.

Langdon took a swig of the soda and swallowed, a look of distaste moving across his sharp features. "Oil," he replied. "I think she's leaking."

Night shrouded the beach by the time the paramedics released Langdon. They disappeared to the hospital with the teenager and his grateful father, making Kit promise to get medical help if Langdon showed any signs of illness during the night. A hotel opposite the beach let him change in their guest bathroom and he reappeared wearing his uniform of black shirt and jacket, trousers and smart shoes.

Raki sipped a vodka at the bar and gave Kit a sympathetic smile. "Sorry about the lube," he said. "It sounds like the crates falling off at the moment contain wine and furniture."

Kit nodded and pushed her lemonade sideways. Sickness roiled in her gut. "I kinda don't care right now," she admitted. "It doesn't seem a big deal compared to what might've happened." She hung her head at the memory of the sobbing father as he sat in the ambulance blaming himself. The teenager had waded into the surf after a bottle of Merlot and the rip took his legs from under him.

Langdon leaned his elbows on the bar and slugged a mouthful of Kit's abandoned drink. "All's well that ends well," he said. A wriggle of discomfort betrayed his dislike of going commando and he clutched the plastic bag containing his soaked boxer shorts.

"Yeah, well done Kit." Raki jabbed a fist into her upper arm and she jumped. "Your lube fetish brought us here and put Langdon in the right place at the right time."

Langdon snorted and pursed his lips at the indignant expression on Kit's face. "True that," he admitted.

Kit pouted. "Your fans are approaching," she griped. She tossed her hair and turned aside from the gaggle of tittering girls who edged closer to the bar. They resembled a flock of hungry, persistent gulls with their sights set on a bag of chips.

Raki shrugged. "Is that the same crowd who followed us from the beach?" he asked. "It's because Langdon took his clothes off and showed his muscles."

Kit gagged as the overwhelming scent of perfume and

floral deodorant slid closer. Langdon saw the glint in her eye and panicked. "Don't leave me," he begged. "Please."

"Half your luck," Raki grumbled. "Can I pretend I'm your wing man and you toss me the ones you don't like the look of?"

Kit gasped and elbowed Raki in the ribs. "Women aren't objects!" she snapped. "We're not possessions to pass around."

Raki shrugged and his eyes sparkled with the germ of an idea. "Hey, Langdon. Do you still have your dog collar in your jacket?"

Langdon nodded and a smile creased his face. Perfect teeth twinkled from between his lips. "Yeah!" With an impressive sleight of hand, he reached into his pocket and fitted the white strip beneath his black collar. He spun round in a haze of victory and stopped. The grin faded from his face. Instead of getting rid of them, the dog collar made them even more eager.

The group of women stilled. A collective gasp went up like a prayer to heaven. "He's adorable!" one girl cried. Her straight golden hair and twinkling eyes still carried the flush of youth. Inadequacy crawled along Kit's spine at facing her exact opposite. Sound erupted as the dog collar created a dizzying aphrodisiac among the women. They lurched as one.

Kit lost a shoe and a furry key ring in their hasty exit. The girls followed them to the car park but gave up when Kit cranked the car into reverse and showed no sign of stopping. Her hands shook as she tore along the expressway. Raki sat in the back and sniggered to himself. "They thought you were their stripper," he chuckled.

Langdon groaned. "I dropped my pants."

Raki snorted. "How did you manage that at the same time as running?"

"No. My wet ones." Langdon half turned in his seat

and glared at Raki over the head rest. "I dropped the plastic bag with my undies in it."

"Oh." Raki sounded disappointed and Kit sighed. She glanced in the rear-view mirror as he pulled his phone from his pocket and set his fingers scrolling.

"Sorry you didn't get what you wanted," Langdon whispered. Kit saw his nose wrinkle in the headlights of an oncoming vehicle.

She shook her head. "You knew you wouldn't find any, didn't you?"

He nodded. "Yeah. I didn't think so. But sometimes it's easier just to go through the motions."

Raki let out a whoop of excitement and Kit jerked on the steering wheel. The car swerved and blood rushed to her head. "You idiot!" she raged as the car stabilised. "Don't do that again or you're walking home!" Her hands shook with the flush of a post adrenaline rush.

"Wait until you see this!" Raki stretched his seat belt as far as he could to wave his phone between them. Kit glanced sideways but saw only Langdon's horror.

"What are you looking at?" she demanded.

Langdon groaned. "The Stuff newsfeed online."

Oblivious, Raki started reading.

THE WRATH OF GOD

The Nicola disaster has tonight caused yet more distress as members of the public risked their lives attempting to salvage her contents. As crates tumbled from the stricken ship, a teenage boy fought for his life in the waves for the price of a bottle of wine. Quick thinking Hamilton vicar, Reverend Langdon Watts from the parish of Rototuna, took off his holy orders and swam to save him. Bystanders were treated to the daring rescue as high tide loomed.

Mrs Wallace from Welcome Bay said, "It's enough to make me join a church. Who knew that's what they hid under their cassocks?"

Langdon sank down in the passenger seat and hid his face in his hands. Raki peered at the photograph which headed the article and twisted his lips to resemble a fish. "Langdon?" he said, his voice slow and loaded with foreboding. "Did you know your undies would get see through when you jumped in?"

-9-

Curly Trickery

Sweat beaded Langdon's handsome brow as he read the email on his phone for the third time. Kit stared at her low-fat shake and let her gaze slide across to the jam laden toast being shoved through the hole in Raki's face. The fingers of his other hand tapped an irritating beat on the table. Jam speckled the end of his nose and dribbled off his lower lip. Kit sighed. "I thought we agreed to have breakfast together, so we could talk," she grumbled. "We're meant to get our story straight about last night."

"Too late." Langdon wiped his forehead with the back of his hand and gnawed on his bottom lip. "The bishop's assistant just summoned me to Auckland."

"For a medal?" Raki peered at the end of his nose until his eyes crossed over. "You're a hero." He stabbed at the blob of jam and poked toast up his left nostril instead.

"I doubt it." Langdon heaved out a tired sigh. "She's probably more interested in my see-through undies." His phone vibrated on the table again and he grimaced at the text on the screen. "I know the youth group girls are."

"Sorry." Kit put genuine meaning into her apology. "Will you tell her about the lube hunt?"

"What do you think?" Langdon waggled his eyebrows. "She'll think I'm a sexual deviant and fire me before I've left the building."

"I guess. I've got work, or I'd come with you." An idea crossed her mind and Kit thought she'd hidden it, but Langdon shook his head as he dumped the remains of his breakfast cereal into the dustbin.

"No, Kit. Don't even go there. I'm not trawling the supermarkets of Auckland on a lube expedition for you. I'm officially off the team."

"Damn," she breathed. Langdon left the kitchen and Kit watched him climb the stairs. His long legs disappeared out of view and the bathroom door clicked shut on the landing.

"He's got a lady bishop?" Raki asked. "That's interesting."

"Why?" Something prickled up Kit's spine and she readied herself to defend her sex from a demeaning comment.

"No reason." Raki used his index finger to collect crumbs off the table. A smirk settled on his lips and Kit rolled her eyes, refusing to rise to the bait.

A crash sounded from upstairs followed by a shout. Kit winced. "Damn," she whispered. "I think Langdon's slipped over again."

Raki lumbered upstairs to help his stricken flat-mate and Kit escaped from the house to avoid recriminations. She fired off an apologetic text after parking her car at work and received an image of an angry Langdon sporting a bloody nose. His white dog collar looked wonky in his black shirt and she gave up on the idea of trying to persuade him to check the Auckland supermarkets for lube. If his vicar's clothing didn't draw attention to his task, his injuries would. She repeated her apology and shoved her phone into her handbag.

Cars already lined up beneath the waiting bays as Kit slipped through the mechanics' entrance. The garage's finest engineers stood around drinking coffee to wake themselves up before unleashing their skills on the vehicles. Kit's heels clacked across the concrete surface towards them as she headed for the office. "Busy day lined up," she commented, reaching for her special mug on the top shelf.

"Yup." Jason, the head mechanic, nudged her aside and retrieved the mug from just beyond her fingertips. "We're back to back all morning. Please don't book anything else in, no matter how urgent. We just can't cope as it is."

"I hear ya." Kit spooned decaffeinated instant coffee into her mug and held it under the water heater. Her forearm ached as she waited for the dribble to fill the mug to the top. "This still broken?" Her tone held exasperation.

Jason snorted. "Yup. Management create a flash new waiting room for customers, but we're lucky to get hot water for a brew. What's new?"

Kit shook her head and glanced around at the gathered crowd of disgruntled mechanics. "I'm sorry, guys. It's not fair, I know." She rooted to the back of the fridge and found her carton of soy milk, opening it to sniff the contents before pouring a decent slug into her coffee. "I'll see what I can do," she promised.

Jason squeezed her shoulder beneath his gnarled hand and gave her a smile. "Thanks mate," he said. Kit gave a mini-wave to the only female mechanic in the crew. The girl gave an upward lift of her head and continued staring into the cavernous hood of an older model SUV. The vehicle had spent more time in the garage than on the road and Kit steeled herself for an angry visit from its owner.

She stopped in the doorway to her office to find the servicing manager sitting in her seat. He had his back to her. She tiptoed forward to look at the computer screen.

Temper flared in her chest as she saw him making bids on an auction site. He'd somehow got her password and Kit saw him scrolling through her work emails before flicking back to the auction site.

Sliding her hand into her handbag, Kit slipped out her phone and snapped a couple of images of the back of Paul's head and her computer screen. Leads trailed across the back of his meaty neck betraying the ear buds glued to his head. It meant he didn't hear the click of her camera or realise she'd arrived until she stood over him.

"You're here." He said the words in a disparaging tone as though he half hoped she'd left on Friday with no intention of returning. He glanced at the wall clock, disappointed to see Kit had arrived early. His pale fingers performed a sleight of hand and a green tab shot to the bottom of the screen.

Kit dumped her mug on the desk and stood her ground. She waited until he wheeled himself backwards and rose from her seat. "Morning, Paul," she said, giving him a sweet smile. "The water heater in the kitchen next door is still broken. Did you call the gas plumber on Friday?"

"Yeah," he lied and edged away from her. "I'll call him again this morning."

"That's a great idea." Kit intensified her smile. "Unless you want a strike on your hands."

"Right." Paul edged away from her backwards, turning at the main office door and heading for his own desk across the hall. His straight blond hair bounced against his collar like long grass in a breeze.

Kit pushed both doors into the office closed and stared at her computer screen. Swear words coursed through her brain but she managed to keep them in. With the speed of a touch typist, she pulled up the auction site, guessing Paul thought he'd logged out. He'd kick himself when he realised she'd seen what he was doing. Employees weren't allowed on social media and distracting websites during business hours. Paul wouldn't risk getting caught doing it on his own computer. "Nice Paul," Kit growled. "Real nice."

She studied his series of bids on a two-year-old convertible. As the garage owner's nephew, he had no reason to purchase the car that way and she looked at the listing closer. It was one of their part exchange vehicles, touted both on the auction site and the forecourt for a quick sale. Someone with the username, 'Angus' had shown an interest and asked questions. Kit looked at the list of bids and her temper rose. Paul had upped the bid each time Angus entered another number, usually by around ten dollars. "Price hiking?" Kit breathed. "Is that an actual thing?" She gritted her teeth and brought up Paul's settings as 'Auto-man.' "Well, Auto-man," she whispered, "as a punishment for logging in on my computer to get me into trouble, let's see if you like auto-bidding without a limit." She clicked a couple of settings and glanced up at the front windows.

Eager customers gathered beyond the glass in anticipation of the early opening. Kit changed the email address on Paul's account and added a new password. He wouldn't be able to log into his account to stop the auction running away with his money. The stupid man hadn't set up two-step verification, so wouldn't get an email or text to let him know what she'd done. Every time Angus upped his bid, Paul's would automatically reply with something higher. If Angus wanted the convertible, he'd keep bidding and Auto-man would play to win without being able to stop. Kit logged out of the auction site but left the tab at the bottom of her screen. She figured Paul would reappear once he realised he couldn't log in from his computer.

After sending off an angry email to the IT tech for telling Paul her password, Kit pulled up the software which detailed the day's scheduled work. Then with a sigh, she clicked across the tiles to unlock the front door. She planted a jovial grin on her face as customers keen to deposit their car keys almost trampled her in the rush.

-10-

Curly Begging

'NO!!!' Langdon added three exclamation marks to his text and Kit wrinkled her nose. He'd admitted to taking spare clothes to his meeting with the bishop so he could go shopping afterwards at one of the big malls. He point-blank refused to search for lube.

'Fine!' Kit typed back, shoving her phone into her desk drawer as Paul sauntered back into the office. She reached for the note from the garage owner, Mr Roy and sighed as she logged into his email account.

"You should go for your break now." Paul leaned his backside on the corner of Kit's desk and stooped over her. The action appeared intimidating.

Kit shook her head and eyed the counter. The head mechanic stood with a customer. He leaned on his elbows and commiserated over the astronomical invoice with genuine sympathy. The owner of the Ford SUV withdrew his credit card with a gargantuan sigh.

"Mr Roy asked me to do something for him," she said,

refusing to look up at him. "He's in Auckland today."

Paul leaned forward and snatched the note from under her nose. *"Good morning, dearest Kit,"* he read out loud. *"Please, can you find the last communication from Jameson's Spare Parts? I can't find anything since Janice left. Gratefully yours, J Roy."*

Kit rolled her eyes and ignored the note of jealousy in Paul's tone. She located the relevant email and sent a copy to the printer. Glancing up, she saw Jason staring at the invoice his customer had just paid.

"I'll sort that out in a minute, if you give it here." She held out her hand.

"Don't worry. I'll do it." Jason waved over his shoulder at Kit and typed information into the computer mounted on the counter.

Paul's eyes narrowed in frustration. "You should take your break," he demanded and nudged Kit's shoulder with his skinny paw. He dropped Mr Roy's note on the desk where it covered her keyboard. "Breaks are a legal requirement for all employees." His gaze slid to her computer screen and his pupils dilated at the sight of the auction site's tab nestled at the bottom of her internet browser.

Jason shook hands with the customer and winced as the man's slumped shoulders passed through the doorway. It clicked shut behind him. He spoke to Paul in his gravelly voice without looking back over his shoulder. "Breaks weren't a legal requirement last week when you wouldn't let her eat her lunch," he commented. Oil stained fingers reached into the pocket of his overalls as he turned. He withdrew a peppermint. It looked like it had been in there a while. Jason picked at the welded wrapper, removing most of it before he popped the warped mint into his mouth. He folded his arms and leaned back against the counter. He looked intimidating and hatred for Paul oozed from every pore. "I sent the lads on their tea break," he commented. "The hot water in the workshop is a joke, so I gave them permission to use the customer lounge." The tiniest smirk lifted the right side of his mouth. "Hope you don't mind."

"You did what?" Paul shot off the desk as though electrocuted. "You sent them where?"

"You heard." Jason held his nerve. His height and bulk outclassed Paul's weedy frame and he used it to good effect, pulling himself upright and flexing his fists.

"They can't do that. My uncle will have a fit." The colour rose into Paul's cheeks and he gripped the back of Kit's chair.

Jason shrugged. "He's not here today though, is he? Gone up to Auckland to check on the delivery of those cars that customs want to double check. But he'll be back later. I wonder what he'll think of mechanics not able to make themselves a brew."

"You can't expect customers to sit in the grease and muck of mechanics!" Paul sounded outraged and his jerky actions swivelled the back of Kit's chair, moving her body with it. Three pens and a stapler fell to the floor as she grabbed the table to stop herself spinning. Overwhelmed by the cloying scent of Paul's expensive aftershave, she closed her eyes and waited for the men to stop posturing. Paul's scent sometimes reminded her of someone she'd worked hard to forget and she swallowed and shoved the sense of alarm back into the gilded box in her heart. Her phone dinged in the desk drawer, the notification sounding odd and disjointed amid the testosterone cloud surrounding Kit's head.

"Then you should have called the plumber to fix the water heater!" Jason barked. Kit kept her eyes closed and exhaled as Paul released her chair. She heard his footsteps patter from the room as he ran to minimise his idea of a disaster.

She jumped as a large hand touched her shoulder. Jason's brown eyes stared down at her, his eyelids hooded. Grey hair stuck out in tufts where he'd removed his baseball cap before walking into her office. "Is he bothering you?"

he demanded. His tone held aggression.

Kit swallowed. "He's starting to," she admitted. She resented how small her voice sounded or that Paul had out manoeuvred her into a defensive position. "I thought I could cope just while Piper was away, but I can't." She patted her curls with her left hand.

"You're leaving?" Jason edged nearer her seat. "You can't!"

Kit blew out a breath. "I need to stay for the next month. Then for the sake of my own sanity, I have to look for something else."

"But we can't manage without you!" Jason's voice rose. "You've held everything together since Piper went on maternity leave."

Kit rose and gave herself a mental shake. She flapped her hands in front of Jason's face. "Please keep your voice down and don't tell anyone else." She gnawed on her lower lip. "It's more important than you can imagine."

The sound of footsteps and angry voices distracted them and Jason's eyes narrowed. "Fine!" he snapped. "I'll say nothing for now." He jabbed a stained finger at the door. "But I might consider joining you in the unemployment line."

Kit cringed as he strode into the corridor. His voice rose in greeting to the unhappy band of mechanics evicted from the customer lounge. "One more month," she whispered to herself. "Just one more."

The entrance of a customer bearing car keys drew her attention to the counter and forced her to abandon her desk. She logged his vehicle on the system, tagged the keys and summoned the retiree who cleaned the sale cars and moved vehicles around the site. "There's a station wagon here, Sid," she said, forcing a smile into her voice. "It needs to go to the panel workshop, please." Laying the radio handset back in the cradle, she turned to discover Paul eying her desk with a crazed expression. "Did you call the plumber?" Kit demanded. She swallowed to stop herself adding an expletive at the end of her sentence and reached her desk before he did.

"Yes!" Paul snapped. "But that will eat into my budget."

Kit felt every nerve in her body jangle. "Not as much as advertising for new mechanics," she breathed. She squeezed into her seat despite Paul's proximity, accidentally-on-purpose wheeling it over his toes as she hauled herself closer to the desk. He jumped back, his gaze raking her computer screen for his minimized icon. She knew the moment he'd spotted it as his pupils dilated and his manner changed.

"How are things with you?" he asked, his tone becoming silky and nauseating. "I realise you've had to work harder without Piper running the office."

Kit swallowed. "Harder?" She swivelled her seat to face him. "I always work hard, Paul."

He held his hands out in front of him, his gaze straying to the monitor for a split second. He eased a cheesy smile onto his face. "I didn't mean to suggest otherwise, Katharine," he purred. "You're one of our best workers."

She gritted her teeth and bit back the ready retort. Only her father ever called her by her full name and the sound of it jarred in her chest. One month. Just one more month. Kit inhaled and released the breath. "What time will the plumber arrive?" she asked. "He likes us to put a cone in the car park to reserve a space for him."

Paul crinkled his nose. "I'm trying a new one."

"Oh." Kit frowned. "But Big Dan always does the plumbing."

Paul shrugged. "Not anymore. Aaron is a friend of a friend. He's doing me a deal."

"Right." Kit turned back to her paperwork and allowed herself a faint eye roll. Her phone tinged in her desk drawer again. It occurred to her it might not be Langdon hurling insults, but something more urgent. Her fingers itched to drag it from the drawer, but she resisted. Paul continued to stare at the back of her head and sigh. She imagined his credit card bill hiking higher and higher with every passing minute and permitted herself the smallest smirk. Calling up the invoicing software, she prepared to get to work and hopefully stave off the urgent need to pee until home time. Nothing short of a fire or earthquake would make her leave her computer unguarded until Paul's credit card melted.

She wanted him to know what powerlessness felt like for once.

-11-

Curly Deviant

"Langdon, I love you so much." Kit clutched the plastic bag to her chest and tried not to cry. Two willy-shaped tubes of lube rustled around inside it.

Langdon slumped onto the sofa and ran a hand through his hair. "You didn't answer my texts. So, don't say I never do anything for you," he grumbled.

Kit perched on the cushion next to him and rested the bag on her knee. "That's a double negative." She pursed her lips and decided not to push her luck. "What did the bishop say about your nudie swim?" she asked, her voice soft. She tensed and waited for his reply. Raki stood at the stove and his wooden spoon paused in mid-air over his wok. Bean sprouts and other healthy alternatives to take away food sizzled in the heat. "Did she fire you?"

"No, actually." Langdon licked his lips. "I'm getting a curate."

Raki's spoon crashed into the wok and he lurched

around the counter. His feet pattered against the floorboards. "You're sick. Oh, that's terrible."

"Huh?" Langdon squinted up at him. His next thought appeared visible as alarm spread across his face. He checked his hands and yanked his tee shirt down to inspect his downy chest. "What? What's wrong with me?"

"Nothing." Kit inhaled a Yoga breath, sucking in peace and breathing out stupid. "A curate is a bit like a vicar's assistant. Not a cure. He's not sick."

"Oh." Raki dipped forward and held out his right hand. Langdon took it and tolerated the hearty handshake. "Congratulations." Raki patted his own chest. "Much relief."

"Wow." Kit forced a smile onto her lips, pleased her flat-mate's day hadn't gone as badly as hers. "So, it wasn't about the see-through underpants then?"

"Fortunately not, although she saw the article. She focussed on the rescue rather than the naked reveal. The women in the admin office kept giggling and talking behind their hands. It made me uncomfortable." He pouted, creating the perfect image of handsome broodiness. Kit suspected the women found him charming anyway and his daring rescue had just sent him to the top of the chart for most eligible bachelor. Poor Langdon seemed oblivious. Kit's brow furrowed as she watched him squirm, sensing tension emanating from him in waves.

"Spit it out," she sighed. "You're moving out, aren't you?"

"No!" Langdon seemed perplexed by her conclusion. He rubbed his hands together and the awkwardness hiked up a notch. He turned in his seat to face her.

A knock at the door punctuated the moment and Raki disappeared into the hallway with his wooden spoon. Kit stood and reached into the bag, extracting one of the delightful purple tubes. "Thanks so much for this," she said. "It's the best thing that's happened to me all day."

"Oh." A stranger stood in the doorway leading from the hall, an overnight bag clutched in his left hand and a suit carrier resting over his forearm. He looked like a mirror image of Langdon, tall, imposing and handsome. But for all of Langdon's blond good looks, God had endowed this man with the darker version. Penetrating brown eyes stared at the lube in Kit's hand and his brow furrowed. "Would you like me to come back?"

"For what?" Kit stared at her improvised hair gel and back at the man. A dirty thought crossed her mind and she drew herself up to her fullest height, still not reaching the crest of his shoulder. She pushed a look of indignation onto her lips, though the thought was entertaining. She dropped the lube into the plastic bag with its mate. "A hairdressing session?"

Langdon's squirming ceased as he rose to stand next to her. A bean sprout lost its battle to cling to Raki's spoon and hit the floor with a plop. He stared at the odd gathering from just behind the visitor. His eyes flicked from one person to another as though watching a tennis match. Langdon cleared his throat. "Kit meet Jerry. Jerry meet Kit."

"Hi Jerry." Kit frowned.

"Hi Kit." Jerry nodded. Then he dropped his bombshell. "I've got more gear in the car. What should I do with it?"

Raki flicked his spoon and the last bean sprout performed a beautiful arc over the counter and landed in the sink. "Oh, wow." Raki snorted and Kit stared at him. He jabbed the rounded end of the spoon at Langdon. "I get it now. Oh dude, you're in so much trouble."

"What? What?" Kit demanded. She gritted her teeth and closed her eyes. "I've had a terrible day. Somebody tell me what's going on."

"I'm the new curate." Jerry's voice sounded low and rumbling against the bare walls of the lounge. "Langdon suggested I rent a room here."

"What room? Where?" Exasperation furrowed Kit's brow and her lips pulled into a hard line. "It's a three-bedroom house and three people live here." She whipped around to glare at Langdon. "What do you suggest, Vicar? Should we wall-mount him?" Her head jerked backwards. "Oh, I get it. That's why you went lube shopping for me. For a moment there I thought you actually cared."

Jerry cleared his throat and joined Langdon in a competition for Most Awkward Vicar. "I heard a sleep-out mentioned. I know nothing about the involvement of lube."

Kit's jaw dropped open. "The junk room on the back of the garage? He'll bake in summer and freeze in winter. Don't you like him, Langdon?"

"I just panicked." Langdon gripped her forearm and the plastic bag dangling from her hand rustled. The tubes of lube clanked together in a purple-willy-shaped dance punctuated by clunks. "I thought the bishop intended to fire me and instead, she gave me a curate. I just said thank you, agreed to everything and ran for my life."

"And you agreed to Jerry living here without thinking to mention it to me first?" Kit's jaw tightened until her teeth ground together. Jerry stood in her peripheral vision like a statue, as though concerned someone might actually wall-mount him if he moved. Or do something involving purple-willy-shaped lube which he might not like.

"But everything is up in the air," Raki contributed. "The house is for sale."

"Ah!" A look of victory spread across Langdon's perfect features. "The house is sold."

"Sold?" Raki ventured nearer with his dripping spoon. "Who bought it?"

"The rental agent said the landlord told them the new

owner wanted to manage the property himself. And we can stay here."

"Yey!" Raki threw up his spoon and Kit watched a drip of clear fluid fly up into the air and land on the sleeve of Jerry's tee shirt.

"Yey," she repeated, but without Raki's enthusiasm. News of the house sale presented her with a raft of problems, not to mention the shower the old owner still hadn't fixed. He wouldn't do it now. She exhaled and her shoulders slumped. "The sleep-out needs an overhaul and neither the old landlord nor the new one will want to fix it. I doubt it's even habitable."

"Not a problem." Jerry delivered a hundred-watt smile which shone right through Kit's limp objections. "I used to work in my uncle's building firm in the school holidays. As long as the structure is sound, I'll fix it up at my own expense." He flexed bulging biceps and grinned.

Kit groaned and sank onto the sofa. "That's not right," she sighed. "You can't pay to fix something which will benefit someone else financially. It's not ethical."

"It's fine." Langdon's hand steered towards Kit's tumbling curls and then he thought better of it. His palm swerved at the last minute and rested on her shoulder. "I'll help. It's a marvellous result. An absolute answer to prayer."

"How?" Kit squinted up at him.

"We can split the household bills four ways instead of three and the new landlord can collect an extra person's rent. And we get to stay together. It's a win. I'll see if I can get some details of the new owner and hunt up a contract for Jerry."

"No." Kit made her reply sound determined. "I'll do it. I'm head tenant."

Langdon withdrew his hand and winced. His cheeks pinked with embarrassment. "Sorry. Yes, in my excitement I overstepped. I apologise. You're the head tenant. We'll leave it to you." He clapped his hands together and strode towards Jerry. Their handshake looked genuine.

Kit imagined the delight of Langdon's parishioners, having not one but two perfect specimens of God's capable handiwork sent to minister to them. It almost made her want to go to church just to witness their reaction. At least the church's proximity to the supermarket meant if the older members became overwhelmed by their hotness, one of the youth group could run for the public defibrillator.

Kit listened to the sound of Langdon's happy chatter resonating from the hallway as he led Jerry through the back door. "I already looked at the sleepout. There's room for a bedroom and a small sitting room."

She pressed her face into her palms and groaned as another section of her life spun out of control.

"Kit?" Raki's voice sounded soft and loaded with compassion. "What's really the matter?"

She sat up to face him and found him squatted in front of her. The reduced sizzling indicated he'd paused his cooking to talk to her. A sense of gratitude welled in her chest and tried to force its release as tears. She gave a sad snort. "How do you always know?"

Raki shrugged and grappled at the cushion either side of her knees to stop himself overbalancing. "Dad's a psychiatrist," he said, ruining the illusion. "I know a whack job when I see one."

"Nice. Thanks for that. I'm cured." Kit straightened her blouse and noticed the coffee stain on her sleeve. Paul had tried everything to get her to leave her desk, even soaking her with instant decaf. He'd scurried into her seat like a rat up a drainpipe the second she'd picked up her handbag to leave. Langdon's gift of lube had cheered her up until she realised she'd been bought off.

Reaching into the handbag by her foot, Kit grappled her phone free. She found the image of Paul using her computer and turned the screen to face Raki. He shrugged without understanding and took the phone. "What am I looking at?" he asked.

"My boss, logging onto my computer to bid on our cars being put through auction sites." She sighed. "I've done a really stupid thing."

"Ohhh." Raki dragged out the sound. "He's schilling. That's illegal."

"Never heard of it. The IT tech told me to change my password when I emailed him to complain. I changed it right then, so Paul can't log into my computer when I'm not around." Kit swallowed. "But in the heat of the moment, I changed the email address on Paul's auction account and the password. Then I set his credit card to auto bidding. He's tried everything to get back onto my computer." She checked her watch. "About now, he's realising he can't stop it and is ringing the bank to cancel his credit card."

Raki's eyes widened. "Remind me never to get on the wrong side of you," he breathed. "You realise that's probably an offence, like fraud or something?"

Kit let out a whine of anguish. "I can't lose my job, Raki," she breathed. "I'm living on the edge as it is. What can I do?"

Raki squatted in front of her, knees bent and his bare heels touching the floor. He employed the practice when he needed to think hardest. He closed his eyes and Kit waited in hopeful anticipation. When his eyes snapped open, she held her breath and her lips pursed into a delicate 'o'.

Raki pushed himself upwards without using his hands. "I don't know what to suggest," he said. "It's a bummer."

Kit groaned and tipped sideways, pushing her face into a limp cushion. "Mr Roy is back from his trip to Auckland today," she groaned. "I'm going to see him first thing tomorrow and confess."

-12-

Curly Consequences

Jerry spent the night on the sofa. His long legs dangled over the edge and he snored loud enough for Kit to hear him in her upstairs room at the end of the hall.

She slumped at the dining table with a mug of coffee clutched in her hands and the weight of the world on her shoulders. She couldn't face breakfast. "I can't get fired," she breathed into the steam. "I can't get fired."

"Call in sick," Raki suggested. "I would."

Kit gave him a look of disgust. "You don't work. You're a student."

Raki shrugged. "Then you need to see your boss and face the music."

Kit nodded and snatched her phone from the counter. She'd left it downstairs in her misery and its battery light shone red in warning of its imminent death. Fear mocked her as she showered in the main bathroom and padded to her bedroom in a towel.

Ten minutes later, Langdon gave his all too familiar

screech of dismay as he stepped in a puddle of sticky flaxseed gel on the bathroom floor. Kit didn't even have the energy to apologise. Her car did bunny hops on the way to work in protest at the cheap grade petrol she'd had to pump into it and she arrived without her usual sparkle.

The mechanics gathered outside the rear entrance, lunch boxes in their hands and their jackets still over their overalls. Kit's heels dragged against the concrete as she took fairy steps towards doom.

"The door's locked." Jason leaned against the brick, a cigarette dangling from between his lips. He pulled it free and blew smoke to the side in a practiced action.

"Then open it." Kit frowned and stared at the closed door as though it offended her. "I can't be late. Paul will birth a cow if I'm even one minute past my start time."

Kelly giggled. "Can you call us over to watch?"

"Don't do this to me." Kit raised her hand to shield her eyes and peered through the glass. Nothing looked out of place in the workshop's untidy anteroom. She tutted and imagined the chaos outside the service bay with vehicles piling up as owners fought to drop them off and get to work. Jason's cigarette smoke wafted under her nose and Kit choked on the fumes. "You can't smoke here," she coughed, waving her hand in front of her face. "You'll set off the alarms."

Jason shook his head and his eyes glittered with mischief. "The electrician installing the new alarm system turned it all off yesterday. There's a fault. He's coming back today to fix it."

Dougie let out an irritated huff. "Does Mr Roy know he did that? They can't just turn the alarms off. What if somebody finds out and the place gets robbed?"

Jason rolled his eyes. "We couldn't set the other alarm, remember?" he barked at the older mechanic. "It kept going off and we got too many call outs. That's why we're getting a new one."

"I'll walk around the outside and ask one of the sales guys to let us in. I need to see Mr Roy, anyway." Kit eased herself away from the dispute. A glance at her watch showed the hands moving past the half hour. Paul would already be fuming over the auction site debacle. He must know she'd done it. Her shoulders drooped. Her lateness might not garner a mention alongside her other sins.

Kit's heels clattered against the forecourt as she rounded the building. The first thing she saw was the sold sign stuck to the windscreen of the convertible. She swallowed and felt her heart thudding its way through her chest wall. Fired. Destitute. Forced to put her hair in a Permanent Ponytail because she couldn't afford Curly Approved products.

Kit's hands shook as she clutched her bag and clattered towards the main doors of the car showroom. She gasped as a tall man stepped out in front of her. "Sorry, Miss. You can't go in there."

Kit took a step back and lifted her head to look at him. He towered over her, a police issue vest covering his ample torso. "But I work here," she said, her voice losing any sense of authority. "The back door's locked and it's made me late." A delicate latch broke on the filter in her brain and connected her voice box directly to her thoughts. "I'm gonna get fired and run out of lube. And the bloody vicar kept me up all night." Kit clapped a hand over her mouth as the policeman's eyes widened. A tiny smirk lifted the left side of his lip.

"You still can't go inside, Miss." He reached in his vest pocket and his fingers pulled out a notebook and pen. "But I'd like to ask you some questions."

The sound of sirens cut him off in the middle of asking her name and date of birth. The loud and screeching entourage of flashing lights and uniformed personnel brought all the mechanics to the front of the building. They milled around, adding their irritation to that of the deluge of angry customers wanting to abandon their vehicles for repairs or servicing. Jason smoked five cigarettes in the half an hour they gathered outside. He sent an apprentice to buy him more from the dairy across the road and the boy returned with nicotine and gossip.

"Someone's dead," he said, pouring coins into Jason's outstretched palm. "That's why the cops are here. The security guard found the body as he opened the workshop."

"Who is it?" Kit demanded. Nervous fingers reached up to snag a curl from next to her left ear. She coiled it, a comforting, calming action which busied both her hand and her thoughts. "What happened to them?"

"Dunno."

"Brad! You're useless at finding out information." Kelly pouted. "Let's work out who's missing. Then we'll know." She stood on tiptoes to count the staff milling around the forecourt. She used her fingers, swore and started again. "Gordy keeps walking around," she huffed. "I've counted him three times."

A nervous twitch tore at Kit's upper lip. Nausea roiled her morning coffee around her guts. Paul's flash Audi wasn't parked in its usual space and she tried to stop her mind working through possible scenarios. Shaking fingers grappled in her handbag for her phone. She experienced the overwhelming urge to speak to her mother.

The uniformed officer waited nearby and watched as Kit hauled the device free. He stood with his legs splayed and his arms behind his back like a sentry. The vest accentuated his build and veiled him in an air of authority. Away from work he probably looked like anyone else in their early thirties. Another glance at his strong features and muscular physique made Kit reconsider. He'd look imposing in or out of uniform.

With her cheeks flushing hot at her inappropriate thoughts, Kit distracted herself by pressing the button to wake up her phone. A blank screen faced her and she groaned.

"Problem?" Jason's gruff voice made her jump. He pushed another cigarette between his lips.

"My phone died. I forgot to charge it." Kit's heels dragged against the concrete. "I can't call anyone."

Jason shook his head and lit a cigarette. "This is chaos," he grumbled. "We'll never catch up on our scheduled work." He jerked his chin at the line of cars spewing out onto the main road and stretching back beyond the traffic lights. Uniformed officers strode between the cars trying to send the furious customers away.

Everyone froze at the sound of a gunshot and Jason hissed in annoyance. "Backfire," he groaned. "It's that bloody SUV again." Kit followed his gaze to the main road where the offending vehicle sat in the line of traffic headed towards the garage.

"But there's nothing wrong with it!" Kelly gasped. "I took it apart yesterday. It took me hours!"

"It's just old." Dougie's grizzled head turned to eye the truck. "Her husband needs to get rid of it. I told him that a year ago." The elderly mechanic shifted his feet and farted. Kit stared at him but nobody else seemed to have noticed and Dougie showed no sign of wishing to excuse himself.

"His wife loves it." Jason qualified the sentiment with another stab of his cigarette in the direction of the SUV. He squinted to look at the driver and winced. "That's her bringing it in now. She looks angry."

Kit sighed and put her head in her hands. Paul was dead and the police would assume she'd killed him. Her phone had died and hidden the incriminating photograph behind its battered casing. They'd think she was the secret bidder and even if she could prove otherwise, she'd still fraudulently locked a dead man's credit card into a schilling scam. Her knees started knocking and her heart yearned for her mother. Or Langdon. His vicar's garb seemed to guarantee him access in the most unlikely situations. Kit pursed her lips and wondered whether Langdon and Jerry might garner more authority.

"You okay?" Kelly touched her arm and Kit swallowed.

She collected herself and forced her grimace into a smile. "What do you call more than one vicar?" she asked. "Is it a brace of vicars or a duo?"

-13-

The Knotty Issue

Kit shrieked as a male hand landed on her shoulder. She tottered sideways on her heels and screamed again once she identified the hand's owner. "So, this is where you're hiding!" he snapped. The policeman started edging his way through the throng of displaced employees at the look of genuine horror on Kit's face.

"Why is she screaming?" Paul's head swivelled on his neck like an owl and Kit screamed again as his grip tightened. When the policeman arrived, she launched herself at him and clung to his vest.

"What's the problem here?" The officer straightened his spine and puffed his chest out. "Are you bothering this lady?"

"Yes!" Kit squeaked. "He bothers me all the time. I can't take anymore." She heard the weakness in her voice and despised it. This wasn't her. She was strong and capable. She didn't need a man to fight her battles. A quick squint up at the policeman saw his face infused with pure enjoyment. She'd made him feel like her hero and it seemed uncharitable to rob him of his moment. He patted her back with a gentle rubbing motion and Kit left her dignity on the concrete between her feet for a blessed moment longer.

"Is this true?" the officer growled. "You bother her all the time?"

"I'm her boss!" Paul put his hands on his hips and thrust out his own puny chest. "I'm allowed to."

"Sexual harassment is against the law." The policeman reached behind him and jangled his handcuffs. Paul inhaled like a raging bull and went on the offensive.

"My uncle owns this garage. He owns every franchise of Roy's in the damn country. You can't tell me what to do!"

"Sir, you need to calm down!" With a clever sleight of hand, the officer slid Kit around his body and took a defensive stance between her and Paul.

Kit pressed the bridge of her nose between her finger and thumb and heaved out a sigh. The mechanics backed away from the apoplectic Paul as one, used to his unpredictable temper and not in the mood for a slice of his wrath. Jason spotted the arrival of the coffee truck on the other side of the dual carriageway and he tugged at Kit's sleeve. "Come on," he whispered. "I need a brew."

Kit almost broke her neck trying to dodge the traffic. The mechanics slid across the road like water snakes through algae, but she wasn't used to taking her life in her hands for caffeine. A car honked at her as she clip clopped across the last lane and leapt up onto the kerb. She joined the back of the line before remembering her depleted bank account. Making an excuse, she sank into one of the white plastic chairs scattered nearby. The mechanics joined her around a rickety plastic table which swayed in the wind. Jason arrived with his drink last and plonked a cardboard cup in front of Kit. She gave him a look of appreciation and resisted the urge to kiss his gnarly cheek. "Thank you," she mouthed.

"Does Paul really bother you?" Kelly leaned forward and the table rocked. Dougie rescued his mochaccino before it spilled.

Kit sighed and viewed the concerned faces gathered around her. She shook her head. "Not like you're thinking. He just gets on my case all the time about silly things." She inhaled and felt the black cloud resting over her head start to lose its grip. "He's said several times that his wife's friend is looking for work. I get the feeling he wants to give her my job. If he can get rid of me, it'll make his life easier."

A chorus of protest surrounded Kit and her ego gave a pathetic flutter. Kelly shook her head. "That's constructive dismissal." She slapped the table with her palm and it shuddered on its spindly legs. "Mr Roy would never allow him to treat you like that."

"No, he wouldn't. He's a great bloke," chimed the gathered men.

"I think we should all go to see him," Kelly stated. She jerked her chin in the air, a ring leader among bandits. "Tell him what's been happening in the workshop. He needs to know that Paul's harassing Kit and won't spend money on fixing things. If he won't sort it out, I'm quitting."

"I don't know." Jason shook his head and shifted in his seat. "Do we really wanna get on the wrong side of Paul? He's not going anywhere, is he?"

A series of angry honks disturbed the rumble of rush hour traffic as a group of salesmen crossed the dual carriageway in search of coffee. They nodded and waved to the mechanics before bunching together around the coffee truck's window. Jason leaned back on two of the chair's plastic legs and Kit held her breath and waited for the crash. "Hey, Gordy!" he shouted.

"What?" The man ventured no closer than two metres as though afraid his pristine suit might get contaminated by

Jason's grease stained overalls. He spotted Kit and Kelly and a spark lit behind his eyes. "Yeah?" His attitude changed a little with the presence of female audience members.

"Who died?" Kelly offered no dignified preamble. "When can we get back to work?"

Gordy winced and glanced back at the flashing blue lights across the road. "It's Mr Roy," he said in a lowered tone. "His wife woke to find he didn't come home last night. She said he wanted to work late because he was checking something out.

"Mr Roy!" A collective gasp split the air. Everyone stared around at each other in dismay.

"Well, that's that then." Jason ground his cigarette beneath his heel, his tone ominous.

Kelly pressed her fingers over her lips. "Paul will take over, won't he? This is the end." She scraped her chair back with her calves and it tottered on its plastic legs. "I'm going home," she hissed. "You coming Jax?" She jerked her head at another mechanic at their table. Her boyfriend rose and grabbed both their drinks.

"Yeah." He gave a smile which contained a mixture of regret and gentle support. "We can work for my uncle."

"Guys, guys!" Jason rose and spread his arms wide. "Don't do this to me. Paul might not take over the garage."

"Dream on." Dougie gave a gargantuan sigh. "I'm near retirement. No point me going elsewhere. I'll keep you company."

Jason sank into the chair with a growl. "I'm touched," he snarled, though he didn't sound it.

Kit sipped her coffee and watched the sunlight bounce off one of the curls framing her face. She tried to distract herself with something cheerier. "It's time for another henna treatment," she sighed as a police officer intercepted Jax and Kelly half way across the car park.

-14-

Curly Cops

The group hung out at the coffee truck while police officers gathered their names and addresses. They demanded driving licences to verify the information given and Kit cringed as she handed hers over. The cop from before blinked and looked at Kit's twice before handing it back. His gaze lingered over her surname. "You should get this renewed," he stated. "It doesn't look like you."

"No," Kit mused. "Because I no longer have frizzy hair and a weight problem?"

The officer's cheeks flushed pink and he turned away. His brown eyes flickered with something akin to regret. Kit inspected the photograph of herself as she'd looked in her early twenties. She'd hated herself, but the photograph reminded her of how far she'd come. Sorting her hair out a few years earlier had been the very start of her transformation into someone she liked when she looked in the mirror. Almost. Exercise and diet had done the rest.

Piper's arrival at the office had introduced her to the WWC and she pursed her lips at the thought of her friend. She winced. "Jason, is Piper's number in your contacts' list?" she asked. "My phone is dead."

He nodded and lifted his device from his pocket. Unlocking the screen, he handed it over. Kit took it with a grateful smile and found Piper's number.

"What?" Piper sounded shocked and then silence made Kit wonder if the call had dropped. "Oh." Her friend sounded devastated. "But he's so lovely. It's not fair." The wail of a baby sounded in the background. "This is terrible."

"I know. I didn't want you to hear it second hand." Kit licked her lips. "My phone's dead but I'll talk to you later." She disconnected the call and handed the phone back to its owner.

Jason raised an eyebrow. "You didn't break the news about Paul."

Kit shook her head. "She's devastated enough. Anyway, she doesn't know Paul. Mr Roy brought him in after she went on maternity leave. I hoped he'd leave once she came back, but somehow I don't think that was ever his plan."

"Mr Roy's or Paul's?" Jason's lips quirked upwards in sarcasm.

"Paul's." Kit sighed. "I just needed to stay a little longer. Doubt that's a possibility now."

"Nah, just wait and see." Jason inspected the logo on his cigarette packet and wrinkled his nose.

The lights of an ambulance flashed as the heavy truck picked its way through the traffic, leaving the garage with poor Mr Roy's body. Hope flickered in Kit's heart. "Maybe he's alive," she gasped. "An ambulance, not a hearse. Look. They put their lights on."

The police officer snapped his notebook closed after finishing with Dougie. He winced. "Sorry, Miss. He's definitely dead. The mortuary didn't have a spare car and the ambulance was already here. They're using their lights to get through the traffic is all."

Kit slumped in her seat. "It's not fair," she mused, echoing Piper's words. "I swear there wasn't a nicer man on the planet. Why do all the good men die too young?"

"Sixty," Dougie commented. "Same age as me." His lips turned down as he entertained morbid thoughts. The policeman turned away. He lowered his chin and spoke into his radio in infuriating tones, so Kit couldn't eavesdrop. Dougie droned on, listing the similarities between himself and their boss. "Mr Roy was a complete technophobe though," he said with a sigh. "I'm a bit more modern."

"Can we go back now?" Jason eyed the garage forecourt across the street and ignored Dougie's chuntering. "We've got regular servicing and a group of twenty ex fleet vehicles to get ready for sale."

The officer raised a hand to halt Jason's ready list of jobs. He nodded at a voice in his ear piece and narrowed his eyes. "There's no work today," he said with a shake of his head. "You just need to go home."

"But my car's in there." Kit rose as Paul helped two of the police officers roll the heavy gates into place across the street. She swallowed in panic. "How do I get home? I live in the middle of nowhere!"

"Do you have anyone you can call?" The police officer's boots scuffed against the concrete.

Kit shook her head. "No. My phone is dead and all my contacts are in it. Poor Mr Roy would have hated this fuss, wouldn't he?" She gave Jason a wan smile.

"Yep." Jason's features softened. "I've loved working for him." He snatched his phone from the table. "I'll call my neighbour for a ride home. Want us to drop you off too?"

Kit shook her head. "No, don't worry. I live miles out of town."

She watched as Jason rose and set off in the direction of the nearest dairy to replenish his depleted stash of cigarettes. He lifted his phone to his ear and she saw the back of his head shaking. The other mechanics and the salesmen followed likewise, leaving Kit alone at the plastic table. Scattered chairs surrounded her like flotsam and she just sat with nowhere else to go and nothing to do.

Chair legs scraped against the concrete as the police officer sat down opposite her. "Want me to run you home when I'm done here?" he asked. "You can sit in the front and then folk won't assume I've arrested you."

Kit shrugged. "I'm not sure. You seemed to have an issue with my appearance. It might be a long journey."

The cop exhaled and tapped the fingers of his left hand on the table. He kept the thumb of his right hand hooked in the front of his vest. "Sorry," he said. "It came out wrong. I regretted it the moment I said it, but you didn't look like you wanted to hear my apology."

"So, now I'm a former fat girl and easily offended?" Kit's lips quirked upward in a smile.

The officer snorted. "All the above." His brown eyes crinkled at the corners in permanent laugh lines. A white scar above his upper lip betrayed some sort of smack in the mouth at an earlier juncture. Kit wondered why it hadn't made him more careful.

"Okay. I'd like a ride home, please," she conceded. "But it's quite far north of Hamilton."

The cop checked in with the police controller and the garage's remaining personnel watched open mouthed as Kit crossed the dual carriageway with the uniformed officer and climbed into the passenger seat of the squad car. She noticed Paul's Audi parked along the street and shook her head. "Of course he wouldn't get his car impounded," she breathed.

"What?" The cop stopped at the traffic lights and gave

her a sideways glance. "Pardon." He corrected himself with a smirk, reaching to the dashboard to turn down the chatter from a radio unit.

"My boss. As my granny would say, he could fall into a pile of manure and come up smelling of daisies."

"How so?"

Kit swallowed. After some consideration, she turned sideways in her seat and faced him. "What's your name?"

"Jackson Delaney." He reached his right hand across his chest and shook her hand. His fingers felt work hardened and warm. Black lines in the creases of his palm betrayed an interest in machinery.

"You like cars, Jackson Delaney?" Kit withdrew her hand.

"Very observant, Miss. You should become a cop." He smiled and his face lit up with an inner glow.

"If I tell you something, do you have to keep it to yourself?"

"Like a vicar?" He depressed the accelerator and the car took off after the traffic, heading towards the northern boundary of the city.

Kit had the sensation of bunched power beneath her, as though great speed was just a press of his boot away. "Yeah." She nodded her head with enthusiasm. "I live with two vicars. They have to keep secrets."

Jackson winced and ran a hand over his cheek. Kit heard bristles rake beneath his fingers. He looked tired and she wondered if he was at the end of a long shift. "It doesn't matter." She turned to face the front.

"Is it illegal?" Jackson kept his eyes on the road.

"I think so, although I'd never heard of it until yesterday. I found someone doing something at work and my flat-mate said it is."

"The vicar?"

"No, Raki's a scientist. A very clever one. But he'd heard of it. I hadn't."

Jackson heaved out a sigh. "I can't keep it to myself if it's illegal, Katharine. I'm duty bound to report it."

"Kit." She corrected him and her brows drew into a frown. "So, I shouldn't tell you unless I want to do something about it?"

"Yeah. Sorry." Jackson reached into his police issue vest without looking and withdrew a business card. He handed it over. "Have a think about it and call me."

"Okay." Kit felt tiny in the front seat of the squad car. Machinery covered the dashboard like a control room. She sighed and darted a sideways look at the officer, surprised to find him watching her through the corner of his eye.

"Promise?" he asked, his voice little more than a whisper.

She nodded, doubting she would ever dare call the phone number on his card. She pocketed it and allowed her gaze to stray to the man's hair. Dark and springy, he'd flattened it beneath his cap. Flecks of grey peppered his neat sideburns. Tiny curls waved to her as they attempted to wriggle free from the constraint of his cap. Kit smirked and he shot her a look of confusion. "What?" he demanded.

Kit snorted. "I was just imagining putting lube in your hair," she replied. She clapped a hand over her mouth and stared through the side window for the rest of the journey.

-15-

Zombie Curls

Raki stood at the kitchen sink with a hammer in his hand. Jerry's legs protruded from the cupboard underneath. It looked uncomfortable.

Kit paused in the doorway and stared at them. "What are you doing?" she demanded. She pointed a shaking finger at Raki. "Put that down! Don't you remember what happened last time?"

"He's fixed your shower." Raki's face broke into a wide grin. "Now he's mending the leak under the sink. Then he's promised to fill the crack in my ceiling. This is just wonderful. It's like a makeover programme on the telly."

Kit closed her eyes and let her head fall forward. "Thank you," she sighed.

"It's nothing." Jerry extracted his long frame from the cupboard and nodded to Raki. "Try it now," he said. Raki's eager fingers turned the tap and he closed his eyes in anticipation. Jerry wiped the underside of the pipe with a dish towel. "All good," he declared. "Leave the doors open to air a bit and it should dry out. If not, I can put a new floor in the cupboard and she'll be as good as new."

"What was wrong with my shower?" Kit held her breath. She'd sensed it might be something terminal and expensive which was why the landlord had sold the property without fixing it, despite his promises. "I stopped using it as soon as the water started coming out of the wall instead of the shower head."

"Yep." Jerry rose and brushed dust from his tee shirt. "You did the right thing. It's done no damage. The connector blew in the shower head, so the water got trapped behind the unit. As long as you didn't use it, the pump didn't send water to the pipe. It's fixed now." His smile looked genuine and infused Kit with relief. "I enjoy this stuff, don't worry."

"What do I owe you for the connector?" An internal voice in her head told her she couldn't pay him, anyway.

"Nothing. I found a spare in my toolbox. When I've finished refitting the sleep-out, I'll give the garage a tidy. I've found a heap of old tools and some wood turning equipment. Mind if I have a play with it?"

"We found a lathe." Raki's eyes lit up. "And there's power out there. Do you think the new owner would mind if we used the lathe to make stuff?"

Kit shook her head. "I very much doubt they'll care."

"Is something wrong?" Jerry cocked his head to one side like a bird. "You seem upset."

"My boss died. We got sent home." It seemed churlish to add she doubted she'd get paid, not when lovely Mr Roy headed towards the mortuary.

"Oh. I'm sorry." Jerry radiated sympathy. His arms flexed and then dropped as though he'd corrected himself. "Anything I can do?"

"Ohhhh." Raki drew out the sound. "The one doing the schilling?"

Kit snorted. "Is it wrong to say unfortunately not? No,

Mr Roy died. We all liked working for him."

"So, you didn't get to sort out the schilling then?"

"No!" Kit ground her teeth and fought the urge to shout. She opened the door to the freezer and retrieved a small green ball of something encased in plastic wrap. The door hissed as it resealed and a puff of freezing white air hung around her. Kit waved over her shoulder. "I'm going upstairs to henna my hair."

"She's doing what?" Jerry's question rebounded behind her.

"Making her hair redder." Raki seized on the delighted subject of the complicated chemistry of henna usage and threw in a few formulae. Kit reached her bedroom and closed the door on the discussion and the sound of Jerry's polite conversational noises.

Her bathroom looked the same as always, although two giant footprints marked the bottom of the shower tray.

Kit pushed the plug into the sink and ran hot water into it. Dropping the frozen ball into a cleanish glass to defrost, she sat it in the water. Her mattress felt soft and comforting as she sat down and put her face in her hands. "Why me?" she breathed. The thought of Paul lording it over her seemed painful, but not as agonising as the delight he'd take in his first task. Firing her. "Oh well," she sighed. "We reap what we sow." She'd acted in haste with the auction site, her motives driven by anger and a sense of injustice. It threatened to backfire with terrible consequences, but she only had herself to blame.

Kit prepared her hairdressing equipment while she waited for the ball to turn into a paste. She stripped to her underwear, used petroleum jelly on the skin nearest her hairline and unearthed a pair of plastic gloves and a shower cap. The hot water needed replenishing twice before the henna became malleable enough to spread on her hair and in between, Kit put her phone on charge and tidied her bedroom.

"Right then," she breathed, facing herself in the bathroom mirror. The process took twenty minutes. Using a flat edged paintbrush, Kit dabbed the green goo onto the roots of her hair. She massaged it into the back of her scalp where she couldn't see what she was doing and then spread the remainder onto her longer lengths. It smelled earthy and the lemon juice she'd used months ago when she'd mixed up the original batch made her skin tingle.

Slick green paste covered her head, plastering her hair into a series of thick waves. "You look like a green Mr Whippy ice cream," she commented, prodding at a loose curl threatening to break free. "Or someone who face planted in a cow patty."

Encasing her head in plastic wrap proved the most difficult task but afterwards, Kit slapped a throwaway shower cap over the top and tucked the edges underneath. A baby wipe removed stray blotches from her forehead and the tops of her ears. "Good job." She admired her handiwork with approval. "Now wait four hours."

And there it was, the reason most women avoided henna. Four hours of heating up beneath plastic wrap while hiding from the rest of society. Kit wiped up the few drips in the sink and rinsed out the glass. She washed her equipment and left it to dry on a length of toilet roll. Her activity ground to a halt and her mind went into overdrive.

Her phone still showed a black screen and refused to turn on. Kit left it to continue charging and pulled on exercise gear. She stepped into a vest top and wrestled it over her hips, unable to put it on over her head because of the henna. Comfy track pants followed.

A few fluffy clouds dotted the blue sky through the window and she watched them rushed along by a breeze blowing up from the south. Jerry clanked around in the garden, Raki dogging his footsteps with his mouth in constant engagement. Jerry carried sheets of plasterboard from the back of his car and dropped them off in the sleep-out. A sense of impending disaster gripped Kit's heart. She needed to stop him putting in hours of work when it might all come to nothing. If she lost her job, she couldn't afford to stay in the property and that meant they'd need to leave. That was the deal, but she didn't have the heart to tell them. Not yet.

Desperation made her antsy and she fidgeted in her room. She usually made henna days into an excuse to relax, reading a book, phoning Piper or cleaning her room. It didn't matter, as long as she kept her plastic wrapped head out of sight and didn't spread the scent of fermented silage all over the house. Kit picked up her phone again and frowned at the dark screen. She couldn't ring anyone.

Fresh air and sunshine called to her, promising the chance of a clear head and some time to consider her options. Her options. Even the thought made her shudder. If Paul fired her for the schilling fiasco, he'd make sure she left with a bad reference. It seemed unlikely she'd find another job. Fear ticked up her heart rate at the sudden realisation she'd bitten off far more than she could chew by taking on Paul. Jackson's offer of help looked attractive, but all she could give him was hearsay and a random photograph of Paul on her phone. If her phone ever turned back on.

Kit grabbed a red woollen beanie her mother knitted her and clamped it onto her head. It covered the plastic wrap and the shower cap. She looked in the mirror and pursed her lips. "I dare you," she whispered to her reflection. "I dare you to go for a walk out there where you might see actual people." A glance at her bedroom invited the oppression of her problems to crowd in, filling her with woe and foreboding. Kit pushed her feet into trainers and snatched up her keys and wallet. "Fine then!" she said and stuck her chin in the air. "Exercise is the antidote for desperation."

-16-

Bloody Curls

Kit managed to sneak from the house without anyone noticing. Her head itched beneath the woollen hat as it heated up the henna and her scalp. She fought the urge to scratch. Lack of a phone or car felt oddly releasing and she inhaled fresh air and freedom. The country lane opened out before her and she strolled amid the creaking sound of crickets and the flutter of birds.

The sun beat down on the red beanie and the henna made Kit's scalp prickle as it heated more than usual. Traffic increased, forcing her to cross the road and face the flow to avoid being run over. A bus drove too close and a whoosh of hot air and exhaust smoke made her cover her mouth with one hand while clinging to the beanie with the other. Her watch informed her she'd walked for an hour and still had another three to kill. Tired and with a growing thirst, Kit resisted the urge to turn around and pressed on towards the outskirts of Hamilton and a corner dairy where she could get a drink.

The former country store stood on the outskirts of Gordonton. Houses engulfed it as residential developments gobbled up the ground at a terrific speed. The city of Hamilton spread like a toxin, chewing up the tiny townships in its periphery and re-branding them as suburbs. Kit waited opposite the store to observe the shoppers as they came and went. She'd hoped to see only the shopkeeper, but her hopes fell at the volume of people popping in and out for milk and bread.

Kit inspected the contents of her wallet, finding a couple of gold dollar coins hidden in the lining. She winced and figured she'd have enough for a child-size carton of juice if she was lucky.

The dark interior of the shop hid her from view as Kit slipped to the back of the store. Tall fridges lined the back wall, lit from within to showcase their wares. She examined the coins in her hand and selected a small box of orange juice, hoping it contained enough liquid to take the edge off her thirst.

A group of primary school-aged children clustered around an adult near the colourful section containing chocolate and boiled sweets. They resembled sharks as they circled the source of the cash with expectation and loud enthusiasm. Kit counted five children of mixed age and sex, all sporting Afro style curls. One wore so many erect ponytails, she resembled a camellia bush in full bloom. Kit touched her red beanie with the knuckle of her thumb and winced as the straight-haired blonde woman laid boundaries in the face of her children's ravenous sugar frenzy. Henna day wasn't the day to offer curly advice.

Kit edged around the throng as the children's complaints started. They bandied about accusations of unfairness as the blonde woman set strict budgets. The line at the checkout cleared and Kit fixed a smile onto her lips and readied herself to greet Mr Rashid. Her mouth opened as he acknowledged her with a strange upward tilt of his head. "Bad hair day?" he demanded with a cackle. "You don't change, not since you work here after school. Always bad hair day." He jabbed a finger at her unusual head covering. "Take hat off. You want job. I give you job. Mrs Rashid not so good. You come work for me. Without hat."

Kit swallowed and released a sigh through her nose. The conversation had been the same for the last twelve years, minus the reference to her hat. "Thanks," she said. Her fingers fumbled the juice box and the money on top of the latest edition of the local newspaper. It felt good to know someone wanted her, although she needed more than minimum wage to fund her latest secret disaster.

Mr Rashid pressed digits on the ancient cash register and avoided snagging his fingers in its temperamental drawer. "Take off hat," he insisted. "Then work for me."

A high-pitched scream split the airwaves behind Kit and almost blew her eardrums clean out of her skull. "Mum!" the voice wailed. Another joined it and then another. Then a gasp.

"That woman's brains are leaking everywhere," a childish voice muttered. "Is she a zombie?"

"Zombie?" Kit turned around to see ponytail-girl backing away. She kept hold of her mother's arm and tugged. Hard.

"I don't like zombies. Mum! Mum! I don't want lollies anymore." Her voice rose to a scream.

Kit put a hand up to her beanie as a tendril of dread slithered into her heart. Her fingers felt wetness on the cuff of the hat just beneath her left ear. She gave an audible groan as she inspected the runny green sludge covering her hand. The super-heated henna had started to leak through the plastic wrap, shower cap and woolly hat. "It's just hair dye," she said, trying to look appealing as she turned to address the family. "I got too hot, so it's leaking." She blinked as a drip landed on her nose.

One of the boy children dropped his handful of goodies in the aisle and backed away. His slender index finger lifted to point at Kit's face. "She's melting!" he screamed. "We're all gonna catch it." Pony-tail girl lifted her wail another few hundred decibels and the mother flushed a dangerous shade of puce.

-17-

Curly Conversion

"No more tears. No more tears." Mrs Rashid wound fresh plastic wrap around Kit's head and gave it a hearty slap over her forehead. She ripped open a packet of cheap shower caps and fitted one over the top. "All better now," she soothed, her eyes narrowed in concentration as she dabbed at Kit's stained neck and cheeks with a baby wipe. "Mr Rashid will drive you home on the way to mosque. All better now." She lifted the beanie and wrinkled her nose. "Little wash," she said. "Make clean. You borrow this." Her gentle olive fingers produced a bottle green hijab and she wound the covering around Kit's head and shoulders. She winked through eyes lined with dark Kohl. "You come to right place for Muslim head gear," she joked.

Kit sniffed and nodded. "I don't go out on henna days usually. Today, I thought a walk might clear my head."

Mrs Rashid giggled. Her stomach wobbled beneath her simple dress and grey hair peeked from the bun she would hide when she went to serve in the shop. She patted Kit's cheek and smudged the eyeliner mess beneath her eyes. "No more tears," she repeated. "Just like old times."

Kit focused her gaze on the lurid, patterned carpet of the Rashid's simple apartment. They'd raised even boys above their shop before sending each on their way with the keys to a store; a Lotto kiosk or a grocery franchise. Kit clasped Mrs Rashid's fingers as she turned to walk away. "You work so hard," she breathed. "Is it worth it?"

Mrs Rashid slumped into the dining chair next to Kit's. She tilted forward to look into the younger woman's eyes, hardship and wisdom mingling in her chocolate irises. "Yes," she replied. "We make good lives for our children. They'll provide for us when we need it. Our parents back home in India die in comfort instead of poverty. And Mr Rashid needs busy hands." She waggled her right eyebrow and Kit snorted.

"I suppose so," she breathed. "I've made some questionable decisions in the last few weeks and I'm not sure how to dig myself out of the biggest hole."

"Ah." Mrs Rashid closed her eyes and tipped her face upwards like a flower beneath the sun's warmth. "You still see boy?" she whispered.

Kit's eyes widened. "No. Goodness, no. Not for years." Her lips turned down. "He built a better life for himself somewhere else. Last I heard, he ran franchises in Palmerston North and Wellington. He lives in a big, flash house with his wife and children."

"Shame." Mrs Rashid patted Kit's cheek and placed a kiss on her forehead. "Mr Rashid has cousins with many sons. The hijab looks good on you, hey?" She rose and pointed to the kettle in the small kitchenette. "Make nice cup of tea," she said. She squeezed her eyes closed and her caramel skin wrinkled at the edges. "Just like old times. Make the disgusting brown stuff you like."

"Builder's tea." Kit allowed herself to laugh. "That sounds like a plan."

Mrs Rashid swished the dark hijab around her own head in a skilled, fluid movement. She tucked the corner in to hold it firm. "Mr Rashid take you home soon," she promised. "Delivery driver here now. I help him and then he take you." She smiled, blew a kiss from her fingers and clattered down the stairs.

Kit rose on wobbling legs and walked into the tiny kitchen. She looked through the window as a heavy truck pulled alongside the front of the store. Men hopped from both doors and lifted the rear shutter with a series of horrible clanks and one decent career ending clunk. The truck's belly disgorged green crates filled with fresh produce and Kit leaned forward to watch Mr Rashid lead the men inside. She'd liked working at the store through her teenage years. Her finger traced a crack in the corner of the window pane and she sighed. She could ask for some casual shifts when Paul fired her, but it wouldn't pay enough to stay at the house with the boys.

Kit groaned and filled the aged kettle with water from the gushing tap. Liquid dribbled from the join with the counter and ran onto the draining board. She wondered if Jerry might know how to fix it.

-18-

Curly Calamity

Kit grabbed a coffee from the mechanic's kitchenette the next morning and sighed at the sight of the dripping water heater. "Still broken?" she called to Jason.

"Yep." He didn't sound surprised. "But we're not allowed to use the customer lounge because we make it dirty." He pushed his face back under the hood of a truck and Kit shrugged. She counted a whole sixty seconds as the hot water trickled into her mug.

Back at her desk she halted, a frown spreading across her face. Her stapler sat on its side on top of a pile of invoices she hadn't processed. She moved it back into its tray to the left of her screen and lined it up with her hole punch.

"What's wrong?" Gordy's question made her jump.

"My things have moved." Kit reached out for a stray pen and stood it up in the pink holder her mum bought for her birthday. Her nose wrinkled. "Bloody Paul!"

"The police might have touched stuff," Gordy offered. He held out a job sheet with a wince. "They turned the showroom and our office inside out."

"Why?" Kit looked up as a customer hammered on the glass front door. The man's eyes bugged in anger and he jabbed a finger at his watch and mouthed something which included the words *service* and *yesterday*. Kit opened her drawer and scratched around looking for the key, distracted by the scent of gossip on Gordy's lips.

"We assumed he'd died of natural causes," he whispered. "I mean, he was a big guy and he liked his pies from across the road too much. But the cops think someone killed him."

"What?" Kit's voice rose to a squeak as a drawing pin jabbed into her finger. "How?"

Gordy shrugged. "Don't know. That's why they sent us home, so they could treat the whole place as a crime scene."

"A crime scene?" Kit felt the blood drain from her cheeks. She sank into her seat. "Mr Roy? Murdered?"

"Yup." Gordy nodded and jerked his head towards the sheet of paper on Kit's desk. "Get it together, Maguire. Can you schedule that hatchback for the first service today please? I've got a potential buyer."

Kit nodded, but her mind remained on Mr Roy's fate. "Who'd do a thing like that?" she demanded. "He was the nicest man I ever met."

"I know." Gordy wrinkled his nose. "It doesn't seem fair."

"Are you opening that front door today, or will you just wait for them to break it down?" Paul demanded. He strode into the office with a scowl on his face.

Kit returned to scrabbling in her drawer. "I can't find the key!" she protested.

"When did you last have it?" Paul snapped. He turned away from the man hammering on the glass. "Where's the spare?"

"I believe there's one in Mr Roy's office." Kit lowered her voice to a whisper, remembering at the last moment that Paul had lost his uncle. "I'm sorry. I opened the front door the day before yesterday and put the key back in its usual place. Then I locked my drawers before I went home." Her finger tapped the blob of tack she always pressed the key into. It clung to the inside of the drawer still showing a key shaped indent. "I don't understand." Her brow furrowed as she stared at her rearranged desk. "Someone's touched things on my desk." A shiver ran along her spine and she shoved her chair backwards a few centimetres. "They've been in my drawer and touched my stuff." She swallowed as the implications ran through her mind and she reached for her handbag in the bottom drawer. "A policeman gave me his card. Maybe I should phone him and asked if they took the key."

"You need to open this door!" Paul shouted. The angry customer threw his keys at the window and they clanged against the glass and dropped to the floor. Kit watched the man stride away from his parked car and head towards the main road. "Great!" Paul snarled. Another customer followed the first man's example, dropping his keys on top of the bunch. He shook his fist at the window and glanced at his watch.

"What's all the shouting?" Jason appeared in the doorway to the workshop, his brow furrowed in concern. Black grease left a dark smudge across his chin. Curious mechanics crowded behind him.

"She won't open the door!" Paul yelled as another set of keys dropped onto the pile and the owner hurled abuse through the glass about being late for work.

"I can't! My key is missing!" Kit stood up and pushed her palms against her ears. "Everyone stop shouting. Poor Mr Roy is dead!"

A hush fell over the office and Kit heard the sound of boots scraping against the tiles. She sensed the mechanics leave one by one and felt a light touch on her shoulder. "Kit," Jason whispered. She looked up to see him shake his head. His hand fell to his side and he too turned away; his gaze fixed on something behind her.

"We can't find the key!" Paul lowered his voice and Kit watched him press his lips against the keyhole. "Don't just throw your keys on the floor. We don't know whose car belongs to who. What about contact numbers?"

"Enough!" The voice held authority and Paul froze. Kit's hands slid from her ears and she turned to face the newcomer.

Mr Roy Junior stood in the doorway leading from the workshop, blue eyes sparkling beneath dark lashes. His brown hair looked windswept and a paisley tie hung over his shoulder as though he'd just battled a strong breeze. Kit held her breath and turned her gaze to the floor. She examined a crack in the tiles caused by Piper dropping a mug of coffee the day she went into early labour. Pursing her lips, she waited, not wanting to look at Alec's fine-boned features or the muscles rippling just beneath his shirt. She wondered if he still owned the St Christopher necklace she'd given him for his twenty-first birthday and dismissed the thought. His wife would have made him dispose of it.

"What the hell is going on?" His tone held bemusement and Kit imagined the thoughts running through his intellectual brain. "My father just died," he snarled. "Paul, why are you behaving like a moron?"

Kit turned her face aside to mask the inappropriate smirk lifting her lips. Trust Alec to nail it in one. Paul made a dash for him, almost skipping across the room with his arms outstretched like a confused extra from a zombie movie. "Cousin!" he gushed. "I'm so sorry about Uncle Jonas." He wrapped his arms around Alec's ample chest and buried his face in his neck. Kit closed her eyes to distract herself from the hilarious look of disgust on

Alec's face. Jonas Roy. She busied herself with processing the well-kept secret of Mr Roy's first name. He looked like a John or a Jeremy. But Jonas. Who knew?

Paul. Paul obviously knew. And Alec. Kit swallowed at the film reel zapping across her inner vision. Naked Alec. Alec telling her he loved her. Alec's goodbye note from the day before her father's funeral. She pushed away the better memories and allowed anger to replace them.

Paul ended the embarrassing embrace and Kit winced at the sight of tears in his eyes. "She's lost the door key." He resumed his irritating whine and accompanied it with a finger jab in her direction. Kit released the breath clogging her lungs.

Alec's gaze slid to her face. "Where is it, Katharine?" he asked.

She winced at the sound of her full first name. Its usage had died with her father and those who knew the fat, frizzy version of her former self. She'd morphed into Kit as though shedding a skin and no one had stopped her. "I don't know." Her voice wavered. "I locked it in my drawer as always the day before yesterday. Someone moved things around my desk and took the key." She avoided eye contact, not wanting to lose herself in his stunning blue eyes. Her knees knocked together with the force of her trembling and she focused on a stray paper clip nestled at the bottom of her monitor. Another thing out of place because she didn't leave it there. Her fingers itched to move it as Alec spoke.

"Maybe the police shifted things around. Who else has a key to your desk?"

"Perhaps Piper has one," Kit whispered. Her fingers writhed behind her.

"Who's Piper?" Alec frowned.

"The office manager." Kit glared at Paul. "The real one. She's on maternity leave." The flush of red in Paul's cheeks gave her a little satisfaction.

Alec shrugged. "I'm meeting all the managers in the board room in five minutes, Paul." His gaze flicked back to Kit's face.

Paul glared at Kit and scurried from the room. His back straightened and his sense of importance ramped higher at his inclusion in a managers' meeting. Kit swallowed and reminded herself she hadn't been treated like a naughty schoolgirl for a very long time. She forced her chin upwards, not wanting to let Alec reduce her to it at the age of twenty-nine. Her throat gave an involuntary gulp as she assessed her assets after almost three decades of living. She owned a bright yellow car older than herself and an impressive shoe collection. She forced fake sass into her spine and attitude. "I'll search for the key," she promised. "It must be here somewhere." Reaching into her bottom drawer, Kit poked in her handbag for a tissue. Jackson's business card fell out onto the floor.

"How have you been?" Alec's tone lowered as Paul's footsteps receded to leave them alone. Clanks and whirring came from the workshop as the mechanics started work.

"Fine." Kit fingered the smooth white cardboard and peered at Jackson's surname. "Senior Sergeant Jackson Delaney," she mouthed. The name had a ring of familiarity.

"Dad mentioned you often." Alec drew near enough to rest his backside on the corner of her desk. Kit winced and reminded herself that ownership had technically reverted to him by default. His desk, not hers. She turned the card over and fought the urge to scream. Her brain emptied of smart retorts at the look of sadness in Alec's eyes. "He said you were wasted out here. We talked about a contract last time we spoke. He wanted to make you his personal assistant. I think he felt lost after Janice retired."

Kit closed her eyes and released a long breath. Her knees wobbled and she sank into her seat. Someone else banged on the front door. "I would have liked that," she whispered. "I'm very sorry for your loss, Alec. We all loved poor Mr Roy."

Alec nodded and then rose, turning his face away from her. He cleared his throat. "Where's the other key?" he asked, his tone devoid of emotion. "The one to that door." His finger jabbed towards it and the faces peering through the glass. The frame rattled as knuckles rapped hard on the door. Keys jangled against the pavement outside as owners abandoned their keys to the growing pile.

"In Mr Roy's office." Kit frowned. "But I'm not sure where he kept it."

Alec headed towards the door without turning around. He dug his hands into his pockets and the fabric pulled taut against his neat bottom.

Kit closed her eyes to the faces peering through the glass and sealed her heart tight against conflicting emotions. It seemed too easy to pick up where they left off and damn the consequences. Her heart ached at her harsh treatment of its yearning and she stamped out the fires springing up in her stomach. "No, no, no," she whispered.

Keeping Jackson's card clutched in her fingers, she strutted across the tiles to the door and knocked on the glass to get everyone's attention. "Just walk through the showroom!" she shouted. "I'll meet you around there." She jabbed an index finger in the general direction of the hallowed ground where new cars shone under scientific conditions aimed at optimising sales. Grabbing a pen and a notepad, she snatched up the tray from her desk. She tipped out the stack of invoices and tucked the tray beneath her arm, ready to transport the keys belonging to the vehicles abandoned in front of the service centre. A shiver ran along her spine and into the roots of her hair as she considered the missing key and the invasion of her desk.

Kit pushed her handbag back into her bottom drawer and locked the unit. She tucked the key into the lace edging of her bra. After a moment's contemplation, she shoved Senior Sergeant Jackson Delaney's card in after it.

-19-

Curly Calm

Kit glanced up to find Alec leaning against the doorpost of her office. His hair stuck up at the top like a row of alfalfas and dark circles formed beneath his eyes. He sighed; his gaze fixed on Piper's empty chair. When he flicked his interest to Kit, she looked away. "You need something, Mr Roy?" She kept her tone professional, knowing by his sharp inhalation that he'd understood the bite beneath the politeness.

"Have you caught up after this morning?" he asked.

"Yes, thank you." Kit nodded and remained seated, wrapping a tag around another car key. She'd identified it as belonging to the Toyota Camry abandoned in front of the doors at a jaunty angle. Reaching for the radio handset, she called up the retiree paid to drive customers to work after dropping their vehicles for servicing. Mr Roy claimed it saved a fortune on courtesy cars and gave the older man an income. Mike and Sid, the other retiree, also moved cars around the site to save the mechanics valuable time. "Hey,

Mike," Kit said, her tone enquiring. A glance to her right showed Alec still there in her peripheral vision as Mike answered his radio.

"Yup." Mike's voice wavered, followed by the crackle of his handset as he released his call button.

Kit cleared her throat and swivelled her chair to avoid Alec's intense stare. "I've found the key to the Camry."

"Cool. I've just dropped the last customer at work, so I'll make my way back," he replied. "Did Sid manage to move the others?"

"Yes, apart from the two Fords blocked in by the Camry. But they can move now," Kit's thumb shook on the call button, Alec's scrutiny making her nervous.

Mike swore across the radio and Kit pursed her lips. "Bit of a nightmare," he conceded. "Camry's owner calmed down by the time we got back into town. He apologised for his behaviour. Says he hates arriving late because his boss micromanages him."

Kit sighed. "Know the feeling," she muttered, but she didn't say it over the radio. She depressed the button and responded to Mike's observation. "Understandable. See you when you get back."

He chuckled. "Hey, I accidentally gave a homeless guy a ride into town. He just got into the van with the other customers. I've dropped him at the Salvation Army place on Victoria Street. He got a free ride and everyone stumped up a couple of bucks for his breakfast. It cheered the grumpy bugger up, anyway. What happened?"

Kit swallowed. "The door key went missing from my desk drawer. Gordy found the spare in Mr Roy's office safe, so it's unlocked now."

"Okay. See you in about ten minutes. Roger. Out." Mike's voice crackled and then silenced.

"Good radios." Alec made the sentence into a statement, but Kit heard the question behind it. She needed to avoid personal discussion at all cost. Instead, she dived into recounting information from the manual which accompanied the expensive technology.

"They're designed to operate within the city limits, relaying data via the repeater fixed to the apex of the showroom roof."

"I know." Alec sounded irritated and Kit swallowed. "Who do you think researched them and signed them off?"

Kit left the question unanswered. She tapped the keyboard with her fingers, writing gibberish on a document bearing the company header. She flinched as Alec left the doorway and perched on the edge of Piper's desk next to her. Highlighting the gibberish, Kit deleted it, not wanting Alec to see evidence of her discomfort.

"We need to talk." He lowered his voice and she licked her lips, shaking her head so her red curls bounced against her shoulders.

"I don't think so, Mr Roy." She opened a blank email to Jason and a covert look at Alec's handsome face showed him gazing through the front windows into the service car park. She typed the word HELP in block letters and then sent the email.

Alec exhaled and looked down at her, his gaze burning a hole in the side of her face. "You look amazing," he said, lowering his voice. "I love your hair."

Kit swallowed and buried the scream rising into her chest, dredged up from the pit of despair he'd created when he abandoned her. "Thank you." Her reply sounded wooden.

"My father just died, Katharine," he breathed. "Please don't be like this."

"Yes, I'm aware of what you're going through, thanks." She turned to face him. Her jaw flexed beneath the softness of her cheek, the two surfaces forming a paradox of pain.

Alex swallowed and looked down at his hands and his shoulders hunched with the weight of guilt. Kit hated that she still felt enough love for him to want to offer comfort.

The hard edges around her heart objected and she moved away, denying the fingers that itched to stroke his cheek.

A clatter in the doorway revealed Jason. He stopped when he saw Alec and stress lines appeared across his forehead. "Mr Roy," he said, dipping his chin. "Sorry for your loss." His gaze darted to Kit and she sent him a pleading look, relieved by the slight uptick of his head. "Have you got a minute, Kit?" he asked. "I need to explain this invoice to you. The owner's wife is due here to pick up that bloody SUV. I've taken the thing apart myself and can't find anything wrong."

"Sure." Kit offered him a warm smile of encouragement. He ventured closer, a random invoice in his hand. In a single swift motion, he hauled Piper's chair next to Kit's and sat down, placing the invoice on the desk in front of her.

Thwarted by Jason's presence between him and Kit, Alec stood and left the room. His audible sigh drifted back from the corridor. Jason leaned across and snatched back the invoice for replacement mechanical parts. "What did you want?" He lowered his voice and jerked his head towards her computer monitor. "Why the need for a big rescue?"

She shook her head and forced a smile onto her lips. "I thought he might sit there all morning. The drama with the front door key set me back hours and Mike's still on the road. I needed to crack on." She pursed her lips and sighed. "Besides, his dad just died. I don't know what to say to him."

Jason's eyes flickered and he nodded. "Yeah. It's hard," he agreed. The characteristic shutter crashed down to cover his emotions. He rose and pushed Piper's chair back beneath her empty desk. "Are we done now? Is Mike bringing the Camry into the workshop? It's next on the schedule and the owner wants it by two o'clock."

Kit exhaled. "The key is here. Just grab the car from

outside and then Mike or Sid can shift the others." She gave him a smile and dangled the key in front of him. Jason let it settle in his palm and whirled around to leave. Kit listened to his footsteps squeaking along the corridor. He'd seemed brusquer than usual, but she'd abused their secret code for her own ends. He didn't know about her tawdry relationship with Alec and wouldn't hear it from her. She shook her curls and sighed, her mind drifting back to the brief affair.

Seventeen and impressionable, she'd started as the new office girl. Falling in love with the heir to the business hadn't been on her 'to do' list, but she'd done it, anyway. "You were a silly, silly girl," she breathed. "And you're still here. For now, anyway. One more month just to stop you-know-who freaking out," she murmured. "Then we're done here."

The front door clattered and Kit recognised the woman who tottered through on enormous platform heels. Her expensive handbag picked a fight with the closing door and she took a moment to wrestle it free.

"Can I help you?" Kit rose from her seat and took her place behind the counter.

"The mechanic called. Jason something. He said he needed to see me." She tossed her hair and pressed her lips together. Kit frowned as she noticed the sparkle of tears behind her bravado.

"I'll get him for you," she said. Deciding not to summon him over the phone, Kit walked along the corridor to the workshop. Jason stood beneath a station waggon with an apprentice, looking up at something under the chassis.

"What now?" he bit. Kit winced.

"The lady who owns the SUV is here." Her brow furrowed. "She said you called and wanted to speak to her."

Jason stepped out from beneath the vehicle and stared at Kit. He blinked twice. "We had this conversation," he said. "Remember? I said I'd taken the bloody thing apart myself and there's nothing wrong with it."

Kit's lips formed into a neat circle of realisation. "That was real?" she said. "Sorry, I thought you made it up on the spur of the moment."

"No." He shook his head and stepped back under the hoist. "I don't have time to talk to her now. Please can you explain the invoice?"

Kit nodded and turned away. Then she spun back in confusion. "Did you send the invoice through to the front office?" she asked. "I haven't seen it."

"I put it on your desk," Jason said. He stared at her as though she'd missed something.

She shook her head. "No, you brought a random piece of paper with you. I figured you wanted to make it look legitimate."

Jason gave himself a shake and lost his focus for a moment. "Sorry." His tone softened. "Kelly quit for real and she took her boyfriend with her. She said they won't work for Paul. Well, she said the words and her Jax just kinda nodded. So, I'm short staffed. I typed the invoice up on the computer, but you'll need to print it." He turned to her with a look of pleading as insistent as hers earlier. "Please can you get rid of her, Kit? I don't want that truck back here again. She needs to replace it. Maybe tell her that. Nicely."

"Okay." Kit nodded and walked back to the service desk. She saw Alec through the glass surrounding Mr Roy's office. He sat in his father's chair with his elbows leaned on the desk and his head in his hands. She allowed herself a moment of sympathy but kept walking.

"Has he fixed it?" The woman's brows knitted beneath her bleach blonde hair. Kit detected a slight wave, but she'd subdued it beneath straightening irons. It screamed out for Curly love, but Kit couldn't help without an invitation.

"I'll just print off the invoice," she said.

The printer spat out a bill for another couple of

hundred dollars and Kit sat with the woman while she cried in a leather visitor's chair. "My husband says he's had enough," she sobbed. "He wants rid of it."

"I understand, Mrs Cartwright." Kit handed her another tissue and ignored the ringing telephone. "We get attached to things. I love my yellow Beetle, but it's an acquired taste. My flat-mates hate driving it."

The woman heaved out a shuddering breath. "Call me Josie," she said. "I'm glad you understand. The men don't. They treat me like it's all in my head, but it's not."

Kit nodded with emphasis. "It might feel like that, but we all heard it backfire the other morning."

"I know!" Josie's eyes bugged. "But it never does it for Ken. Only me. I think it needs an exorcism."

Kit blinked and contemplated offering Langdon's services. She imagined his expression when she told him and shelved the suggestion. While she was distracted, Josie reached out a finger and touched one of Kit's curls. The Curlies bemoaned such behaviour loud and long as a hideous invasion of personal space. Partners had been dumped for less. "I love your hair." Josie removed her finger after encouraging the tiniest bounce of a red curl. "How do you do it?"

Kit paused and contemplated bothering with a run-down of CR. The Curly Routine. Josie's hair looked welded in place and Kit doubted she would put the work in required to heal it. She imagined the woman spending three weeks of her life wearing a curly nest on her head while her hair transitioned from wrecked to less damaged. She opted for the short answer. "No silicones, no sulfates and no oils unless they're water soluble." Josie's eyes glossed and Kit congratulated herself for not wasting time on the longer answer.

"What else?" Josie persisted. Kit sensed her seeking a shortcut. She turned in her seat.

"Lube," she replied, looking for the shock factor.

Josie's left eyebrow attempted to quirk upward, stopped by the Botox in her forehead. "Which one?"

Kit swallowed. "The purple-willy-shaped one. But I can't find any at the moment. The Nicola wrecked off Tauranga and took the latest shipment with her. The salvage crews can't board her because she's listing too much and the sea is still rough."

"Oh." Josie blinked. "Even the sex shops? What about online? I order stuff from Australia all the time. I got a great little nurse's outfit." She sniffed. "I must wear it tonight before I show Ken this invoice."

Kit's eyes widened and a grin split her face from ear to ear. "Josie, you're a genius."

Josie patted her stiff fringe. "Thanks. I wish that was true. Then I'd know what to do about my poor truck."

Kit shifted to look through the window. "Why do you like that particular vehicle?" She rose to fetch a cup of filtered water from the dispenser in the corner. Josie crossed her legs with a look of discomfort at the tinkling of the liquid into the cup.

"It's perfect for my shopping," she said. Shaking fingers dabbed the tissue across her fake eyelashes without dislodging them. "Big things fit in the back without me needing to flatten the back seats and I love the peg in the front to hang things."

"Hang things?" Kit frowned and contemplated her own smooth dashboard. A place to hang things seemed idealistic. "What things?"

"My handbag." Josie lifted the enormous case embossed with giant purple flowers on a pink background. "I don't want it falling over and scattering my stuff all over the foot well. I break nails trying to pick it up again." She twinkled her fingers at Kit, waiting long enough for her to admire the multicoloured talons. "I just hang it up on my peg." She sniffed into the tissue and then looked around for a dustbin. Rising with the elegance of a hippo on her platforms, she staggered across to the water cooler and dumped the tissue in the recycling bin for cups. She sighed. "I should pay this bill and prepare to give the car up for good," she concluded. "Its days are numbered."

Kit processed the payment and gave Josie a copy of the invoice and her receipt. She smiled up at her. "Would you like me to take you next door to the showroom and introduce you to Gordy?" she asked. "He's got some brand new SUV models just like yours."

Josie shook her head. "They don't have the peg," she replied. "I already checked."

"The peg." Kit frowned and pursed her lips. "Just wait there one moment." She jogged to Paul's office and poked her head through his open door. "Please can you just mind the office for a couple of minutes? I need to go outside with a customer. It's important." She didn't wait to hear Paul's grumbling begin, dashing through the front door with Josie before he even reached the office.

They found Josie's fated SUV in the service car park. Jason had even reversed it into a space, so she could make a fast getaway. Sid had hosed it down and given the inside a courtesy wipe and Kit thumped into the passenger seat. "Show me this peg," she demanded as Josie settled into the driver's seat. Josie nodded, pausing to examine her lipstick in the rear-view mirror.

"It's here." Her manicured fingernail tapped the lever just beneath the radio. Kit held her breath as Josie hauled it out and hung her handbag over it. "Isn't it great?" she said, her lips curving into a smile. Her happiness wilted. "It folds away when I'm not driving. New models don't have one."

Kit pursed her lips as she considered her words with care. She stared through the windscreen at the blue sky. Then she turned to Josie. "That's not a peg," she said, lowering her voice and invoking a sense of conspiracy. "It's the choke. It helps the engine to mix oxygen with the petrol while it's cold. You're meant to push it in after you've gone a few kilometres and the engine has warmed up enough. It warns you by juddering, back-firing and then stalling."

Josie shook her head, determination filling her blue eyes. "It's my handbag peg," she maintained, clasping her fingers around the lever and yanking it out as far as it would go. "I can sometimes fit my grocery bag on it too."

-20-

Curly Cuffs

"That took more than a few minutes!" Paul snapped. He rose from Piper's chair and left a speckling of dandruff over the back. He'd switched on Piper's computer and it showed a credit card statement. Kit's gaze flicked to the screen and back to his face and he leaned forward and exited the website. She swallowed and waited for him to fire her. Every muscle in her body tensed. Any. Second. Now.

A snowstorm of telephone messages covered her keyboard and instead of firing her, Paul waved his hand towards the paper mountain. "The phone didn't stop ringing," he complained. "I couldn't work the switchboard buttons, so I wrote everything down for you." His eyes narrowed. "Some things are gonna change around here."

"Sorry, I didn't mean to take so long," Kit conceded. "The customer took some persuading." Straightening her spine, she pressed her shoulders back. Paul turned away and her head ached from a morning spent anticipating her imminent unemployment. Fear sapped the energy from her bones. "One more month," she mouthed to herself behind his back. "One more month will buy me some time."

Josie's naivety had worn Kit's nerves down to the nub. She'd used Josie's phone to find a website selling vehicle accessories and discovered some hooks suitable for dashboards. Josie ordered twelve and then rang her husband, allowing him to think he'd talked her into buying a new SUV. Kit left her buying a top of the range, showroom model with an elated Gordy who had dollar signs for irises.

She slumped into her chair and started sifting through the messages, looking for a blank sheet to write on. "Sex shop and online," she whispered under her breath. Pulling on her top drawer without thinking, she felt it open beneath her fingers. A pat of her bra made the key dig into her breast. She frowned. The drawer looked just as she left it, but it was unlocked.

Kit stared down in shock, the colour draining from her face. She'd locked it when she went to the showroom to iron out the drama from the lost door key. Paul cleared his throat behind her. "I'll go back to my proper job now," he snarled. "This office is where you're paid to work. Don't leave it unattended again. Let's assume your absence counts as your lunch break." He squeaked away on his sensible shoes without granting her the right to reply.

Just as her shoulders began to slide into a normal position, he pushed his head back through the doorway. "If you see that bloody electrician, tell him to come to me. He still hasn't connected everything up from the other day. Mr Roy asked me to get it sorted. It's the least I can do for him now." Paul lifted his head like a giraffe grazing tasty leaves near the ceiling. Pride puffed out his chest. He stamped from the office and she heard him slam his door.

Kit swallowed and performed a mental check of her drawer. Nothing had moved since she closed it earlier. On a whim, she inspected the shallow tray which occupied the space and contained spare pens, sticky notes and a bottle of headache pills. She used the edge of her fingernail to lift it high enough to see beneath without disgorging its contents. The key to the front door nestled underneath it and she dropped the tray with shaking fingers. The temptation to doubt herself fled in the face of reality. Someone had used the door key and put it back, going to great lengths to make her look like a moron. Kit poked at the pile of messages covered in Paul's crabbed handwriting. Why would he need her front door key when he shot off the premises on the dot of five o'clock every night? He'd leave earlier if he could find a ready excuse. She imagined him returning to kill his uncle and shook the thought out of her head. Too weak. And squeamish to ridiculous levels.

Kit tapped a nail against her front teeth and pondered on the issue. Her routine hadn't altered in twelve years. She left the service centre via the mechanics' door each night, often later than she intended. The security guard did his rounds close to half-past five and secured all external doors. Mr Roy owned the spare which doubled as a master key to every door, but she'd never seen it. Her key remained locked into her drawer from one morning to the next.

Kit blew out a breath. It made no sense for her key to go missing and reappear. A second guard from the security company unlocked the doors for staff in the morning as part of his rounds. He didn't unlock the service centre door because otherwise customers eager to dump their cars would litter the unmanned counter with keys. The car park would have vehicles strewn from end to end in a repeat of the earlier chaos.

Kit printed off a copy of Josie's invoice and trotted to the workshop. Paul glanced up at her with a frown as she sped past him. "This is my job, Paul. It won't take more than a minute," she called as she passed, knowing he wouldn't get up to supervise the front desk, anyway.

In the workshop, Jason bent over a car bonnet, his head invisible. He reached inside for something and his feet lifted so his heels left the floor. "It's here!" he exclaimed with satisfaction. A grunt came from his headless body and he reappeared with a crispy rat dangling from his gloved hand. "That's the smell," he announced. "The engine cooked it. I'm not sure why the owner thought his ex-girlfriend stuffed a take-out in the air filter. He must have a strange diet to mistake this for a burger."

An apprentice produced a dustbin and Jason dropped the rat into it. The little corpse remained sticking straight up like a stiff piece of cardboard. The tail bent at an unnatural angle. Kit waited for Jason to whip off the glove and throw it on top of the rat. Then she held out the invoice. "I spoke to Josie Cartwright," she said. Jason performed a dramatic eye roll and Kit held up her hand. "She's paid the bill and I sat with her when she started the engine. It seems fixed. I left her with Gordy and she's agreed to part-exchange it for a new model."

Jason's eyes bugged. "You're amazing." His lips parted in a wide grin and his arms opened in promise of a bear hug. He took a step forward to enfold her.

Kit tottered backwards, shaking her head. "No thanks. Not until you've washed your overalls. I don't want to smell of a rat."

Jason laughed and dropped his hands. "Your next coffee is on me."

"You bought the last one. I'll let you off." Kit frowned. "Remember when we arrived the other morning and found the workshop door locked?"

"Yeah." Jason nodded. He glanced back at Dougie, who had his head stuffed into a sedan's bonnet. Jason sighed and his shoulders slumped. "It needs winching!" he shouted. Jerking his head towards the apprentice, he sent him in the direction of the older mechanic. "Tell him the problem is underneath, will you? He didn't read the job sheet properly."

Kit took a breath and tried again. "Don't you have a key to the side door?"

Jason shook his head. "It's a fire exit. We press the bar to go out, but there's no key to come back in. The security guard checks the workshop from the inside and props the door open with that old oil drum. I get here early, so he's usually doing it when I arrive. The sales guys don't like us walking through their flash showroom in our grease. I don't open the roll doors until we're ready to start bringing the cars in. Why?"

Kit glanced across at the door still propped open. It often stayed that way all day, despite the roll doors facing the service car park being wide open to the elements. "Right." She pursed her lips, remembering the feel of the bar beneath her fingers when she left late and the sound of the door slamming behind her. She nodded. "Sorry. I knew that."

"What's this about?" Jason stepped closer and lowered his voice.

Kit whispered, "Someone went into my locked office drawer and removed the front door key. I just checked and they let themselves into the same locked drawer to put it back. Do you think I should tell the police?"

Jason shrugged and screwed up his face. "Could you have misplaced it?" He asked the question and Kit imagined a police officer drawing a similar conclusion.

"Maybe." She sighed. "I can't bear to think someone used my door key to get in and kill poor Mr Roy." She blinked and lowered her voice to a whisper. "Gordy said the police think it's murder. Do we know how he died?"

Jason swallowed and his eyes misted. His distress mirrored Kit's. "No. Just that someone killed him." His chin wobbled. "That man employed me straight out of school. He sponsored my apprenticeship when no one else would." He scrubbed at his eyes using a hand stained with grease. Each crack and line of his skin contained the colour black. "He treated me like his family. This is messed up." Jason turned away from Kit and strode across the workshop. He ignored a request for help from a teenager waving a wrench and walked into his office. The door slammed behind him.

The radio blared a pop song from the eighties into the cavernous space and Kit backed away from the clanging of metal on metal, her heart heavy with sadness for poor Mr Roy. She'd heard many adjectives added before Mr Roy's name over the years. Lovely, generous, kind and compassionate. "Good bloke," she muttered, repeating the most frequently used. It seemed unfair that his death had added a different one. *Poor.* Poor Mr Roy.

Kit reached the corridor to find an agitated Paul barrelling towards her. She held her hands up in self-defence. "I'm sorry," she pleaded. "I needed to speak to Jason about that SUV. It's all sorted."

To her horror, Paul snatched at her upper arm, squeezing the skin between his fingers and thumb. "Get in here!" he snarled.

"Take your hands off me!" Kit dug her heels into the floor, finding the action wasted against the smooth tiles. A movement to her right found Alec already on his feet in the glass office and moving towards Mr Roy's open door.

"What the hell, Paul?" he shouted.

Paul ignored him. Maintaining his painful grip on her arm, he swung her through the office door. Kit lost her footing and staggered. She heard Alec enter behind them and stop, his shiny shoes projecting a dramatic squeak into the silence.

Four police officers filled the space behind the counter and Kit gaped. Jackson narrowed his eyes in concern as a colleague stepped forward brandishing a set of handcuffs.

"Katharine Maguire," the officer said in an official tone. "We'd like you to come with us."

Kit heard Alec gasp and saw Paul's jaw harden with satisfaction. She opened her mouth to speak, not surprised when nothing came out.

-21-

Curly Rule Number 7

"Are you Katharine Myrtle Maguire?" The policeman spoke again. The others shifted on their feet, including Senior Sergeant Jackson Delaney.

Kit saw only a Kevlar vest in her eye line. Everything else blurred around the fringes. She winced at the use of her middle name, feeling the sting of humiliation bloom across her chest. Her head jerked forward on her neck in an awkward movement signifying agreement.

"You need to say it out loud, Kit." Jackson's voice came from behind his colleague and his tone sounded soft. She leaned sideways and saw him offer a smile of encouragement.

"Yes," she said. A fearful swallow cut the word in half.

"We'd like you to come with us." The officer in front of her held out his arm as though herding her. She kept an eye on the handcuffs as though anticipating the charge of a loose bull.

"I don't want you to tie me up," she whispered. "I don't like it." She glanced up at Jackson and saw him smirk.

"She's coming with us voluntarily," he stated, moving between Kit and his colleague. "You don't need cuffs."

"This is a murder investigation and she's a flight risk," the other man hissed.

Jackson bumped into him without regard as he cupped Kit's elbow in his palm. "Do you need to bring anything?" he asked her, his tone kind.

Kit nodded, her head wobbling as though disconnected. "My handbag." Her chin trembled and her voice stuttered. The men's uniforms seemed to fill the room, blocking out the light through the front windows and making her feel trapped and claustrophobic. She jabbed a finger at the bottom drawer of her desk. "It's in there."

Jackson bent and yanked on the handle while still holding her elbow. The whole unit shifted forward on its casters, but the drawer didn't give. He frowned and looked up at her, his body forming an impressive Yoga position. "Key?" he asked.

Kit slipped her right hand into her blouse and the officer still holding the handcuffs bridled. Jackson shot upright at speed and pressed his hand over hers. She felt the warmth of his palm through the thin material of her blouse. "Easy," he said to his colleague. "Take it out slow." he said to her.

Kit released a breath of terror mixed with pure embarrassment. She waited for Jackson to release the pressure on her fingers and then pulled out the key. After a moment's hesitation, she hauled out his business card and laid the warm offerings in his open palm.

"Bag it as evidence," the excitable cop demanded.

Jackson raised an eyebrow in the hush that followed. "It's a drawer key which now has my prints on it." He lifted the key with his other hand and then the wilted cardboard. "And the business card I gave her yesterday." His tone sounded sarcastic and Kit glanced up at the other officer to see him wince. She understood the pecking order as she looked at the gathered men. Jackson was king. She blew out a tiny sigh and forced herself to relax.

Jackson unlocked her unit and retrieved her bag from the bottom drawer. He clasped it under one arm like a rugby ball and slipped his other hand beneath her elbow again. "Let's go," he said, raising an eyebrow at the other officers.

"Lock her up and throw away the key," Paul snarled.

Kit squeezed her eyes closed to stop the tears prickling behind her eyelids. Dread rose from her stomach and occupied her chest cavity, but when she stumbled over the threshold and out into the fresh air, Jackson steadied her.

"Get the car, Fitzgerald," he said to the officer jangling the handcuffs. "And put those away. She's just a wee slip of a girl and she's coming voluntarily."

The word indicated choice and freedom. It set off cloudbursts of hope behind Kit's eyes. She stared up at Jackson's face, her expression guileless and terrified. "What's going to happen to me?" she whispered. "What did I do wrong?"

Jackson turned to the remaining two officers. "We're good," he said. "Tell Detective Lane we'll meet him at St Andrews' watch house."

"You're not going to the main headquarters in town?" the younger of them asked.

Jackson shook his head. "No." He waited for them to move out of earshot and then looked down at Kit. He put his body between her and the glass windows where Paul craned his neck for a better view. "Lane has some questions for you. There's no need to feel frightened. It's best you come to the station with us of your own free will. Okay?"

Kit concentrated on the yellow flecks in Jackson's brown irises as she nodded. She listened while he put her under caution and asked her if she understood. He spoke the whole phrase without pausing and Kit held her breath. TV and movies made it sound familiar enough to join in like a chorus of legalise. She nodded again, correcting the action with a verbal affirmation that she comprehended, even though her brain had gone into shutdown mode and she understood nothing. Then she got into the back of his police cruiser and one of the other officers got in beside her. Jackson drove and Kit watched her handbag strap wobble in the passenger seat with the motion of the vehicle.

The busyness of Te Rapa continued without her involvement. She glanced at the coffee cart across the street as Jackson joined the traffic on the dual carriageway. Monday seemed a lifetime ago and Kit cringed at the difference forty-eight hours had made to her life.

At the small suburban watch house in St Andrews, Jackson put her into an interview room and offered her coffee. Kit sat at a table fixed to the floor and shook her head. "Lane will get here soon," Jackson said, his tone soothing. "Is there anyone you'd like me to call to let them know you're here?"

Kit looked down at her hands and ran through a list of possible candidates. Piper had the baby, Raki wouldn't hear the phone in his laboratory, her mother would have a nervous breakdown and Langdon would die of shame. She shook her head. "No thanks. Nobody."

Jackson gave a sympathetic squeeze of her shoulder and his smile appeared sad. Kit glanced up at him, her eyes filled with tears. "That's police brutality, Officer," she whispered as Jackson removed his hand.

He tutted and gave her a surreptitious wink. "You bet ya," he replied.

Detective Lane arrived in a rush. He slammed a binder on the table between them before introducing himself. Tufts of white hair covered his head and a grease stain on his open-necked shirt showed a late fast food breakfast somewhere. "Did they offer you a lawyer?" he demanded through lips so thin they hardly showed.

Kit nodded. "Yes, thank you. I don't need one."

"Fine. As long as they asked if you wanted one." He opened the binder and fiddled with a mobile recording device. Then he loaded into a formal spiel filled with legal phrases and words Kit always assumed she'd never hear. Her heart raced and deafened her with the pounding it produced in her eardrums.

"Where were you the night before last?" Lane asked. A tick showed in his cheek as he checked his watch.

Kit swallowed and picked through her thoughts. Fear muddied her ability to recall what she ate for breakfast even that morning. "I don't remember," she replied. She glanced up at him, panic in her wide eyes. She lowered her voice to a whisper. "It's all gone."

Lane took a breath and shifted in his seat. "Run me through your day from the moment you woke up." He smiled as though trying to offer help.

Kit nodded and wracked her brain. "Monday," she said. The memories flooded back. "I went to work and the mechanics were upset because the water heater didn't get fixed over the weekend. I found my manager using my computer when I arrived. He was schilling."

"Whoa! What?" Lane raised a hand. "Back up a second. He was what?"

Everything spilled free from Kit's lips, Paul's behaviour, what she did with the password, her conversation with the IT tech and Jerry's arrival. Everything. Lane leaned back in his chair and stretched.

"So, you'd have a motive for returning after hours," he said. His thin lips pursed and disappeared completely.

Kit shook her head. "I didn't have a key with me." She frowned and shrugged. "There are security guards, anyway. I didn't need to go back. Changing the login details meant

I couldn't get back into the auction site. Paul didn't know that. I kept the website's tab open on my browser at the bottom of the screen. He kept coming into the office to look over my shoulder. He couldn't see that I'd logged out of it. I managed to stay at my desk all day and closed down my computer before I went home. I'd changed the password to log in to the garage's server and didn't tell the IT guy what I'd changed it to. He'd need to go in as an administrator to find my new password and tell Paul, but I saw him leaving at the same time as me. I think that's how Paul got my password in the first place. From the IT guy, although he didn't admit it in his email."

"Do you have any evidence your boss is schilling?" Lane's eyebrows knitted into a series of deep crevices topped by bushy white overhangs.

"I took a photo on my phone," Kit admitted. "It showed him sitting at my desk with my screen and the auction site in the background. I showed it to my flat-mate, Raki."

Lane nodded. "Where's your phone now?"

Kit groaned. "It died. I can't seem to get it to charge. It's in my handbag, outside with the custody sergeant."

Lane jerked his head upwards, exposing a parallel line of grey whiskers beneath his chin. They looked like railway tracks furrowing through his white stubble. "Very convenient," he remarked. He glanced at the notes he'd taken on loose sheets of a refill pad. "So, you helped your flat-mates with the sleep-out until late? Can they corroborate this?"

Kit nodded. "Yes. Two of them are vicars."

Lane blanched and she realised how ridiculous her alibi sounded. She sighed as Lane studied his notes. Victory sparkled behind his blue irises as he lifted his head. "So, why do we have camera footage of someone matching your description entering the service centre?" he said. He watched her face for acknowledgement.

"What?" Kit frowned and shook her head. "I've never gone back to work after hours. And I didn't think the cameras were working."

"Didn't you?" Lane waggled a bushy white eyebrow. "Well, they are it seems. Just the burglar alarm and fire system that developed a problem." Satisfaction spread across his face and his thin lips appeared in a narrow smile. "I bet you wish you'd known that when you went back to work to commit murder."

Kit gaped and a hideous hole opened up in the tiled floor of her imagination. She willed herself into it.

-22-

Curly Conspiracy

Jackson drove her home in a police car and Lane sat in the passenger seat. His fingers clutched the warrant issued by an irritated judge coaxed off the golf course at Horsham Downs just seconds after he'd fluffed a shot.

Jerry opened the front door to the house, his dark hair covered in a layer of dust. His gaze settled on Kit and then the army of uniforms surrounding her.

"They took my keys," she mumbled as an explanation. "They want to search the house."

Lane held the warrant in front of Jerry's face and he took it in fingers speckled with paint. His brow furrowed as he read the conditions and his gaze veered back to Kit. "What am I involved in?" he asked, his tone sincere.

Kit burst into tears.

The police officers searched the house from top to bottom. Jerry called Raki and Langdon to let them know and they arrived half an hour later to compound Kit's humiliation.

After the boys gave statements, they all sat in the lounge with Kit and listened to feet tromping around upstairs. Jackson stood in the doorway to the hall. He faced them with his hands clasped behind his back like a soldier on parade. Occasionally, Lane escorted Kit upstairs to verify something and then returned her to her seat.

"What are they looking for?" Langdon demanded for the tenth time. His eyes flicked to the ceiling and he frowned. "Why are they in my room?"

"Scared they'll find your dirty magazines?" Raki joked. The look of disgust on Langdon's handsome face silenced him. Jerry grinned behind a fake yawn and winked at Kit.

"They're looking for evidence that I killed lovely Mr Roy." Kit swallowed.

"How did he die then?" Raki leaned forward.

Kit glanced sideways at Jackson and saw his gaze fixed on the view through the kitchen window. He watched a group of officers head to the sleep-out. "I don't know," she whispered. "I don't know when he died or how. First thing I knew about it was Gordy telling us all at the coffee truck. Up until that moment, I just knew someone died, but not who. The shopkeeper across the street told the apprentice when he went to get Jason's ciggies."

"How did the shopkeeper know?" Raki asked. "Maybe he did it."

Kit blew out a breath. "I don't know. Detective Lane made me repeat everything over and over until I started to forget what really happened. He tied me up in knots and then told me they had video footage of me letting myself back into the office after work."

"When after work?" Jerry ran a hand through his dark hair and left it sticking up at the front. It resembled a cockerel's plume and bounced as he spoke. "We cleared the sleep-out until midnight. I vouched for you with that detective when I gave my statement."

"Me too." Langdon sighed. "I don't think we spent time even five feet from each other all evening." He wrinkled his nose. "The dust is still in my sinuses."

Raki nodded. "I sneezed yesterday and all this stuff came out. I looked at it under a microscope. Do you want to know what it was?"

"No!" they chorused, except Jerry who looked interested. Langdon raised a hand.

"Never ask him laboratory type questions."

"I thought you studied chemistry," Jerry commented.

"I do." Raki nodded with enthusiasm. "That's my post graduate study. But my bachelor's degree covered micro-biology and biochemistry. I've specialised for my PhD."

"Nice." Jerry gave a nod of approval. "Very useful." He leaned forward and rested his elbows on his knees. His attention turned to Kit. "There must be other cameras on the premises. What about footage from those?"

Kit swallowed. "They didn't mention any. The cameras focus on the showroom and the new car yard. There might be one in the compound where the second-hand cars are. There's definitely one over the service reception door because someone tried to break in last year."

Heavy footsteps thundered down from the upstairs level. Lane appeared in the doorway and waited for Jackson to ease aside. He made a bee line for Kit. "Where's the cap, Miss Maguire?" he demanded.

Kit frowned. The Curly in her bridled. "Curlies don't wear hats," she said. A fire sparked in her chest at Lane's effrontery and she channelled pure Chairwoman Pam. "Rule number seven. Don't you spread gossip that I wear hats. You'll get me thrown off the committee for accusations like that!"

"What?" Lane bent at the waist as though hard of hearing. "What are you saying?"

"She. Never. Wears. A. Hat." Raki spelled it out for him, trying to offer assistance. He tugged his poker straight fringe. "It's against the WWC Rules."

Lane stood up straight and shook his head. "WWC? And you don't own any form of headgear?"

"Women With Curls," Raki murmured. Lane ignored him and focussed on Kit.

She pursed her lips and nodded. "A red knitted beanie my mum made. I use it when I henna my hair." She kept silent about the hijab Mrs Rashid lent her, hoping the officers mistook it for a headscarf on the washing line under the porch.

Lane looked wired, his eyes round and his pupils dilated. He'd scented the success of a closed murder investigation. "You what?" he demanded. "A beanie. Is that all you own?"

More footsteps thundered down the stairs. A young officer stood in the doorway with a plastic bag raised in gloved fingers. "Found this, Sir," he said. "We think it's weed."

Lane's eyes narrowed and his lips quirked upward in victory. Langdon gulped, but Raki released a squeal of laughter. "It's Lawsone. 2-hydroxy-1,4-naphthoquinone," he giggled. "Or also known as hennotannic acid. It's a red-orange dye present in the leaves of the henna plant or Lawsonia inermis." He grinned at Kit and his eyes widened. "How many conversations have we had about this?" He waggled his eyebrows. "It's your worst nightmare, someone mistaking it for weed."

Kit's gaze tracked to Jackson. She watched him eye the bag of green dust and look across at her. His brow furrowed. "It's henna," she confirmed. "I get it from the bins at the bulk buy shop. If you need to test it, please can you just take a little and leave me the rest? I don't have any left in the freezer and the store was running short."

Lane jerked his head at the young officer. The man's cheeks flushed pink with pride and he dropped the henna into an evidence bag. Kit sighed. She watched her Curly Routine come under threat. No henna and no lube. No money to buy either at this rate. She sighed and stared at the floorboards between her knees. Permanent Ponytail might become a factor in unemployment and a sojourn in prison.

The front door clicked as the officer went to put his spoils into the police car. "It sucks to be me," she breathed.

"The cap, Miss Maguire!" Lane sounded frustrated and his eyes bulged in his face. "What did you do with the cap?"

"What cap?" Kit's legs straightened as her body snapped upright. She beaked her face into Lane's and he took a step back at the flare of redheaded temper in her eyes. "I've told you already; I do not own any hats apart from the red beanie Mum made for me." Kit's index finger jabbed at the washing line under the back porch. The red hat waved in a light breeze. "I washed it after I dyed my hair. It's out there."

Langdon released a low groan as all eyes turned to the window. A twin of his lost undies from the night of his Tauranga harbour swim dangled front and centre. The beanie cosied up to a leg of the boxers. Thudding overhead betrayed the officers searching Kit's wardrobe. Hysteria bubbled in her chest at the thought of strange male hands sifting through her knickers and drawing wrong conclusions about her sacred stash of purple-willy-shaped lube. Her mind went into free fall again and her chest locked.

Lane shook his head. "No. We're looking for a baseball cap. One with the Chief's logo on the front of it."

Kit's neck recoiled. "Rugby?" Her lips curled upward into a snarl as she gasped out the words of Kiwi sacrilege. Indignation gave her an edge over the debilitating fear gnawing her bones. "I hate rugby. Why would I own a cap with a local rugby team on it?"

"Oh." Raki blanched and Kit turned to stare at him. He

swallowed and pursed his lips. "I have a Chief's baseball cap. But I can't find it."

All eyes turned back to view Kit's horrified expression.

-23-

Curly Suspicions

Jackson drove Kit back to the police station, but she didn't get the smart interview room in St Andrews. The charge room at the police headquarters in Hamilton looked bleak, the walls painted an institutional grey. Kit stood before the front desk, peering up at the sergeant. Jackson hung close, the dark hairs on his bare arms tickling her skin as he moved. She glanced down at his angular wrist, grateful for the contact as other people under arrest paid her too much interest.

"Nice hair," a drunk warbled. He staggered against the officer leading him through to the cells, using the opportunity to leer at her. Kit swallowed and locked herself inside a cocoon of protection, staring at a notch in the worn countertop as she provided wooden answers to the sergeant's questions. Jackson lifted his arm in her peripheral vision and she changed her focus to his wristwatch. The glass looked cracked and as she stared at the ornate dark hands, she saw the time showed as just after ten o'clock. A glance at the wall clock behind the sergeant read three. Kit's brow furrowed.

"You don't understand, or you do?" The sergeant tilted his head.

"Sorry?" Kit's eyes widened and she darted a frightened look at Jackson.

He licked his lips as the sergeant sighed and his shoulders slumped. Wiry and fit, the man looked fed up, both with her and his life. Jackson raised a hand to halt the coming tirade of irritation. "It's okay," he said. "Kit, you're here for questioning but you haven't been charged yet. Sergeant Addison just showed you all the items from your handbag and he'll keep them safe while you're speaking to Detective Lane. Just like at St Andrews watch house. Got it?"

Kit nodded, the lump in her throat making speech difficult. She turned her hands over and stared at her fingers. The officer had scanned her prints and told her she'd been added to the police database. The sergeant stared at her with expectation and she croaked out a wavering, "Yes."

"I'm ready." Lane appeared from a doorway leading to the rest of the building. "You can sit in, Delaney."

Kit experienced a wave of gratitude as Jackson cupped his palm beneath her elbow. The sound of muffled hammering began on the other side of the door the drunk had gone through. Garbled shouts followed. She sent a silent and belated prayer to heaven that she'd escaped that particular fate. For now.

"This baseball cap is a problem for you." Lane went straight for it after concluding the formalities. "Are you sure you don't want a lawyer?"

Kit shook her head. "I can't pay one," she said, her tone sad.

Jackson's lips parted and his gaze burned holes in the

side of Lane's face as he sat next to him. As though feeling the heat, Lane repeated his earlier advice. "We can provide one for you," he said.

Kit exhaled. "I did nothing wrong. My father believed in the justice system. I guess I should too."

Lane frowned. "Your father?"

Kit nodded but offered nothing else. If they checked their records, his name would come straight up. They'd been on the same side, after all. Cancer had gnawed away at the skilled prosecution barrister in record time, taking him the day after he won his last big case. Kit cringed. He'd also embedded one simple truth into her brain and she heard his voice as though from the grave. "Never talk to a cop without a lawyer present."

"Let's get on with it," she said with a sigh. An index finger pointed to her hair. The curls had survived her terrible day and even though she didn't get to banish the brittleness of the lube at morning tea time, gravity had performed the step for her. Graceful red ringlets jingled as she turned her head. "I have not used a hat since 2011," she stated, her voice strong. "I own one beanie type woollen hat which I showed you drying on the washing line. It went into the wash because I wore it after using henna on my hair. It helps to heat the henna and advance the chemical reaction. The bag you took containing green powder will test positive for pure henna. I don't use inferior products." Kit shook her head and her bouncing curls emboldened her. "Raki says he owns a baseball cap with the Chief's logo, but I've never seen him wear it. I didn't borrow it, use it or kill poor Mr Roy wearing it." There it was again. *Poor* Mr Roy.

The detective folded his arms and observed her with an unblinking expression. When he leaned forward, he changed angle like a reckless driver switching lanes on the expressway. A reluctant passenger in his game of chicken, Kit felt her neck tense with emotional whiplash. "Let's go back to why you started schilling," he said. His lips quirked upward in victory. "And why you chose to send a notification to that particular email address. Did you see it as an act of revenge, Katharine?"

The colour faded from Kit's cheeks. She sensed it leave and a chill remained in its wake. "I thought he might know what to do," she whispered. "I would have sent it to Mr Roy Senior, but he didn't know how to open emails."

"So, it wasn't an act of spite?" Lane sat back in his chair and it creaked beneath his weight.

Kit shook her head. "No," she replied. But she didn't sound certain.

-24-

Curly Shock

Detective Lane released her and Jackson drove Kit home. The atmosphere in the car remained subdued for the length of the journey to Gordonton. The powerful vehicle cruised to a stop in front of her driveway and Kit clasped her handbag against her chest. Lane handed everything back to her, minus her phone which he seized as evidence.

"Thank you." Kit shot Jackson a weak smile and pulled on the door release. "I know you didn't have to drive me home." She pursed her lips and the door creaked open.

Jerry pushed an ancient lawn mower in shaved stripes up and down the front lawn. The scent of grass and freedom filled Kit's nostrils.

"I knew your dad." Jackson spoke as her feet touched the scrubby grass on the verge. "He was a good man."

Kit nodded and gave the door a push, listening to the resounding click as she turned away. The engine gave a whine as Jackson depressed the gas pedal and eased the heavy vehicle onto the road with the briefest flash of an indicator bulb.

"What did he say?" Jerry left the mower running and walked across the neat stripes to her side.

Kit sighed and offered him a smile tinged with sadness. She didn't want to talk about her father, lacking the energy to deal with the void which thoughts of his death threatened to drag her back into. Burying Jackson's loaded comment, she forced a smile onto her face. "They let me go," she said, her tone ominous and at odds with her expression. "For now."

Jerry blinked and watched the police car's tail-lights flare as Jackson engaged the brakes at the end of the narrow lane. He wrinkled his nose. "So, how do we fix this?" he asked. The mower belched in the background and disgorged a cloud of grey smoke. "Hold that thought," Jerry shouted as he ran back to fiddle with the choke.

Kit stared at the scrubby grass snipped into submission and sighed. The previous owner had employed a man with a ride-on mower to keep the lawns and verges neat, adding the cost to their rental agreement. She swallowed and pursed her lips, realising she hadn't given the house sale much thought over the last few days. Giving herself a mental shake, she avoided the lines of chewed grass spat out by the ancient mower and walked along the driveway and up the porch steps. She clutched her handbag to her chest, afraid Lane might pop out of the bushes and snatch it back.

Raki met her in the hallway, a feather duster in his left hand and a grimace on his face. "Don't get mad," he started and Kit paused before kicking off her stilettos. "Don't leave them there." Raki pointed the duster at her discarded shoes. "Jerry made a shoe cupboard." His other hand stroked a tall cabinet knocked together out of sun faded pallets. Three drawer fronts bisected it. Brackets fixed it to the wall and Raki hauled on one of the mismatched handles. The drawer became a flap and dropped down to a forty-five-degree angle. "This is yours," he said, pride in his voice. "I picked the handle for you." His fingers stroked the gaudy, crystal effect knob. "I'm in the middle and Langdon has the bottom." Kit glanced at the other two drawers. A metal, business-like handle finished Raki's drawer and Langdon's looked bare. "Langdon wasn't here. He still needs to choose."

Kit nodded and forced a smile onto her lips. Raki's enthusiasm didn't contain its usual ability to infect her. "It's lovely," she said, her tone flatter than she intended. The other ninety-three pairs of shoes in her wardrobe wouldn't fit in, but she appreciated the thought.

"Jerry let me use the handsaw," Raki said. His irises betrayed a hidden fire and his fingers twitched against the handle of the feather duster. "I liked it. We're gonna make even more stuff from the pallets we hauled from the sleep-out."

Kit bent to lift her shoes and dropped them into her open drawer. The hinges made an oily squeak as she pressed it closed. The wood felt smooth and she sympathised with its weathered appearance. "I like it," she concluded, gratified by Raki's eager grin. Her face clouded. "Why would I get mad?"

Raki's lips twisted. He turned his body to block the door to the open plan lounge. "About that," he began.

Kit pushed past him and halted in the doorway. The former jumble of furniture had moved since she left the house in the back of the police car. The huge, floor to ceiling bookcase Marian gave her last birthday no longer occupied the three metres of wall space. Instead, it served as a barrier between the lounge and dining room spaces. Kit whirled around to face Raki. His lips flattened into a line. "Jerry braced it against the ceiling," he offered. "It's earthquake proof now." His colour paled. "I told him you'd go mad."

"This is a rental!" Kit squeaked. "You can't just start banging things into walls."

"We didn't bang, we screwed," Raki corrected.

"I don't care if you banged or screwed!" Kit's voice rose.

A throat cleared behind her. "I can come back," Jerry said. Kit spun in time to detect the faint trace of a smirk on his lips. He flapped a hand towards her. "I hope you like the changes."

"Changes?" Kit croaked out the word. A shaking finger pointed to her bookcase. "You screwed my birthday present to the ceiling."

"It's secure. I found a beam." Jerry's smile looked guileless and Kit ran a hand across her face, not trusting herself to speak. She saw in their drastic home improvements, a bungled attempt to both please and distract her. She glanced around the room and waited for her heart rate to lower.

"The cops made a right mess," Raki said. He waggled the feather duster. "We put everything back, but Jerry suggested we took the opportunity to improve things. We stopped it looking like a warehouse and made it cosy."

Kit inhaled and released a controlled Yoga breath. "Thank you," she sighed. "I think I like it."

The ignored garage and sleep-out had disgorged a veritable treasure trove of household items. Kit's favourite armchair nestled in the new corner created by the bookshelves. A blanket hung over the back of the chair and a lamp with a wonky shade sat on the shelf within reach. It emitted a soft glow which offered comfort and seclusion. Kit sank into the chair and stuffed her hands beneath her thighs to stop her fingers trembling. Other little items from a bygone era decorated the room and gave an eclectic feel. A Singer sewing machine table graced the space beneath the window, a cracked vase sitting on top.

"This is your reading nook," Raki said, indicating the chair and shelves. "For when the cops give your henna back and you have four hours to kill while dying your hair." He jerked his head towards the opposite wall. Kit's eyes widened at the sight of the gaping hole.

"What did you do?" she breathed.

"Jerry ripped the plasterboard off," Raki announced. "Did you know it hid an open fireplace?"

The shake of Kit's head showed she didn't. Words failed her. She swallowed and put her weight into her thighs to stop her knees knocking together.

"It's fine," Jerry reassured her. "My uncle just ripped a mantle and hearth out of an old construction site in Auckland. He'll drop it off at the end of the month when he passes through on his way to Rotorua." He paused and his brow furrowed. "Are you feeling okay?"

"I don't know." Kit's chin wobbled and she blinked away threatening tears. "Is the kitchen still there? Can I fetch myself a drink of water without getting lost?"

"We didn't touch the kitchen yet. I'll get you a drink." Raki bounced away, the fly-a-ways from his straight hair forming antennae at the back of his head. Kit heard him clattering in the kitchen, fetching a glass and running water from the tap which no longer leaked. She felt a wave of gratitude towards Jerry for swooping in and organising her life.

"What's that ringing?" Jerry pushed his shoulders back and cocked his head. Raki paused in front of Kit with the water.

"Yeah, I can hear it too," he said. They stared at each other for a moment, trying to pinpoint the sound. Then he slapped his forehead. "It's the land-line," he said. "Nobody ever rings that." He sauntered into the hallway and lifted the receiver from the hook on the wall. Kit could just see him through the doorway as he settled the receiver over his ear. "I bet it's those scammers pretending the computer we don't own has developed a bug. I'll get rid of them." Placing his index and middle finger between his lips, he let out an impressive, eardrum busting whistle.

"I think that's probably illegal," Jerry mused. "If he damaged someone's hearing, they could sue him."

Kit groaned at his use of the word illegal and paid the rest of his sentence no attention. Thoughts of Lane's dogged determination sprang into her mind. She jumped in surprise as Raki gambolled towards her, the long, coiled cord from the receiver trailing after him. It caught against the back of the newly situated sofa and Raki jerked forward like a crash test dummy. The phone flew from his fingers and pinged back into the hallway. "It's your boss!" he hissed. "Sorry. He's shouting, but he might not be angry. Just deaf."

Raki chased after the phone and Kit rose on knees which felt less like joints and more like elastic bands. Her movements looked awkward and Jerry put out an arm to steady her.

Kit straightened her spine and forced dignity into the upward tilt of her chin. She remembered Paul's enthusiasm at her predicament and gritted her teeth. Raki stuffed the receiver into her hands as she reached the hallway but stood facing her. When she turned, Kit discovered Jerry at her back. Surrounded by concern, she spoke into the phone, trying not to let her voice reflect her foreboding. "Hi, Paul," she said, infusing lightness into her tone.

"Katharine." Alec's voice rumbled in her ear, a slight elevation to the pitch after Raki's whistle.

"Alec." She swallowed.

"You haven't answered your mobile. I'm inviting you

to a formal meeting tomorrow at ten o'clock," he said. "A letter went out in today's post. Bring a support person." The dial tone followed the click of him terminating the call.

Kit turned to her loyal flat-mates, dread snaking a hand around her throat and squeezing. "He's firing me," she croaked, dropping the receiver into Raki's outstretched hand.

-25-

Curly Questions

"I'll come with you to your disciplinary meeting tomorrow." Jerry ran a hand over the dark stubble gracing his chin. "I'd be honoured if you'd consider me your support person."

Raki's eyes widened. "Maybe we all should go."

Kit sighed and sank into the deep cushions of the sofa. Her father's familiar aftershave seemed to shroud her in a protective aura. She ran a finger over the worn fabric and drew comfort from his memory. The tremor in her legs lessened. Her mother had donated the sofa and two chairs to the flat-mates when she bought a new suite with Kenny. "I'll be okay by myself," Kit said. "I've done nothing wrong."

A look of something passed between Raki and Jerry. The latter raised his eyebrows. "Is there anything we can get you now?" he asked, his tone soft. "You've had a day of shocks."

Kit nodded and heaved out a tired breath. "I have.

There's one thing I won't mess up though. Raki, please can I borrow your laptop and go online?"

Jerry made coffee, Raki fetched his laptop and logged into the Internet for Kit, then they both returned to their previous tasks. The mower started up outside with a roar and Raki flicked the feather duster around the door frames and light fittings. Kit listened to him sorting out the contents of a drawer the police had upended on the kitchen counter.

"You okay?" His question made her jump and a guilty expression passed across her face. Kit swallowed. "You should know what I'm searching for," she said. "In case the police come back and seize your laptop. They already took mine. And my phone."

Raki's eyes narrowed and he grinned. "As long as you're not looking for places to hide the body." He clapped a hand over his mouth and flapped the feather duster. "Eek! They didn't bug us, did they?"

Kit raised the first genuine smile in hours. "I don't think so. But you should know that I'm searching online for lube."

"Got it." Raki bent to snag a ball of grey fluff discarded by the duster. "I don't mind. Have you found any?"

Kit shook her head and her red curls bounced. "Most websites are showing it's out of stock."

"Aw sorry." Raki wrinkled his nose. "Good luck. I've vacuumed upstairs and I'll do downstairs soon."

"Oh, but it's my week." Kit's eyes widened. "Langdon will grumble if I don't take my turn."

Raki shrugged. "I'm on bathrooms this week. Just do those instead. We need a new roster if Jerry's living here, anyway. He won't sleep in the house, but he'll use the kitchen and bathrooms." The mower belched and Kit rose to look through the front windows.

"I don't know," she mused. "He seems to have taken on the household repairs and outside work. I'll talk to him.

Perhaps he'd rather do those jobs and we can just carry on with our old roster for inside the house."

"Okay." Raki returned to his dusting.

Kit's eyes widened five minutes later and a sparkle returned to her blue irises. She used the online telephone directory to locate the number she needed and then made a call from the hall phone. "Oh, hi Debbie," she said as the WWC secretary answered. "Is it possible to use the group credit card to purchase the stock for our meeting?" Kit's face fell with Debbie's reply.

"There isn't one." Debbie's mouth made slapping sounds as though she answered the phone with her mouth full. "Why do you need it? Come round and I'll give you the cash."

Kit released a breath. "I don't have my car at the moment and anyway, I need to shop online. The shipwreck in Tauranga means there's no available stock in New Zealand."

Debbie scoffed. "Do we want to encourage the girls to try a product they can't get for themselves? I'd rather we used accessible items, otherwise it makes for misery. Remember that incident with the macadamia conditioner?"

Kit pressed her forehead against the wall. She felt like banging it but restrained herself. "I remember," she murmured. "The lube situation will improve, but I need to source it from Australia for the next meeting." She stood up straight and the solution brought her immense release. "Actually, postpone the meeting. Or slot someone else in and I'll pick it back up once the supermarkets are stocking it again." A weight rose off her shoulders. She had no intention of picking it up again. No way. No how. "Pam can do it instead. I've always wondered how she does that pineapple shake thing to get the ends to coil."

Kit heard a noise through the receiver. It sounded like grinding teeth. She pulled it away from her ear and tapped it before listening again. Her heart sank as she realised she'd identified the noise just fine. Debbie spoke through gritted teeth. She'd obviously swallowed her mouthful in a hurry. "We do not postpone meetings or demonstrations," she asserted, her tone firm. Kit winced, remembering one unfortunate woman demonstrating how to put wet hair into a tee shirt Plop. She wore a dressing gown and someone had to help her bend over. The women ate cake and drank coffee while the Curly returned to bed to continue recovering from her hysterectomy. Kit imagined they'd all turn up during prison visiting hours to see her demonstrate the wonderful uses for lube. She groaned and the sound echoed along the hallway and reverberated up the stairs.

"Use my credit card," Debbie snapped. "I'll claim it back from the WWC current account. Here's the number and don't go over a hundred dollars."

"Wait!" Kit cried as she ran into the lounge in search of a pen. She spotted one on the coffee table, but the phone cord pinged her backwards as her fingers almost reached it.

"I don't have all day!" Debbie snapped. She'd started eating again and Kit held the phone away from her ear to avoid sounds resembling a washing machine percolating into her eardrums.

"Just wait! Please!" Kit begged. She sat the receiver on top of Jerry's shoe cupboard and ran around the downstairs like a maniac. The pen on the coffee table didn't work. There were always pens lying around, but Raki's thorough clean-up had banished them to some far away, hidden drawer. Or the dustbin. Kit found a permanent marker in the knife drawer and made a few delicate spots on her arm to ensure it worked. She ran back to the hallway to find Jerry hanging the receiver back in the cradle.

"What did you do?" she cried. "You just hung up on the secretary of the WWC.

Jerry frowned and jerked his head at the phone. "I

thought all that slurping and heavy breathing was a dirty phone call," he replied.

Kit groaned. "That was Debbie eating her dinner!" She stamped back to Raki's laptop. She searched for Debbie's number in the online phone book again and memorised it long enough to dial it.

"You hung up on me," Debbie snapped.

"Sorry. Misunderstanding." Kit narrowed her eyes and pursed her lips in accusation at Jerry. He'd removed his boots on the porch but left the door open as he returned to slap the soles together to dislodge the clumps of damp grass from the crevices. He appeared oblivious, but something in the set of his shoulders made Kit wonder if he wasn't just a little bit more devious than she'd given him credit for.

Whump! Whump! Whump! His soles slapped together and echoed around Kit's ears. She edged nearer the door and tried to close it with her foot as Debbie rapped out a series of numbers from the front of her credit card. After discarding the idea of writing on the wall or Jerry's new shoe cupboard, Kit scrawled the digits in giant handwriting along her forearm. Debbie ended the call after reiterating the date for the next meeting and cutting Kit off mid-sentence.

Jerry left his boots outside and closed the front door behind him. His dark eyes widened in surprise to find Kit leaning against the wall. "You feeling better?" He stripped his grass stained tee shirt over his head to reveal abdominal muscles able to rival the torso Langdon kept hidden beneath his vestments. Balling the fabric into his hands, he asked her, "Do we put all our washing in together, or each do our own?"

Kit peeled her gaze away from defined pectorals and forced herself to look at his face in a bizarre role reversal of chauvinism. She gulped. "We're on mains water now.

And nobody wants their clothes swishing around with Langdon's socks."

"Fair enough." Jerry lifted his arm and used the dirty tee shirt to dry sweat from between his shoulder blades. Kit blinked and continued leaning against the wall until after he'd gone.

"What you doin'?" Raki clumped down the stairs carrying the vacuum cleaner. He reached the ground floor and bent to fit the plug into the socket. He glanced up when Kit didn't answer.

She shrugged. "I think I just ogled a vicar," she replied. "How sad is that?"

"Poor Kit." Raki slipped an arm around her shoulder, his task momentarily forgotten. "I thought you wanted to stay single."

"I do." She looked up at him with a sad smile. "But some days are harder than others."

Raki gave her a squeeze and let go. "You've always got us," he called over his shoulder. The vacuum cleaner roared to life and Kit retreated to her bedroom with the laptop.

She spent an hour ordering ten tubes of lube from an Australian supplier using Debbie's credit card. The website refused to play fair, spitting out her address because it didn't recognise the New Zealand rural post code. Eventually it accepted Marian's and she made a mental note to let her mother know she'd get a surprise delivery of a discreetly wrapped parcel of sex lube in the next week. No sense letting Kenny get overexcited.

Settling her head on her special, Curly Approved silk pillowcase just to rest for a moment, Kit woke up in the early hours with gritty eyes and a taste in her mouth like an old flip-flop. She shed her work clothes and clambered under the covers in her underwear.

-26-

Curly Companionship

Kit sat in Jerry's passenger seat and blew out a breath through pursed lips. Her heart hammered in her chest and she tried to get control over her state of hiking agitation.

Paul stood in the showroom talking to Gordy. He waved his arms as he spoke and Gordy's shoulders slumped deeper with every syllable from Paul's open mouth. Kit inhaled. "There he is. Little ray of sunshine."

"Looks like a character," Jerry commented. He lifted his hand and ran strong fingers through his dark fringe. "Interesting choice of clothing," he mused. "He looks like an M & M."

Kit snorted and peered through the windscreen at Paul's outfit. In tune with his elevated status, he'd donned a complete suit made from electric blue fabric. Expensive brown shoes and a matching brown waistcoat completed his ensemble. "He does look like he's got a chocolate centre," Kit giggled. She swallowed and the smile slipped from her lips. "I should go inside and meet my fate." She swallowed. "Do I look okay?"

Jerry smiled and his dark-eyed gaze coasted over her hair and face. "You look stunning," he replied.

Kit lifted a hand to touch the ringlet nearest her left cheek. She'd taken special care over her appearance, using more of her precious lube than advisable in the current shortage. She dropped her hand and flapped it at Jerry's dog collar. "Has Langdon asked you to start early?" He didn't reply and panic back-lit Kit's blue irises. "Please can you do your praying thing for me? I know my mum believes in God, but I can't tell her about this."

"I will." Jerry leaned sideways and laid a large hand over the fingers writhing in Kit's lap. "But you know you can pray for yourself, don't you?"

Kit swallowed and pursed her lips. "I think God's still angry," she confessed. "He won't answer me."

Jerry smiled and squeezed her fingers. His expression softened and his eyes glittered with kindness. "Perhaps it's you who needs to stop feeling angry with him," he whispered. He glanced at the clock on the dashboard, but his comment left Kit reeling. She was angry with God. For many things, but one in particular. Her father's death had rocked her world and she'd remained in a victim's state of righteous injustice. She couldn't see it changing any time soon.

"Come on, Miss Maguire. Let's get this farce over with." Jerry released her hand and unwound his tall body from the vehicle. The door clicked shut before Kit could catch a breath.

She spun from the car with a hiss of annoyance, tangling the strap of her handbag around the seatbelt. "I don't need a support person," she said, her panic rising as Jerry walked around to stand in front of her. He bent to free her handbag. "Langdon's orders," he said. "He wanted to come himself, but he's booked to speak at the high school this morning. We had a flat meeting last night and I'm your alternate representative. Raki thought the full rig might cause a stir." Jerry patted his black shirt and his fingers reached up and twitched his white collar.

"You had a flat meeting without me?" Kit's brows furrowed in dismay. Then her mind switched to her impending doom and her eyes widened. "I should go in alone. There are things I don't want you to know. Stupid things I've done."

Jerry blinked and he tilted his head to view her sideways. "You didn't kill your boss or make fake auction bids though?"

"No!" Kit's voice lifted enough to catch Paul's attention. He snapped upright and his eyes narrowed like a hungry dog spotting a crumb. Kit glanced at him and cringed. "No. Not that. But I had a relationship with someone at work many years ago and there's also the little matter of the new email address I put into the auction site for Paul's schilling account." She gulped. "Majorly dumb."

Jerry shrugged and fitted his customary good-natured smile onto his face. "So, now I know," he said. He opened the rear door and pulled a pad and pen from his back seat. Slipping his large hand under Kit's elbow, he tugged her around the back of the car and set a course for the open showroom doors. "Let's go."

Gordy escaped to his desk as Kit's high heels clattered over the metal runner which the huge doors fitted into when closed. Paul's eyes bugged and his lips parted at the sight of Jerry's dog collar. The curate dwarfed him, making him appear even more like a tiny M & M. As Kit led the way towards Alec's office, Paul turned and scurried behind them.

Alec saw them through the glass surrounding his office and stood to open the door. His eyebrows rose into his fringe at the sight of Jerry. When his gaze tracked to Jerry's hand on Kit's arm, he frowned and his lips pursed. "Come in," he said, gesturing towards seats set up around a circular table at the back of his office. Mr Roy's messy filing and his huge peace lily had disappeared.

Kit shuffled around the table to allow Jerry to take the seat next to her. He laid his pad and pen on the table next to his mobile phone. Her heart sank as Paul trooped in and closed the door with a click. Kit's mind turned it into the clang of a jail cell. Paul placed himself on the other side of her, leaning over as he settled in his chair.

"Murderer!" he hissed through the side of his mouth.

Kit's lips parted and she stared at him. The quick wit inherited from her father escaped before she could call it back. "Like you're murdering that suit?" she retorted.

Oblivious, Alec sat opposite Kit and shuffled papers in front of him. Dark lashes fluttered over his vibrant blue eyes and he heaved in a sigh as though finding the task difficult. He smiled at Jerry, displaying perfect, expensive dental work. "I'm Alexis Roy," he said, leaning across to shake Jerry's hand. "I didn't catch your name." Alec's gaze flicked to Kit and she kept her composure as he formed wrong assumptions about their relationship.

"Reverend Gerald Kirsch," Jerry replied. His handshake made Alec wince. He indicated the pad and pen. "I trust you don't mind if I record our meeting?"

"Not at all. This is Paul Roy," Alec said. He waved his arm towards his cousin and Paul stood to lean across Kit. She shrank back against Jerry so hard she almost tipped him off his chair.

Jerry cleared his throat and ignored Paul's outstretched hand. "I don't think the presence of Mr Paul Roy is appropriate," he replied. "Not under the circumstances."

Paul withdrew his hand as though slapped. "What?" he shouted. "I'm her manager. I got the evidence together for this complaint."

Kit's heart sank. She knew Alec could suspend her on

full pay while the police conducted their investigation, but an accusation of auction rigging with credible evidence meant the immediate termination of her contract. Not for the first time, she cursed her useless phone with its incriminating photograph.

Sticking to Jerry's side, she reached a hand under the table and seized a wad of smooth trouser fabric in her fingers. A sense of security and safety infused her and she relaxed. Jerry's large palm covered her fingers beneath the table. Glancing up, Kit saw frustration and disappointment bud in Alec's irises. She realised in that moment he still liked her.

Grasping hold of the figurative rope Jerry threw her, she straightened her shoulders and pulled it tight around Paul's neck. "I don't want him here," she stated. "I have evidence of my own. It compromises my position to have him present." She glanced sideways at Jerry, looking for help.

He cleared his throat. "You have a duty of care to your employees, Mr Roy," Jerry said. His voice rumbled with a low, gravelled quality. "Mr Paul Roy has harassed Miss Maguire for an extended period of time without repercussions and put her health in jeopardy. It's unfair to allow him to take part in any form of disciplinary action."

Alec's lips parted in shock and he stared at Paul. He lowered his voice. "What did you do?" he demanded.

"Nothing!" Paul exclaimed. He remained standing from Jerry's rebuff of his handshake. Kit spotted the price tag still hanging from his inside pocket as he waved his arms in the air. "She's a rubbish admin assistant," he blustered. He engaged in a bit more arm waving and his spit sprayed onto the glossy table surface as he protested.

"That's not true!" Kit argued. She jabbed a finger at Alec. "You said Mr Roy wanted to make me his personal assistant. He wouldn't do that if I didn't work hard and prove reliable."

Alec squirmed in his seat and Kit suspected the meeting hadn't gone as he'd planned.

Jerry looked at his watch and scraped his chair backwards. Kit's body shuddered with the effort of not plunging through the gap that appeared between the chairs. "This meeting is over," Jerry said. "It creates an unfair bias against Miss Maguire." Lifting his phone from the table, he fiddled with the screen and slipped it into his breast pocket. "I'll transcribe the notes from this recording and send you a copy. Are you ready, Miss Maguire?"

Kit blinked and snatched her handbag from beneath the table. She rose, not understanding what just happened.

"That's an illegal recording!" Paul screeched. "You can't do that!" He reached across Kit to make a grab for Jerry's front pocket and knocked her back into her chair.

Jerry's face darkened and he raised a long index finger and stuck it in front of Paul's nose. "How dare you assault Miss Maguire!" he snapped. The timbre of his voice ricocheted around the glass office. "Mr Alexis Roy gave permission for me to record the meeting before we started. I specifically asked."

Alec swallowed and ran a hand across his forehead. Sweat beaded near his hairline. "I thought you meant write it down," he conceded. His hands spread in front of him in placation and defeat. "This isn't going quite how I anticipated. Paul, I think you should leave." His gaze flicked to his cousin and to Kit's surprise, Paul dropped into his seat and folded his arms like a petulant child.

"Oops, still recording. I pressed the wrong button." Jerry tapped his breast pocket. "I'd just like to note that Mr Paul Roy refused to leave the meeting. I'll add that to the transcript along with a note to explain that he assaulted Miss Maguire." Jerry stretched his fingers out to Kit and she took them, using his strength to help her rise on wobbly legs. Snatching up his pad and pen as he squeezed from behind the table, Jerry strode towards the door, trailing Kit after him.

Her heels clattered over the tiled showroom floor and Gordy looked up from his paperwork. His down turned lips radiated misery. Assuming Paul's elevated status was the culprit, Kit shot him a weak smile of consolation. Jerry barrelled towards his car and she clip-clopped behind him, her tight skirt restricting the movement of her legs.

Gordy's sidekick stood by Jerry's car and he looked up as they approached. "Hey, Kit," Barry said, his smile genuine. He pointed towards the old, red Mustang. "This is in incredible condition. Will you let me make you an offer?" His lips paused at the sight of Jerry's dog collar, but his car-worship overrode any hesitation. "Is this yours?"

"Yep." Jerry nodded with enthusiasm. "I took a gap year after graduating from law school and toured the States. There are models like this just rusting in back yards. It cost me nothing to bring it to New Zealand because an emigrating friend had some room left in his shipping crate."

"Law school?" Kit released his hand. "Before God-school."

"Yep. I worked as a lawyer for ten years. I'm older than I look." Jerry's eyes twinkled with amusement. He turned towards her. "Oh, you should grab your car while we're here. You don't want the M & M to clamp it out of spite."

Kit swallowed and backed away. Her fingers shook as they hauled her car key from her handbag. She inhaled and blew out the breath, still confused about what just happened in Alec's office. She walked to the far side of the car park and skirted the boundary fence, wanting to slip out of the compound without seeing Jason or his mechanics. A deep sense of shame infused her soul, even though she knew she'd done nothing wrong.

She approached her yellow Beetle from behind it. The

sight of its rounded wheel arches and bubble shaped roof sent a lump into her throat as she held in her distress. Kit knew she'd feel better once she climbed onto the ancient leather seats and started the engine, drawing comfort from the tick-a-tick-a of its Volkswagen engine.

"Katharine." Alec Roy stepped out from behind Jason's filthy SUV. His lips pursed into a thin line. "We need to talk."

-27-

Curly Cringe

"I have nothing to say to you, Alec. Just leave me alone." Kit's fingers fumbled and she dropped her car key onto the concrete with a clang. Bending to pick it up, her heart rate increased to send blood pounding through her head at the sight of Alec's shoes moving closer in her peripheral vision. "Just go!" she gasped. "Do you want me to scream for Jerry?" She rose and fitted the key into the lock. "Leave me alone."

"I know you didn't kill Dad." Alec exhaled. "It's ridiculous. If you'd gone to see him about the schilling, he'd have sat down and talked to you about it. He had a soft spot for you, Katharine."

Kit's driver's door made a guttural creak as she hauled it open and tossed her handbag across into the passenger seat. Her shoulders slumped and every muscle ached. "I didn't go to see him about the schilling because I wasn't doing it!" Her words emerged through gritted teeth.

Sighing, she rested her forehead against the roof of her car. "You broke my heart, Alec. Just a note saying sorry and a casual mention by one of the sales guys that you'd moved to Palmy to take over a franchise there. You reduced our relationship to a quick, dirty fling right when I needed you the most. You made me keep our relationship a secret because you played me, Alec. I was the gullible teenage office girl and you were the boss' son. It sounds like a cheap romance novel. You made me feel worthless." Kit said the words and swallowed, as though hearing them for the first time. He hadn't made her feel worthless; she'd let him.

"I'm sorry." Alec took another step forward. "It was twelve years ago, Katharine. We need to sort out what's happening now." A tone of desperation entered his voice and Kit frowned. He'd dismissed her pain in a single sentence consisting of five words and her old name.

Inhaling through her nose and breathing in courage, Kit stood and pushed her shoulders back. "My name is Kit," she said. Her father called her Katharine and he hadn't done that for over twelve years. "I wouldn't know where to start schilling and didn't even know such a thing existed until my flat-mate explained. He's told the cops that and they have evidence of my innocence if they can retrieve it. And I didn't kill Mr Roy. I couldn't lift a finger to hurt that beautiful man. So, leave me alone, Alec. Please. I'm sorry for your loss and all your pain. But leave me alone."

Alec tried to speak over her tirade several times. She recognised the moment he gave up and took the conversation in a different direction. He didn't even try to understand her grievance with him. "I need you to come back. Be my personal assistant." Alec took another step nearer, naked hunger in his eyes. "I saw the letter in Dad's stuff when I tidied the office. We both know you need this job."

Kit scoffed. "Are you joking?" Her heart gave a fleeting skip at the thought of him sticking around and not returning to Palmerston North. She squashed it with a trailer load of bitterness and regret. "One minute you're dragging me into your office with a support person to fire me. The next, you're offering me a promotion?"

"It wasn't like that." Alec's lips tightened. His fingers twitched and she knew him well enough to see him itching for a cigarette. "I wanted to get to the bottom of things. Properly. I knew when the email came through that something was wrong. I watched the auction for that convertible and it went too high." His fingers reached up to touch a bouncing red curl in Kit's fringe. His shoulders slumped as she jerked her head back. "I phoned the IT guy and he said you were worried about your login being compromised. You told him Paul did it. I'd already set off to Hamilton early the next morning when I got the call about Dad."

Kit shook her head. "I changed the password on the auction site as well as the email address. You didn't know the new one."

Alec shrugged. His hair ruffled in a gust of wind and he settled the straight layers flat with his palm. "I just clicked the button to say I'd forgotten my password. It sent a link to my email address and I put in a different one."

"Right," Kit conceded. "Do you still think I did it?"

"No." Alec dismissed her fears with a shake of his head. "Why did you send it to my email address though? Why not my dad's?"

Kit heaved a sigh and stared down at the toes of her patent black stilettos. "He didn't open his emails. Janice used to open them for him and print them. Then he read them and just phoned people. He didn't like his computer." She pursed her lips and allowed the flood of sadness to fill her chest cavity. Mr Roy was gone, deleted from the face of the earth as though he never existed. She took a step forward. "How did he die, Alec? He didn't suffer, did he?"

Deep furrows appeared in his forehead and his nostrils flared. Genuine pain filled his eyes. "He had a heart attack, but the cops found signs of a struggle. Bruising. Stuff thrown around. He sustained injuries which make them think he got into a fight with someone. The medical examiner said the heart attack came last, so yes, he died frightened and in pain."

"That's terrible." Kit placed a hand over her mouth. "He didn't deserve that."

"No, he didn't." Alec looked down at Kit and a void opened behind his eyes. "Now I'm stuck here in Hamilton trying to sort everything out. Help me?"

Kit swallowed and felt her heart thaw at the misery resonating behind his words. "Okay. But please will you tell the cops I'm not schilling? They think it's a motive for me to kill Mr Roy."

Alec winced. "The cops will find out you didn't do it, Katharine. They're not stupid."

"But you could tell them," she urged. "You could tell them I didn't do it and they'd drop their interest in me."

"And transfer it onto my cousin." An air of finality entered Alec's voice. Family before fealty. Kit gulped and stared up into his eyes. She shook her head and pushed her car door open wider, shock lodging like a stone in her gut.

Alec let out a huff of irritation and frowned. "Don't be like this," he said. "If it's not you, then it's him. My family need no more grief right now." His voice rose and Kit heard aggravation creep into his tone. She dropped into her driver's seat.

"You're not your father's son," she hissed. "You're nothing like him." She locked her door against Alec's grip on the handle, firing the engine and cranking the gear stick into reverse with a grinding sound.

Tearing backwards out of her parking space, Kit saw Alec leap back in shock as she almost ran over his shiny shoes. "You stupid idiot!" she yelled at her reflection in the rear-view mirror as she made the turn onto the main road. "You just let him shaft you a second time."

-28-

Curly Sergeant Major

K it paced the lounge with her fingers clasped behind her back. She sensed her frantic behaviour alarmed the boys. Taking a deep breath, she turned to face them. A collective cringe met her gaze as they huddled on the sofa in a line of long legs and rounded knees.

"Right!" Kit said, lowering her pitch from hysterical to piqued. She aimed an index finger at Raki's innocent face. "You need to find that baseball cap. If that's all the cops have got to add credence to their ridiculous video footage, then let's find it and prove it doesn't contain my DNA."

"You gave a DNA sample?" Jerry's eyebrows waggled. "Without a lawyer?"

Kit groaned. "I did a lot of stupid things under duress, Jerry. The detective kept threatening me with court orders and warrants. I know I'm innocent, so I just gave them what they wanted."

"Classic mistake." Jerry wrinkled his nose and glanced

sideways at Langdon. "You know not to do that, don't you?"

Langdon's blond head jerked backwards and he edged away from Jerry. "I don't imagine finding myself in that situation!" He shot a glance at Kit and cringed. "Sorry. You didn't deserve to end up there either."

Kit nodded to acknowledge his apology and continued her circular pacing. "Jerry, acting as my lawyer, can you get a look at that video tape?"

Jerry scratched his chin. "I'll see, but you need to plan for the worst, Kit. I don't think they'll give you access to it."

"What can I do?" Langdon wrinkled his nose and the bruising from his black eye appeared darker. Kit's brow furrowed.

"Ponder this," she said, performing another three strides in a circle. Motion sickness kicked in and she swayed on her feet as though she'd just left a merry-go-round. She blinked and continued. "Who killed Mr Roy and why?"

"What?" Langdon's jaw dropped open. "That's not fair. Can't I just look for something around the house? I'll help Raki look for his cap."

Kit slumped into her reading chair with a gargantuan sigh. "This is all too hard," she groaned. "Someone used the key from my desk drawer to get back into the garage after hours. They either stole it while my back was turned or used a spare key to get access to my desk. That means the killer is a colleague. They hid their face beneath a baseball cap and despite my alibi, the police still think it was me. Perhaps this mystery woman got into a fight with Mr Roy and hurt him. But there are only two other women who work at the garage and they're nothing like me. They're a lot older. One walks with a limp after a line dancing accident last year and the other leaves at lunchtime."

"Okay." Langdon twinkled his fingers over his knees,

treating them like piano keys. He stared at the ceiling. "So, either one of the men dressed up as a woman or it was a customer." He stared at Kit. "Do you keep your drawer locked at all times?"

She blew out a breath. "Not during the day because I'm never far away. But I always lock it at night before I leave." Her fingers twitched as though acting out the task. "I take my handbag from the bottom drawer and lock the whole unit with the front door key inside it. Then I leave."

"Do you remember if your drawer was locked when you returned to work after the murder?" Langdon cocked his head.

Kit buried her face in her hands and tried to remember. She ran through the scenario in her head. "I got to work, Gordy came in to ask me to schedule a service and got talking about Mr Roy's death." Her eyes widened. "No! It wasn't locked! Things had moved on my desk and it distracted me. I just pulled the drawer open without thinking about it and everything inside looked rearranged. Someone suggested the police might have searched it. Then a customer hammered on the door and Paul went nuts." She lifted a hand to her throat. "The police would have broken it open if they believed it was important. Or demanded the key. They haven't mentioned it."

Jerry lifted his giant hand and after a moment's hesitation, Langdon high-fived it. "Good work," Jerry said. "Let's go back to the customers. Would they even know that's where you kept the front door key?"

Kit winced. "No, but look, the day I discovered the front door key missing, I didn't leave the office. I stuck close to my desk all that day to stop Paul getting onto my computer and finding out what I'd done with the auction site."

"Right." Langdon nodded and scratched at the stubble on his chin. "No one broke into your desk after hours just to get the front door key because if they broke in, they were already in. I think you're right. It's a colleague. Would you have noticed it missing when you locked up the night Mr Roy died?"

Kit nodded. "Yes. The tack looks kinda naked without the key." Her head bobbed up and down and her curls bounced. She blew out through her nose. "And I kept my drawer locked while the key was missing and yet found it unlocked when the key turned up again. Whoever took it didn't put it back in the same place as though they wanted me to think I'd made a mistake."

Raki shuffled forward on the couch, perhaps deciding Kit looked less rabid. Langdon's eyes narrowed to slits. "You're sure there isn't another key to your desk drawer?"

"I don't think so." Kit's head rocked forward and back, getting slower as she realised she didn't know for sure.

"What about when you had a sick day?" Jerry asked. "How did they unlock the front door then?"

"I'm never sick," Kit replied. "And I've never needed time off for anything, except my dad's funeral. Mr Roy closed the garage that day and they all came to support me." She swallowed. Not all of them. "But Mr Roy had a master key. Gordy found it in the safe. We'd never used it before the other day."

Raki let out a snuff. "Why would someone go to all those lengths to get your door key from a locked drawer when there was a master key in your boss' office?"

Kit wrinkled her nose. "Only I knew about that one. You'd need the combination to Mr Roy's safe and Gordy had that. I didn't."

"Why did you know about the spare and nobody else?" Raki leaned forward.

Kit tapped her chin with her index finger. "Mr Roy mentioned it when I first started at the garage twelve years ago. I got to work earlier than anyone else and opening the front door is in my job description. He mentioned there was a master key in his office if I ever got into difficulty.

He didn't say where and I've never needed it."

"What about the security company?" Raki asked.

Kit nodded. "They have a master key. The security guard locks up at night and a different guard unlocks in the morning. They don't unlock the service entrance because the customers will just dump their keys everywhere. I use my key in the morning." She swallowed. "I did use my key. Past tense." Her face sank into her hands. "I no longer have the key, a desk or a job," she groaned. "What will I do?"

"Take the job the new boss offered," Raki suggested.

Kit's vehement head shake hurt her neck. "No way!" she exclaimed. "He'll save Paul before he steps up for me. I don't want to work for a man like that. He knows the truth but is content to throw me under the bus!"

Jerry puckered his lips and extracted himself from the sofa cushions. He left a dent and Langdon put a hand out to stop himself rolling into it. "First thing's first," Jerry announced. "Let's find this baseball cap. Then you need to ask Piper if she had a spare key to your desk hidden somewhere in your office."

The phone in the hall sent out its pathetic ring tone from the receiver on the wall. Kit shrank back into her seat. Raki loped across the room and lifted the receiver, waiting for a moment before speaking. Kit groaned as he pulled the curly cable and stepped back into the lounge. "It's for you," he said. "Your mum says she's calling the cops because Steph's gone out for a run. She thinks she's having a mental breakdown."

-29-

Curly Calamity

"She's not suicidal, Mum! She can go out for a run if she wants to." Kit punched the air in victory for Steph. "Good on her wanting to improve her health."

"I wondered if you'd go out and look for her." Marian's words formed a staccato beat in Kit's ears, signifying her mother's uptick towards panic. "She might have suffered a heart attack with the extra weight she's carrying. And why won't you answer your mobile phone?"

"It's dead," Kit said, omitting its current residential status with the New Zealand police force. She took a deep breath and tried not to grind her teeth. "She only left five minutes ago. Even a coronary takes longer than that. If she doesn't come home before dark, then call me and I'll go for a drive. Actually, call me anyway. If she's not sweating, then she's meeting a boy around the corner because she doesn't want you or Kenny to know." Kit said goodbye to Marian and ended the call.

Jerry clattered in the kitchen, hauling a glass from a cupboard and running it under the tap. He jerked his head at Kit as she leaned on the counter. "I spoke to my father. We can't get access to the video footage until the discovery part of the process. That angle is a bust."

"Discovery?" Kit frowned.

"Yeah. It comes after the police charge you for murder and send you through the magistrate's court for processing. The defence gets full discovery of everything in the prosecution's armoury before a crown court trial. They don't need to show us anything before that."

"Oh." Kit rested her chin on her forearms. "Why did you call your dad?"

"He's Gerald Lawrence QC." Jerry took a slug of his drink. "Well, the senior one. I was Gerald Lawrence QC Junior."

Words failed Kit as she looked up at the capable hands clasping the delicate glass. "So, you knew the answer anyway." Her voice sounded flat.

"Yeah. Sorry. That's not the only reason I called him. I'm no longer a practicing lawyer, Kit. I'm a curate. He's agreed to act for you if you need him. He's good."

"Thank you." Kit's mood plummeted even lower. "I can't afford a lawyer, especially not one of his calibre. I recognise the name. Wasn't he splashed all over the news about four years ago for defending gang members? He said everyone deserved a fair trial."

Jerry swallowed. "That was me." His eyelashes fluttered and he stared at the tiled floor. He looked like he might be counting tiles. "And I still believe that."

"Oh, gosh," Kit groaned. She pressed her forehead against her wrists and closed her eyes. "It's so hard to believe in the system, but I'm left with no choice."

"It's a good system." Jerry leaned his hip against the other side of the counter. A large palm landed on Kit's back and a soporific stroking motion moved across her muscles. She experienced a wave of gratitude. Men who didn't touch her curls were rare. "It will spit you out because you're innocent, Kit. Don't worry."

"And if it doesn't?" She lifted her head to watch Jerry's expression.

He didn't falter, leaning across to kiss her forehead in a way that felt neither inappropriate nor seedy. "Then you have the Messrs Gerald Lawrence QC at your free disposal." He set his glass on the counter and gave her a wink. "Don't put that in the dishwasher, I'm coming back for it after I've filled the cracks in the ceiling of the sleepout." With a last squeeze of her shoulder, Jerry stalked from the room and the back door clicked shut behind him.

Kit moped around the kitchen listening to Raki and Langdon turning out his bedroom to look for the baseball cap. She entertained herself with their muffled argument about the best way to fold a sock. The Yellow Pages gave her Piper's home telephone number and Kit rang her using the land-line in the hallway.

"Yes." Piper confirmed the existence of another key. "I kept it in that little tin in my desk drawer in case you ever lost yours. I don't think I ever used it. Have you lost yours?"

"Don't worry, I just needed the spare for something."

Langdon yelped as Raki dropped his laundry basket on his foot and then they argued about the lifespan of boxer shorts with holes. The volume rose in the hallway and Kit wedged a finger in her ear and said goodbye to Piper. It dawned on her that she was wasting valuable hours of potential freedom she might one day regret not putting to better use. Grabbing her car keys, she fired up her yellow Beetle with a particular destination in mind.

Mr Rashid waved to her from behind the counter as Kit entered the dairy. She winced, wishing she could make her purchase with his more understanding wife. Tracking to the aisle selling tampons, condoms and lubricants, Kit took a circuitous route to make sure she saw nobody familiar. As the last customer pushed a stroller laden with groceries through the door, Kit made a dash for the lube. "Rock it, girl," she whispered, bolstering her courage. "It doesn't matter what other people think of you. This is a Hair Emergency Code Red."

Kit's fingers trembled with anticipation as she lifted the last tube of purple-willy-shaped-lube.

"I see you!" a voice boomed. An Indian sounding voice. Kit screamed and threw the lube into the air, grappling to catch it again as it twisted and began its precarious descent. She fumbled it but managed to save the plastic container from bursting open on the hard floor.

"Mr Rashid!" she snapped, clutching the precious lube to her breast. "What are you doing?" She looked around but couldn't see him.

"Watching you through my new camera," he replied. "And speaking through the speaker. What do you think to my security improvements?" The speaker above Kit's head crackled and hissed over Mr Rashid's Punjab accent.

Kit spun on her heel and noticed a glass dome in the ceiling. She stuck her tongue out.

"What are you doing in the sexy aisle?" Mr Rashid asked. His voice held the lilt of humour. Kit heard the clatter of footsteps crossing the threshold and the front door beeped to warn of incoming customers. She shoved the purple-willy-shaped lube under her shirt and marched towards the front of the shop.

"Not funny!" she hissed as she lifted her shirt to reveal her spoils. "And I'm not putting this on the counter for you to hold up and shout to Mrs Rashid for a price check."

Mr Rashid's smile involved all his facial muscles and left his large teeth welded together at the front. He waved his brown hand at her. "Oh, don't be so sensitive." His head bobbed from side to side and his straight, black hair shuddered. "Nothing wrong with a little lubrication. I am being very pleased you have a boyfriend."

"I don't have a boyfriend!" Kit stage whispered. "I use this on my hair."

Mr Rashid's eyebrows rose and fell like a furry Mexican wave. "I know a lovely Muslim boy with strong teeth and a reasonable income. Good sense of humour and I know for a fact he likes romantic bush walks."

Kit's eyes narrowed. "Does Raj know you've been stalking his Tinder profile again?"

Mr Rashid's head bobbled faster. "No and you won't tell him." He flapped his hand at the lube. "On the house, on the house," he gushed. "For your hair." His exaggerated wink looked more like a nervous tic. He lifted his left arm and rubbed at his sleeve. His face creased in a scowl. "Stupid old age," he grumbled. "Pins and needles."

Kit sighed. She turned sideways to smile at the overweight customer browsing the nearby confectionery aisle before shoving the lube down the front of her pants. "Don't suppose you've got a plastic bag?" she asked Mr Rashid with a wince.

His wide, alarmed eyes and slow head shake accompanied an inability to remove his gaze from the bump in the front of Kit's pants. Then he laughed and pointed, jerking his head at the chocolate buying customer who jumped back with a guilty look on her face. "She looks like a lady-boy, no?" he demanded.

Kit spun away, but not before the woman's brow furrowed in confusion. Shock spread across her face as she spotted the lump. "That's disgusting in a public place!" she exclaimed. She shelved the multipack of artery cloggers without care and wobbled from the shop. Mr Rashid watched the potential sale walk through the front doors with a shrug. The security buzzer beeped twice as she left as though confused about whether she represented one or two people.

"You did that," Kit said, loading her voice with

accusation. "You just lost a sale."

"She'll be back." Mr Rashid shrugged. "She's just teasing herself with the chocolate fish. She has a weakness for dairy milk. Jumbo size."

"You're a very wicked man," Kit sighed. "I remember your fat-jokes well."

"Ah, but they are being successful." Mr Rashid leaned a hand across the counter and pointed right at Kit's flat stomach. "You is skinny now."

"Not because of the humiliation." Kit's tone rebuked him; the sentiment wasted. "People have to want to lose weight, get fit and fix their hair issues." Her index finger strayed to her fringe and she slipped it through the coils of a ringlet. She glanced at the newspaper headline facing upward from the counter. It showed an image of the fated ship, Nicola. She appeared even more lopsided than when Kit saw her in person. "You have no idea how much stress that ship has put me under," she grumbled. Looking up, Kit blinked in surprise.

"Mr Rashid?" She spun around in confusion. "Where did you go?"

A guttural groan came from behind the counter and Kit leaned across the stack of newspapers. Mr Rashid lay on the rubber mat in front of the cigarette cupboard. He clutched a shaking hand to his chest and his lips flattened to pain filled white lines.

-30-

Curly Friends

Kit leap-frogged the counter, belly flopping the last few centimetres and sending the newspapers scattering across the shop floor. The lube shot from her pants and rolled towards the fridge. "Mr Rashid!" she gasped, dropping to her knees.

"Pain," he groaned. "Pain." His eyelids shuttered and his brown skin adopted a grey hue. "My arm."

Kit's fingers scrabbled in her pockets, remembering the location of her phone before the panic took hold of her limbs. "Please, don't die," she hissed. "Please, don't die." She reached for Mr Rashid's collar and tried to loosen the buttons. He stopped clutching his chest long enough to slap her fingers with his right hand. "I'm trying to help you!" Kit complained. She sat back on her haunches. "Are you having a heart attack or just messing around?"

Mr Rashid groaned again. "Don't feel so good. Ache in my chest and arm."

"I'll get help." Kit rose and cast around for the battered

phone which used to hang behind the counter. She lifted it and pressed zero to make an internal call to the apartment upstairs.

A rough male voice answered. "Yeah?"

"Raj, Raj!" Kit gasped. "Is that you?"

"Yeah. What's happened? Where's Dad?"

Kit glanced down at Mr Rashid. "He's on the floor. He just collapsed. Please, can you call an ambulance while I check on him?" She pulled on the phone cord and grimaced. "I can't dial emergency and reach him at the same time."

"Okay." Raj sounded capable and clipped. "I'll do it now. I'm on my way downstairs."

Kit sank to her knees next to the stricken Mr Rashid. "Let me put you in the recovery position," she said. A memory of distant first aid lessons returned and her hands went to work, bending Mr Rashid into the approved position.

"I don't want to be a pretzel," he grumbled.

"Shut up or I'll tie you in a knot," Kit retorted. She frowned when he didn't reply, the lack of a retort both uncharacteristic and unnerving. "Are you still with us?" she said, her voice trembling. Mr Rashid nodded, his cheek rubbing against the dirty rubber matting. Kit heard the rumbling of feet against the stairs and held her breath, desperate for help to appear.

Raj Rashid raced through a side door, a body like Adonis and silky dark hair swept off his forehead. His muscles rippled as he leapt the counter and joined Kit on the floor, bearing no resemblance to the skinny teenager she used to work with after school.

"How is he?" Raj demanded. He nodded to the voice piping through the phone against his ear. Kit saw his fingers shaking. The image brought back a flood of misery at the memory of her father's lingering death.

"He's stopped insulting me," she whispered. Her brow furrowed. "It must be bad."

"Dad, Dad." Raj nudged his father's shoulder and received a groan in reply. "He's not talking," he said to the emergency operator. "A friend put him in the recovery position."

Kit swallowed as he classified her as closer than she imagined. It hurt her heart in a peculiar and unexpected way. Reaching out, she rubbed her fingers over Mr Rashid's ratty green cardigan in a comforting motion. Not a former boss or an acquaintance. Friend.

"Help is coming," she whispered to him. His eyelashes fluttered and he drew his uppermost knee in tighter to his stomach. His teeth began to chatter and Kit stripped off her light jacket and laid it over his torso. "Don't worry about anything," she whispered. "Help is coming. Try to hold out for them otherwise Raj is giving you mouth to mouth." She saw his lip curl up a fraction and heaved a sigh of relief. His sense of humour hadn't gone yet. She smoothed her palm over his shoulder and tried to rub away the pain in his left arm. When she reached for his wrist, his hand lifted and his fingers closed around hers.

Raj continued to answer questions, leaning around Kit to check on his father. "He's not as grey," he said into the phone. He slipped an arm around Kit's shoulder and rested his chin on top of her head. It created an open line of communication through which he channelled his terror and misery. The door buzzer sounded and they both jumped. Raj kept the phone against his ear and popped up to see over the counter. "We're closed," he said to the person who'd walked into the shop. "I'm sorry." He jerked his head towards the door and Kit heard grumbling and footsteps.

"I'll lock the door," she murmured. Raj backed up so she could rise and step past him. He took her place by his father as she lifted the hatch built into the counter and stepped back into the shop. It took seconds to cross the familiar concrete floor and close the front door. Kit reached up to secure the top bolt with a sense of deja vu, feeling it slide into place in obedience to her fingers.

"Wait there to let the paramedics in?" Raj's voice caught and Kit swallowed. She heard him trying to rouse Mr Rashid without success. Tears rose from a place she'd buried deep in her psyche and prickled behind her eyelids. She closed her eyes and stood behind the door, listening for the sound of sirens and willing them to hurry.

"Kit?" The muffled call accompanied rapping on the door and she opened her eyes. They widened at the sight of Paul standing a few centimetres from her face. "Open the door!" he insisted. "I need to buy milk. This isn't funny!" He cupped a hand over his eyes and peered through the glass.

"Sod off!" Kit shouted. Irrational rage bubbled like lava in her stomach. "Go away!"

"I need to get in." Paul's familiar whine lit a match in her brain. "Open the door."

"Go away!" she reiterated. She accompanied her words with the slap of her palm against the glass. Paul's head jerked backwards.

Kit gaped in surprise as a woman tugged at the sleeve of Paul's lurid blue suit jacket. A woman with blonde curls and heavy makeup. "Let's go, Paul," she pleaded. Her gaze flicked to Kit and she paused. "It's closed. We can get some at the supermarket."

Paul turned away with a snarl. His stiff-legged gait took him stomping back to his car.

Cindy swallowed and her lips tightened as she acknowledged Kit with the slightest upward jerk of her head.

-31-

Curly Stand-in

Paul's car remained in the disabled parking spot outside Mr Rashid's shop. He kept the engine running and glared at Kit through his windscreen. The ambulance arrived and parked behind him, preventing him leaving even if he changed his mind.

Kit unbolted the door and admitted the two paramedics. Then she locked it. They introduced themselves and she led them to where Mr Rashid lay behind the counter. The emergency operator ended the call with Raj, leaving him free to speak to the paramedics.

"He's saying his left arm hurts," Kit said. Her fingers writhed together in front of her. "We were chatting and he said he had pins and needles. I looked away for a second and he'd collapsed when I looked back." Mr Rashid lay motionless on the floor, but Kit saw his eyes squeezed together. It gave her hope. He was alive, but either in paroxysms of pain or humiliation.

The female paramedic fixed a cannula into Mr Rashid's

inner right arm, after unwinding it from the recovery position. Kit stepped back from the small space to allow them room to work. They fixed up monitoring equipment and rapped out instructions to each other in hushed voices.

Raj stood next to Kit, hopping from foot to foot on the other side of the counter. "I told him to slow down," he hissed. "Mum begged him to visit the doctor months ago. He said he did, but you know him. I bet the old fart lied." He gnawed on his lower lip and Kit felt her stomach flip.

"This is awful," she breathed. Reaching up, she covered her face with her hands. "This is terrible."

A strong arm snaked around her shoulders and Raj pulled her into his side. "No, it's not as bad as it could have been. At least you were here and managed to get help. Imagine if it happened when the shop was empty. He could lay there and the gits around here would just loot the shop until they'd taken everything he owned." Raj's sentiments explained the presence of the new cameras.

Kit swallowed and nodded. She jumped as the female paramedic stood. "I'm nipping outside to grab the stretcher from the back of the van," she said. "Do you want to stop people trying to get in?"

Kit nodded. Another round of knocking on the door echoed through the shop. She followed the woman to the door and released the bolt, standing in the gap as the paramedic jogged to the ambulance. Paul shot from his driver's door and accosted her as she hauled the stretcher onto the road.

"I think she's a serial killer," he spat. He turned and jabbed a finger in Kit's direction. The other thwarted customers gathered in the car park and turned to watch the free drama. "She's killed once already this week." He fixed his hands on his hips and oozed fake importance. "You should call the cops."

"I'm not discussing this with you," the paramedic

replied. She locked the legs of the stretcher and slammed the ambulance door. "Thanks for your information. I'll pass it on to someone."

"But you don't understand!" Paul spun around and followed her. "She's a killer. I bet she did it."

Tears welled in Kit's eyes. His accusation, coupled with the whispered conversations taking place behind hands in her peripheral vision, destroyed a chunk of her hard-won confidence. The paramedic gave her a sympathetic smile and paused as Kit fumbled the bolt closed above the door. "He's just an idiot," she said, her tone soothing. "Mr Rashid's heart is in difficulty. From what his son says, it's been happening for a while."

Kit nodded and stared at the worn concrete beneath her feet. "Will he get better?" she asked, her voice sounding faint.

The paramedic leaned sideways and squeezed her shoulder. "We'll take him up to the hospital and he'll get the assistance he needs there. You did well putting him into the recovery position and calling for help. Don't beat yourself up." She smiled and Kit managed a watery one in return.

It took mere moments to get Mr Rashid onto the stretcher and load the various monitors on with him. Time had seemed to stand still and yet when Kit looked at her watch, she saw over an hour had elapsed. Her realisation of the time explained the increased number of knocks on the bolted door. The paper boys had arrived. Mr Rashid groaned and waved his right arm towards the back of the shop. Kit frowned and shot a look at Raj. "The paper delivery," she hissed. "Do they still leave it outside the back door?"

"I don't care. I'm going with my dad." His lower lip trembled. "The business means nothing without him."

Kit glanced back at the stretcher and found Mr Rashid jerking his head at her. His brown face looked grey and sick against the white pillow. A groan punctuated each jerk of his head and Kit's heart sank. The business meant everything to him. She sensed Raj's declaration caused him a different kind of heart pain. The shop encompassed Mr Rashid's identity. He was the owner of the dairy on the corner of Main Street and Gordonton Road.

"I'll take care of everything." A sigh accompanied the slump of her shoulders. She waved a hand of dismissal at Raj. "Go with your father. I'll manage."

Unlocking the front door admitted a tide of irritated customers. The paramedics waited until the flow steadied before pushing their way out to the ambulance. Kit directed the paper boys towards the back of the shop with instructions for filling their own bags. "One chocolate bar each if you do a good job," she said, her tone firm. "Fast as you can and I'll give out the chocolate. Don't help yourselves."

The customers milled around the store, snatching up their wanted items at speed and causing a backlog at the cash register. Kit managed them with ease, settling into the familiar busyness with an air of competence and calm. The paper boys lined up along the front of the counter, their upturned faces eager and their eyes bright. After looking around at the others, the largest boy spoke. "We're done, Miss. Clark's bringing the extras for the newspaper stand." He jerked his head towards the rack next to the counter. A crumpled copy of yesterday's news lurked in the bottom.

Kit paused while the nearest customer punched her pin number into the credit card machine. She gaped as a pair of spindly legs appeared at the end of the personal hygiene aisle. The Roman sandals emerged first and then grey school shorts, an almost non-existent backside and a bent body. It appeared in reverse, the head coming last. "Why is he walking backwards?" Kit demanded. The line of customers stopped gossiping with each other to stare.

"It's heavy." The biggest boy frowned and pursed his

lips as though Kit should know better than to ask such a stupid question.

Kit sighed as the tiniest boy in the crew tugged on the rope binding the newspapers together. He grunted, groaned and sweated his way backwards across the shop to the counter. His mousy hair stuck up at weird angles on his head and his arms hung limp by his sides. By the time he'd tugged the stack to its destination, he looked like he needed more than a sugar rush to get him back on his bicycle. Kit pointed at the stack and back to the row of watching boys. "It didn't occur to you to help him?" she asked, sighing even before she received the answer.

They looked around at each other as though it hadn't entered their heads. Then the largest boy spoke up. "Can we have our chocolate now?"

Kit heaved in a breath. "Fair's fair," she agreed. "You did what I asked." Bending down behind the counter, she emerged with an armful of chocolate bars. Big ones.

"Wow!" Clark breathed. His eyes widened to the size of tea plates. "Awesome!" He needed both hands to accept the bar from her.

The other boys grabbed their unexpected treats and disappeared; the clattering of bicycles interspersed with the crinkling of foil wrappers. Kit turned her attention back to serving the customers and hoped the boys didn't check the expiry date. Mr Rashid only kept goods behind the counter for one reason.

The remaining customers either complained about the delay or asked after Mr Rashid. Kit plastered a fake smile on her face and dodged both inquiry and insults with equal grace. After ten minutes, it felt as though she'd never left her spot behind the counter, never had a whole other life elsewhere. And had not been arrested for murder.

The customers filtered away until only one remained. She hung at the back, clutching a carton of soy milk to her breast like a fragile kitten.

"Where is he?" Kit demanded. "He's banned until Mr Rashid gets back."

"Paul's in the car." Cindy's manicured hands pushed the carton onto the counter. "I'm sorry about everything."

Kit snatched the carton and rang the amount into the cash register. The drawer sprang open with a ping and she accepted Cindy's cash. "What are you sorry for exactly?" she demanded. "For being married to an ass or something else?"

Cindy swallowed and withdrew the carton. "I'm just sorry," she breathed. She turned and left, her blonde curls bouncing against her shoulder. Kit observed the shape of the ringlets with a practiced eye and shook her head. The woman needed lube.

-32-

Curly Thoughts

Kit salvaged the tube of lube from the floor and found a paper bag under the counter to disguise it. Her Visa card choked on the small price and forced her to leave Mr Rashid an IOU on a sticky note.

Raj returned as she made the decision to close the shop two hours earlier than usual. "Yeah, I'll help you," he sighed. He pulled the board in from outside and cashed up the money in the register. "I'll lock this in the safe upstairs."

"Did you find your mother?" Kit spoke as she fixed another roll of receipt paper into the credit card machine.

"She went to my brother's place for lunch," he said. His shoulders slumped. "Aban just extended their shop. She wanted to see it."

"Nice." Kit's eyes narrowed and she paused, concerned by the look of misery on Raj's handsome face. "Is it your dad?" she asked. "Did he get worse?"

Raj shook his head and turned to face her. He waved a mocha toned hand, but no words accompanied his movement. "All he thinks about is the shop. His friend on Hukanui Road got robbed last week. Did he tell you?"

Kit sighed. "The security system should have given it away. No, he didn't get the chance to say much before he collapsed."

"He should have two people here at all times, but he won't listen to any of us. If you hadn't stopped by, he would have died."

Kit blanched and she glanced down at the paper bag hiding her lube. "About that." She swallowed. "My Visa card didn't work when I tried to pay for my shopping. I've written an IOU for your dad. Where do you want me to leave it?" She raised the sticky note and it fluttered from her index finger.

Raj snatched it and crumpled it into a ball. "Nowhere," he replied. "It's him who owes you for your time here this afternoon. And for saving his life."

Kit cleared her throat and felt her cheeks pink with embarrassment. "I didn't do much," she argued. "It's not like I gave him mouth to mouth or anything. I couldn't even ring an ambulance."

"You did more than most," he protested. Reaching across the counter, he seized her fingers and gave them a squeeze. "Thank you." His thumb brushed back and forth along the sensitive underside of her wrist and Kit shivered. Hammering on the front door shattered the peace and she dragged her hand away. Her heart beat in a strange staccato.

"We're closed!" Raj shouted at the shopper through the glass. "Sorry." He dropped the blinds and rolled his eyes at Kit. "Come on," he said, his tone sad. "Let's get out of here."

The local pub offered a comforting lull after the drama of the afternoon. Voices rose and fell in gentle conversation, punctuated by the occasional laugh. Raj bought the drinks and returned to the table Kit chose near the fire. Fake flames offered a placebo against the growing chill of evening. "I ordered fries," he said, settling into the seat opposite her. "Wanna share?"

Kit smiled and nodded. But her knotted stomach gave a grumble of misery. She sighed. "Isn't it incredible how one day everything is fine, but the next just turns to custard without warning?"

Raj nodded and sipped his pint of draught beer. The fluffy, white foam gave him a beer moustache which he wiped on the back of his hand. "You can say that again," he concluded. "You just described today."

"Yeah, sorry." Kit's fingers played with a beer mat. "I didn't mean to make it about myself."

"Do it!" Raj demanded. "Give me something else to think about."

So, Kit told him. Everything. She told him about Mr Roy's death, her arrest, Alec, everything. She even told him the thing she hadn't shared with anyone close to her; the reason her bank account lay in tatters. Also, the fact that Mr Roy had the straightest hair she'd ever seen on a human being. "Like a chimney brush," she admitted. "And now he's dead."

Raj waggled his dark eyebrows, his eyes widening at various points of Kit's monologue. He snorted through the story of Langdon finding a drowning teenager instead of lube but waited until she finished to comment. "Lube?" He sounded surprised. "Who knew?" His gaze strayed to her curls and then back to her face. "You know you grew up gorgeous, don't you?" He swallowed and peered into his beer. The foam had flattened, leaving wisps of white along the sides of his glass. "I love your hair."

"Thank you." Kit accepted the compliment though her tone sounded flat. She saw no one in the mirror over the fireplace behind Raj but herself. Frizzy hair. Dumpy. That image overwrote any reinvention of herself as thin or stunning. Her eyes saw a different Kit to the one other people viewed. She sighed and pushed her glass of sparkling water aside, her fingers fluttering as they revealed her inner turmoil. "I'd appreciate any suggestions you might want to make." Her voice sounded small and insignificant against the backdrop of the pub.

Raj's nose twitched. "You need to see the security footage," he concluded. He swilled his glass and swallowed the last dregs. "That's what is keeping you under their microscope. You need to find that woman."

Kit nodded. "The new lodger is an ex lawyer. He says I won't see it until any future trial, unless it suits the prosecution to reveal it earlier."

Raj frowned and a mild expletive crept from his full lips. "That's bad news, Kit," he agreed. "I'm sorry." His fingers reached across the table to clasp hers. She stopped shredding the cardboard beer mat and stilled. "Why didn't you go to university?" he asked. "Why are you working in a garage for a minimum wage?"

Kit sighed and lifted her gaze to the ceiling. Fake wooden beams gave the pub an English appeal. "I don't know," she breathed. "I honestly don't. Dad got sick and Mum couldn't cope. It didn't seem the right time to move up to Auckland. The job at the garage gave me regular hours and meant I could stay at home and help take Dad to the hospital. Then he died and my life just froze. I'm waking up to find that somewhere in between school and now, I've become a felon and I'm no further forward in my career than a decade ago."

"Which is why you're broke?" Raj nodded, his dark fringe dangling into his eyes as he bobbed his head. "It's a little drastic, but I can see why you blew your money like that."

Kit closed her eyes and wished she could switch bodies with someone else for a while. A month might do it. A month to step into another's life and let them deal with hers. Her gaze wandered to a couple staring into each other's eyes over a shared chocolate mud cake. Any life but that one. She knew from experience how messy relationships could get.

Kit opened her eyes to realise she'd moaned out loud. Raj grinned. "It's not so terrible," he soothed. His fingers patted her hand and then let go. "Work for us?" He raised a hand palm facing outwards to stall her protestations. "Just until Dad gets on his feet. Then the world is yours to explore. I'll put you on my payroll and he can square it up at the end. Please, Kit. Help us out?"

The slow nod of her head seemed to happen against her will. Curls relaxed by the humidity bounced against her cheek. "Fine," she agreed. "Just let me check with Jerry if I can legally work while suspended on full pay from the garage. He'll know."

"I'll email you a roster." Relief lessened the lines on Raj's chiselled forehead. "What's your email address?"

Kit's lips froze as the familiar Gmail stuck in her throat. "Oh no!" she groaned. "I can't check it. The cops took my laptop and my phone."

"Borrow mine. I'll log out and you can log into your account." Raj spun his iPhone around to face her.

Kit shook her head and slumped against the chair. "I can't. I set up two step verification. If I try to log in on someone else's device, it will text a code to my phone. Which is dead in an evidence locker somewhere." She ran a hand across her forehead and tried to still the palpitations in her chest. "And the shipping company promised to let me know when they were dispatching my parcel of lube. They'll use my email."

"Oh, whoops!" Raj winced. "Lube?" His mind drifted before Kit could explain, sorting through his own more pressing issues. His phone buzzed and his eyes narrowed as he read a text. "I need to pick Mum up from the hospital. The doctors are keeping Dad under observation overnight before scheduling him for surgery tomorrow." He slapped his thigh and looked up. "I need to go. The fries are all yours when they arrive." He rose and pressed a kiss to the top of Kit's curly head. "Come to the shop tomorrow before we open and I'll sort out wages and all that stuff. Talk to your lawyer and we'll discuss it then."

Raj nodded to the waitress as she approached the table carrying a basket of crispy looking fries. Steam rose from them in a haze which promised burned tongues and lips. He gave Kit a wave and disappeared through the doors in a blur of movement. Kit stared at the sizzling fries and her stomach gave an involuntary lurch. Putting her head in her hands, she released a groan of pure misery which earned her a sympathetic look from the waitress. Mr Rashid opened his shop at five o'clock in the morning. Every morning. Even tomorrow morning. "Great," Kit hissed. "As fast as I solve one problem, another appears."

"Well don't let that problem run away from you." The waitress winked as she set the fries on the table and jerked her head towards Raj's retreating back. "He's a hot problem we'd all love to have."

It didn't seem worth her effort to explain her woes to the straight-haired waitress. Kit was more interested in her hair than Raj's curves. Stunning curls didn't just happen. They demanded a strict showering routine and copious amounts of care and attention. With a sigh of resignation, Kit set an alarm on her watch for four o'clock the next morning and abandoned the fries. She had six hours to get home, pick Jerry's legal brain and sleep. Her life might have turned to custard, but she'd be dammed if her Curly Routine would become yet another unwilling casualty.

-33-

At The Curly Chalk Face

"The Nicola is sinking into the Astrolabe Reef." Raj jerked his head towards the newspaper under Kit's hand. She yawned and glared at him.

"Don't you come in here all chirpy!" she growled. "And stop smiling. It's way too early for that kind of silliness."

Raj snorted. "I forgot you weren't a morning person. Well, get used to it, snowflake. This is your life."

Kit groaned and rested her forehead over the newspaper headline. "It feels like lunchtime."

"Sorry, babe. This is what five o'clock in the morning feels like to those of us who get to share it with the birds."

"I know what five o'clock feels like!" Kit protested. "But I'm usually just getting into the shower, not recovering after refereeing a paper boy dispute!"

Raj wrinkled his nose. "Dad put that chocolate under the counter to send back to the supplier. They duped him with old stock and customers complained about the mould on it."

"I was desperate!" Kit groaned. "Extenuating circumstances."

"And now we're a paper boy down because he spent all night on the toilet," Raj concluded. "So, I'll see you when I've delivered his papers and checked on the other boys. Three of them didn't look too good."

"How long will all that take?" Kit swallowed and pursed her lips. "I don't want to be on my own for hours. That's not what I agreed to when I wrote my resignation letter to my old boss. You promised you'd post it, remember?"

Raj sighed and lifted a sack of newspapers onto his shoulder. "We both know resigning was a case of jumping before he pushed you. I'll do my best, but you'll have to manage, Kit," he said. A yawn punctuated his words and he lifted a white envelope from his back pocket. "I'll post this on the way. Don't forget, I've got my own shop to run as well. Sanjay will come after the breakfast rush at his bakery. He should get here around ten o'clock." He frowned and pointed an index finger at Kit's head. Her resignation letter dangled from his thumb and middle finger. "My family is Muslim, but there's no requirement for you to wear the hijab." He cocked his head and anxiety radiated from his chocolate irises. "You know we're not racist, hey? It doesn't matter that you're a catholic." His lips pursed. "It looks good on you though." Raj spun through the front door carrying his burden and robbing Kit of the right to reply.

She reached up and touched the damp hijab which hid her careful ringlets beneath its bottle green folds. Unable to follow her usual Curly Routine, she'd adapted it. Instead of her old tee shirt soaking up the moisture, she'd improvised using Mrs Rashid's borrowed hijab. A domed mirror in the corner surveyed the shop with its panoramic view. Kit glanced up at herself and admired the way a red curl sneaked from beneath the green cloth. The colour suited her and she cheered up enough to plaster a smile onto her face for the next customer to walk through the door.

Of medium height and middle aged, the handsome man graced Kit with an American accent. He set his carton of skimmed milk on the counter and smiled at her. "Jim Bronson," he said, offering his hand. Hazel eyes twinkled in the overhead lights. "You're new."

"Yes and no." Kit accepted his handshake and then hid a yawn. "Sorry. I worked here many years ago, but Mr Rashid got sick yesterday, so I'm just stepping in for a few weeks." She lifted the carton of milk and read the price tag. The buttons on the cash register squeaked as she entered the digits and accepted Jim's cash. "I'm Kit," she added, handing him the change. "And I don't function well before ten o'clock." Another yawn began at the soles of her feet and involved her whole face.

"Coffee. Strong and early." Jim smiled as he lifted his carton of milk from the counter and stuffed his jingling change into his trouser pocket. "I always make sure there's a mug of coffee ready for my wife before she wakes." He winked, his expression endearing. "That's why I've stayed married for twenty-five years."

Kit sighed. "And that Mr Jim, is why I'm still single."

He cocked his head and frowned. "Why?"

"Because you're already taken," she retorted. Jim's laugh echoed around the shop as he left, the front door clicking shut behind him.

Kit drank her fruit smoothie two hours earlier than planned. She'd hiked up her health kick in case she ended up eating prison food for the rest of her life. Sanjay blasted through the front door just after ten o'clock as Kit chewed through the pink gloop. A carbon copy of Mr Rashid, he skidded to a halt and widened his eyes in horror. "Are you being sick into a flask?" he gasped.

"No!" Kit stared at her container and back at Mr Rashid's oldest son. "It's a fruit smoothie. But I had to make it last night, so the blender didn't wake my flat-mates this morning. The strawberries discoloured in the fridge overnight."

Sanjay made retching noises as he lifted the counter to join her at the cash register. "It looks horrible," he remarked. "Why are you wearing a hijab? Staff don't need to convert to Islam to work here."

Kit groaned. "Your mother lent it to me." She poked a finger through the side and touched the drying curls. They felt crunchy. "I'm using it to Plop my hair," she said. "Please can you mind the shop while I take it off in the bathroom?"

Sanjay's jaw dropped. "You're using a treasured symbol of my culture to style your hair?" His dark brows narrowed into a forbidding line.

Kit swallowed and gave a shallow nod. "I didn't think about that. If it causes offence, I won't do it again. I just started work so early, I couldn't follow my usual routine."

Sanjay released a belly laugh and shook his head. "Still gullible then, Kit? I don't care how you dry your hair. Just keep helping us out, please?" He waved a hand in dismissal and she excused herself, locking the toilet door and leaning against it.

"I don't think I can do this every day," she told her reflection. "Prison might be easier."

Unwinding the hijab from her head took mere seconds, but Kit stayed in the bathroom much longer than she'd intended. Immaculate ringlets tumbled from her crown in stunning waves. "Wow," she breathed. "Who knew I needed to just Plop longer?" She left her curls to air dry and hung Mrs Rashid's scarf over the towel rail. Having great hair renewed her energy and Kit bounced from the bathroom a very different person to the one who crawled in there.

"Your hair looks different." Sanjay pointed a finger at Kit's fringe and she batted it away.

"Never touch a Curly's hair!" she reprimanded. "Especially not before they've Scrunched Out The Crunch."

"Scrunched out the what?" Sanjay paused to smile at a sullen customer buying pain killers. She snatched the box and marched away, complaining about the extortionate price.

"Scrunched Out The Crunch, also known as SOTC," Kit said. She picked up the pricing gun and Mr Rashid's list. "Flaxseed gel and lube make the curls crunchy. It's called a cast. When they're completely dry, I can crack the cast and the curls will look more natural."

"And you do that when?" Sanjay's dark brow narrowed. "I'm leaving at twelve o'clock. The lunchtime rush at the bakery starts then."

Kit touched her curls. "I can just stand here and do it." She glanced at the clock behind Sanjay's head. "What time is Mr Rashid's surgery?"

"My mother just sent a text. The nurses are getting him ready." He bit his lower lip and Kit winced. She knew his pain. It still lurked in a hidden place in her heart. She waved the pricing gun at him.

"I'll nip into the storeroom and price up the tins if you can stand here a little longer. The shelves are looking sparse." Sanjay nodded and as Kit ducked under the counter, she noticed the way his gaze strayed towards his phone. "I'll be quick," she promised.

Kit priced enough tins of tomatoes, peas and sweetcorn to feed a local army before relieving Sanjay at the cash register. He rushed off to take care of his bakery and left her alone in the shop. The rush increased across lunchtime, not helped by angry customers unable to buy their Lotto tickets. "I can't sell them to you," Kit stressed for the hundredth time. "I haven't had the training."

"This is ridiculous!" an elderly man shouted. "I always buy my tickets here! Same numbers, same location, same day of the week and the exact same time. If I don't win this week, I'll hold you responsible!"

"Have you ever won?" asked a younger man in a baseball cap. "Does that strategy work?"

The old man shuffled towards the milk fridge without replying. Kit pursed her lips to avoid commenting on an addiction with such an extended reach as to dictate a man's weekly activities.

A flurry of movement in the camera monitor on the counter caught her eye and Kit paused as she processed a customer's credit card payment. She watched a scruffy teenager in an aisle near the door shove a jumbo packet of confectionery inside his jacket. She swore and the customer followed her gaze as she leaned over the counter and stared at the back of the thief's head. His arms moved as he tried to zip up his jacket before turning around and heading for the door.

"Is he stealing?" the young man asked. He slipped his credit card back into his wallet and pushed it into his jacket pocket. Excitement lit behind his irises and he rose onto his toes. "I'll get him."

Kit held her breath as the man rugby tackled the thief from behind and knocked him flat. They both disappeared behind the shelf and she heard scuffling. "Call the cops!" she begged a woman in the queue with a buggy parked in front of her. The baby watched wide eyed as Kit turned the key to lock the cash register before shoving the small sliver of metal into her bra. Then she leapt the counter with an impressive bottom swivel and landed on her feet. Rounding the shelf, she saw the chocolate thief gaining the upper hand. He sat on top of the hero with his fist raised.

"Don't even think about it!" Kit snatched a tin of minted peas and socked him around the side of the head. The thief groaned and rolled into a ball, covering his ears in fear of further reprisals. The jumbo pack of snack bars slid from inside his jacket, flattened to half their usual width.

"Cops are coming." The mother and buggy appeared around the side of the shelf. She wrinkled her nose at the sight of the two sprawling men and spoke into her phone. "Yes, the shop assistant has assaulted everyone with a tin of minted peas."

"No, no! Don't tell them that!" Kit begged, her voice rising to a squeak. "I defended him." She pointed to the young man lying on his back and staring at the ceiling. His eyes rolled around in his head as though dazed. A packet of cereal on the first shelf wore his baseball cap at a jaunty angle. Its exit appeared to have taken the young man's hair with it. A bald head remained in place.

"I think I broke my back!" he groaned. "I'll sue the shop."

"I'm suing her!" The thief jabbed his finger at Kit. "She beat me up with a tin of minted peas."

Kit stared at the baseball cap as a memory returned. A helpful, liberating memory. A smile broke out and lifted her lips into a maniacal expression. The woman with the buggy backed away and the thief buried his head in his arms.

-34-

Curly Crimes

Jackson stood with his arms folded, his broad shoulder resting against the door post. "Run this by me again?" he demanded.

"He hit me and then she hit me," the thief exclaimed. "I did nothing to deserve it." He rubbed wiry fingers over the bump above his right ear.

Jackson's brow hiked enough to suggest his lack of belief. "Right. You expect me to believe that, Claude? You just came in here to buy chocolate and this dude rugby tackled you to the ground?"

"Yes!" he protested.

Kit fidgeted on the spot. "Can I just make a phone call?" she begged.

"No." Jackson didn't meet her frantic gaze. "Did you tell this man to tackle Claude?"

Kit sighed. "No. I saw the kid put the packet inside his jacket. This guy took off before I could stop him. They scuffled and I arrived to find Claude on top of whatever-your-name-is, so I hit him with the tin." She winced. "I wasn't fast enough and it looks like he'd already hit him."

"Self-defence!" Claude's whiny voice matched his thin physique. "I hit him in self-defence!"

Jackson winced and turned to face Kit. His eyes sparkled with a hidden emotion she couldn't discern. She frowned. "Are you going to arrest me again?"

"Again?" The ex-hero lay on his back on the tiled floor and groaned. "She's a criminal?"

Kit closed her eyes and swallowed. A rustle grabbed her attention as Jackson withdrew his notebook and a pen. The woman with the buggy intervened. "That guy was definitely stealing," she said. "We all saw him." She looked for solidarity to the gathered crowd of customers who'd hung around for the after party. Many of them nodded.

"But he hadn't left the shop." Jackson's expression scrunched up in distaste. "So, technically he didn't shop lift. Yet." He glared at Claude.

Kit sighed. "So, technically, whatever-his-name-is assaulted him? And you think I told him to do it."

"She didn't!" The woman shoved her buggy between Kit and Jackson. "This isn't fair!"

"My name is Bob!" the man on the ground complained. "Why does no one ever remember my name?"

Jackson frowned. He nudged the squashed jumbo pack with the toe of his boot. "Pay for the food, Claude," he ordered. His tone hardened. "Pay up and this will all go away."

"But I didn't leave the shop." Claude's weedy face creased into a grin of victory. Kit's fingers itched to grab the minted peas and whack his head back through his dirty turtleneck.

Jackson folded his arms. "No, but you damaged stock belonging to someone else. That's vandalism. Pay up, Claude."

Kit gave the tall cop a look of appreciation. She

suppressed the urge to kiss him in a wave of gratitude. Her writhing fingers ceased their endless movement and she waited. Claude's watery eyes stared up at Jackson. Spiky, blond hair poked from beneath his hood. "I got no money." He blinked and Jackson's expression hardened.

"So, you were stealing," he concluded. "Why didn't you just run when you got the upper hand on this guy? Why give him a black eye and then go back for more?" Jackson's eyebrow quirked upward in question and Claude blanched. A sigh rippled around the gathered customers as they felt justice teetering towards a slow victory. The pages of Jackson's notebook swished as he flicked onto a new leaf. "I'm advising Miss Maguire to issue a trespass notice against you. You can't come back to this shop again until that notice is lifted. If you attempt to enter the premises, she's entitled to call the police and I will arrest you. Do you understand?"

Claude nodded. A hand reached up to touch the bump on his head. "What about my headache? Can I press charges?"

"You can try," Jackson replied. He flipped his notebook shut and fitted it behind his Kevlar vest. "The civil court might listen to you. It's against the public interest for me to arrest anyone for assault when you came in here intending to shop lift." He glared at the man stretched out on the ground like a Popsicle. "You were trying to make a citizen's arrest, weren't you?" he asked, his tone loaded. The man nodded. "And Miss Maguire tried to defend you by hitting the thief." Jackson's eyes narrowed at Claude. "I suggest you both get up and go about your business."

"My back's broken." Bob let out a chilling moan and waved his hands in front of his face. "I'm paralysed."

"Get up, Bob," Jackson growled. "Last week you tried to sue the council for the loose flagstone you tripped over. Before that, you wanted to sue a traffic warden. Just get up."

Bob shot up like a marionette with its strings yanked from above. "I couldn't get the glue from his ticket off my windscreen!" he protested. "That's criminal damage." He jabbed a finger in Kit's direction. "She didn't even say thank you."

"Thank you!" Kit's voice rose in exasperation. Hysteria tinged the higher notes. "Everyone just go away. I need to make a phone call!"

Jackson blinked and Kit sensed she'd hurt him. She pointed at him. "Everyone except you. I need you."

The woman withdrew her buggy and gave Kit a surreptitious wink. The customers shuffled back to the queue, managing to maintain the same order they'd been in before the drama started. Jackson browsed the aisles while Kit served them. The clock caught her eye and she wondered if Mr Rashid's surgery proved successful.

"What did you want?" Jackson dumped an energy drink on the counter and dug in his trouser pocket for coins.

Kit waved his money away. "Mr Rashid would want me to let you have it," she lied. Mr Rashid would wring the last breath out of his own mother.

"I'm not allowed to accept gifts." Jackson's eyes crinkled in the corners. "Or bribes."

Kit huffed, exasperation causing her to bristle. "Whatever!" she snapped. "There's video footage of the whole incident. Mr Rashid had cameras installed. If you'd like to come back later when Raj gets here, he can show it to you."

"Don't worry. I believe you."

Kit's lips straightened into a thin line. "That makes a change. Have you seen the video footage from the service centre which supposedly incriminates me?"

Jackson's lips twisted. He popped the tab on the drink and fizzy liquid bubbled free. "Maybe," he replied. "Why?"

Kit's shoulders slumped. "Does it look like me? Really?"

Jackson sipped his drink and sighed. "You know I can't

answer that. What did your lawyer say?"

"That he won't get access to it unless the case goes to trial. But I know it's not me. I just don't know how to prove it."

Jackson wrinkled his nose in sympathy. "I have to be careful what I say." He lowered his voice. "I can't damage the case Lane is building."

"Against me?" Kit swallowed. "Of course, against me. He has no one else." She chewed on her lower lip and frowned. "I need to ring my flat-mate. I know where his hat is. He wore it home to Christchurch last week and I bet it's still at his parents' house. That's what I wanted to tell you. Do you think that might help?"

Jackson winced. "Not really. You could have got a cap from anywhere and disposed of it straight afterwards. Most criminals don't just throw evidence in their own dustbin. Searching your house was a long shot." He lifted his chin and Kit noticed a spiderweb of thin scars dotted beneath his stubble.

"So, I can't help myself. Is that what you're saying?" Panic burned its way up the back of Kit's neck and into her head. "I just have to wait until Lane charges me with murder?" She waved a hand in front of her. "I feel it hanging over me like a dead weight. I've lost my job and ended up back where I started." The newspaper crinkled beneath her forearms as she leaned on the counter. "I'm living in a nightmare."

"I know. And I'm sorry." Jackson adjusted his police issue cap on his head and more dark curls poked from beneath amid salt and pepper grey. "Just hold tight. I know you didn't do it. We need to wait for Lane to prove it."

Kit nodded. "Thanks. And thanks for believing me. I guess I need to find the woman who went into the office after hours. I know she had my key and that someone else put it back when the garage opened again the day after the murder." She strummed her fingers on the newspaper. "If

I can find her, I'll be able to prove my innocence."

"No." Jackson laid a warning hand over Kit's fingers. His palm felt warm and he squeezed her hand. "You're not to interfere. Lane will lock you up in a heartbeat. It's also dangerous. A man died, remember."

"Yeah." Kit nodded. "A really nice man."

-35-

Curly Crush

"Oh, yeah!" Raki slapped his forehead and leaned on the kitchen counter. Blue stains covered his fingers and nobody dared ask what he'd been mixing up in his chemistry lab. "That's right. Mum washed my cap. I'll phone her and she can take it to the local police station."

"It doesn't matter." Kit leaned her chin on her forearms. The bar stool twisted beneath her as she shifted to get comfortable. "Jackson said it won't help. I need to find the woman from the security video."

"Jackson told you to do that?" Jerry's lawyer-antenna shot upright in disbelief. "Tell him to do his own investigating." He adjusted the dog collar at his throat as though struggling with which version of himself to let speak.

"Kit's right." Langdon stopped stirring his soup on the hob. "Find the woman. Solve the mystery." He dug an index finger into the pan and tasted his strange brew. "Pumpkin and cheese. Good advice, Jerry."

"From your former life as a chef?" Kit let the sarcasm percolate her words and Jerry grinned.

"Just a tourist," he said with a smile. "Let's look at the day all this started. What happened to make someone need to sneak into the office after hours?"

"The schilling! The convertible!" Kit shot backwards off her seat. Jerry caught her as she tumbled. Excitement drove her as she bounced around in front of him. "Paul's the murderer! He couldn't stop the bidding and the security guard wanted to lock the garage. He took the key meaning to come back later. Maybe he thought I'd sent proof to Mr Roy and wanted to check his computer. They argued and he killed him!" Kit bounced from foot to foot. She punched the air with her fist.

"It doesn't work," Jerry said. He wrinkled his nose as he put out Kit's fire. "He'd assume you put in your own email address. Most people would want to watch the outcome and see how much it cost their victim. It's just a fluke you didn't care."

"So, who's the woman?" Langdon demanded. "And why did he need her?"

Kit paused in her celebration. The cogs beneath her red curls whirred. Then her eyes widened. "Someone Google Blackhawk Security!" she demanded. Her hands flapped in front of her. Raki pulled out his phone and kept everyone waiting while he peered at his blue fingers.

"Oh. How'd that happen?" he mused. His brow furrowed. "Less indigo next time."

"Just do the search!" Langdon groaned. He returned to his simmering pan.

Raki fumbled around on his phone screen, his fingers knobbly and deft. "It's a website and software programming company," he stated. "Why?"

"That's who Cindy works for." Kit clicked her fingers. "Her father owns it. I bet she's a programmer. Paul brought her in after hours to try to stop his credit card bidding on the website. I'm guessing they tried to get into my computer. She said she was sorry. That's what she meant."

"Why not just cancel the credit card? Paul could tell the bank he lost it, or someone stole it."

Kit shook her head. "No, that would initiate an investigation by the credit card company and the police. He couldn't risk that because he was schilling with it. The credit card company would contact the auction website and the whole scam would come out in the open. He didn't want that."

"But Lane told you he had footage of a woman. He didn't mention anyone going into the garage with her." Jerry tapped his fingers on the counter and frowned.

Kit snorted. "You met him. Does he strike you as the kind of man to keep a dog and bark for himself?" Her lips curled back in a sneer. "I bet he gave her the key and told her to sort out his mess."

She paced the dining area and then slumped into her reading chair. Unable to settle, she stood up and paced for a while longer. Her feet ached from standing in the shop all day. She glanced at her watch and thought about poor Mr Rashid. Raj had relieved her just after the school rush at three o'clock and his father had still been in surgery.

Kit glanced through the front window and stared at her yellow Beetle sitting on the driveway. She tapped the end of her nose with her finger. "The car," she breathed. "Who bought the car?"

"What car?" Jerry stared into the bowl of soup Langdon laid in front of him. "What are the black bits? I don't remember black bits in the recipe."

"Peppercorns," Langdon said. He winced as his conscience got the better of him. "Actually, I don't know. They just appeared."

Raki peered over Jerry's shoulder and gave a shudder. "It's the Teflon lining from the saucepan," he concluded. "It needs throwing away."

Kit stopped pacing as the boys bowed their heads over the steaming bowls as though praying. They debated the soup's safety while Raki added his professional opinion that it wasn't. "I'm just nipping out," Kit said. "This won't take long."

The boys continued their discussion about Teflon and whether sieving the soup would remove the black bits well enough to make it edible. Kit slipped from the house and fired up her yellow car.

She drove to her mother's house first and found Kenny at home. He answered the front door with a mince and cheese pie clasped in his hand. The pastry flakes clung to his beard. "What?" he demanded with his mouth full. "She's not at home. Her and Steph went bra shopping." Kit looked into his eyes and wondered for the millionth time how her mother had replaced her intelligent father with humanity's missing link.

"Nice," she replied. "I'm glad I missed it. Please can you tell my mother there's a parcel due to arrive? It's for me. She doesn't need to open it."

Kenny waggled bushy eyebrows. "Finders keepers," he sang. Then he slammed the door in her face.

Kit took deep breaths in through her nose and out through her mouth. She kept her gaze focussed on the door knocker until her teeth stopped grinding together. "You don't know how much I want to kill you," she hissed. Instead, she made herself a promise. If it looked as though they would convict her of Mr Roy's murder, she'd nip back and bludgeon Kenny to death. "Might as well get my money's worth," she snarled.

Kit imagined various satisfying scenarios as she drove to her next destination. They all ended in Marian's devastation and she shook her head in defeat. Her journey took her into Hamilton and she found herself going against the flow of rush hour traffic. She'd wasted time driving to Marian's house and had missed her opportunity to satiate her curiosity. Te Rapa road was grid locked and Kit thudded the steering wheel with her palm. The security guard finished locking the main gate of Roy's Motors as she sat in the queue to turn right. "Noooo!" she groaned.

A slender figure crossed the road in front of her, navigating the traffic as he strode to the other side of the carriageway. Kit cursed her car's lack of electronics as she sprawled across the passenger seat to wind the window down with the handle. Too late. Gordy's lanky legs took him to safety on the pavement and he walked across the car park opposite and into the dairy.

Not wanting to admit defeat, Kit made a risky manoeuvre. She edged into the middle lane with her indicator flashing, forcing the queue to a halt to let her move into the stream of traffic. Someone honked their horn and she winced and waved an apology in her rear-view mirror. "Sorry," she called.

The traffic picked up speed and the wind whistled through her open passenger window. Unable to close it again, Kit tolerated the way it whipped her curls around her head like Medusa. She imagined trying to maintain her Curly Routine in prison and hopelessness set in. While others brewed illegal alcohol in the toilet cistern, she'd have to find a way to make flaxseed gel by rubbing flammable objects together and igniting her farts.

It took ten precious minutes for Kit to circle the block and push her way into the car park belonging to the dairy. She jammed on her handbrake and leapt from the car. Her sandals clacked against the concrete as she dodged vehicles and jogged across the car park. At the front door of the dairy, she ran into a hard chest.

"Sorry." A steadying hand rested on her back as she bent double. "Kit?"

She glanced up with a groan to see Jason peering down at her. "Hey," she managed, her breath tight. "Is Gordy in there?"

"In there?" Jason spun around and appeared to stare into the dark interior. "No. Why?"

Kit forced herself to straighten. "I need to ask him something."

"I heard what happened." Jason winced and twisted the cigarette packet in his fingers. "Everyone knows you didn't kill Mr Roy."

"Thanks." Kit gave him a rueful smile. "Perhaps you'd like to give the detective a call and let him know." Her brow furrowed at the reminder of the handcuffs and Lane's desperation to close the case. She studied Jason's craggy features and decided to confide in him. "I'm not sure if you're aware, but I caught Paul schilling on my computer a few days ago. I suspect he'd been doing it for a while. His bets involved a convertible which Gordy had up for sale online. Do you remember it?"

Jason pursed his lips. He closed his eyes and tilted his head back in a characteristic thinking pose. Then he nodded. "Blue? About two years old. We banged a panel back out before it went up for sale. That one?"

"Yes!" Kit bounced on the balls of her feet with excitement. "That one. Paul pushed the bids much higher than the car's worth and another bidder matched him. I kinda made it impossible for Paul to pull out of the auction." Kit frowned and ran her teeth over her lower lip. "I think Mr Roy found out. Paul tried to stop the auction by borrowing the key to the office door and sending his wife in to hack my computer. I think Mr Roy caught her and Paul killed him." The story sounded lamer with every word Kit uttered. Paul just didn't fit as a murderer.

"Hang on there!" Jason held up a palm creased with black lines from years of handling grease. He glanced around him as customers entered and left the dairy. "You can't say things like that without proof, Kit!"

"I'm getting proof." Her eyes sparkled. "Gordy can tell me the final auction price and who bought the car. He'll know because once the auction ended, he'd deal with the paperwork. I saw him go into the shop."

Jason shrugged and shook his head. "He's not in there. I would have seen him."

"Damn," Kit breathed. "I got caught in traffic and missed him." She stared across the road at the high gate surrounding the garage compound. "Do you know his address?"

"No, but I've got his number." Jason reached into the pocket of his dark blue boiler suit and dragged out his phone. "I can text it to you." His fingers pushed buttons and he glanced up with an eyebrow raised in question.

Kit shook her head. "The cops have my phone. I haven't replaced it. Sorry. Just give me the address and I'll visit him at home. Hopefully he won't mind."

"Not on your own." Jason frowned and wrapped an arm around her shoulder. "He might get the wrong idea and then you're there alone. It's dumb. I'll find out where he is and then come with you."

Kit wriggled free of Jason's arm on a pretence of lacing her sneaker. She dropped to one knee and pondered his odd comment. Gordy had never shown the slightest interest in her. "It's a stupid idea," she said, standing upright and jangling her car keys. Her hair felt like a rat's nest beneath her fingers and she just wanted to go home. The thought of another dawn start at Mr Rashid's shop the next morning robbed her of energy. She needed to ring Raj from the house phone and ask how the surgery went. Then she wanted an early night. "I'll catch up with him another time."

"Hang on." Jason dragged his phone from his ear and tapped her shoulder. "He's still at work." He nodded as though Gordy could see him and frowned. "Oh. Okay. I'll text when we get there." Stained fingers pushed his phone back into the deep pocket. "I thought you wanted to see him."

"Not tonight." Kit licked her lips. "And I'm definitely not going into the garage."

"But you've done nothing wrong." Kindness infused Jason's features and his lips quirked upward in a soft smile. "It's not fair. I'll nip across and ask him. You wait here."

"Thanks." Relief flooded Kit's body. "I'll wait in the car." She turned to move away and then halted. "Why would Gordy get the wrong idea about me if I turned up at his place? He's married."

"Dunno." Jason shrugged. "He talked about you last week in the pub after work, but not in a good way." Jason winced. "You know what I mean?"

"No." Kit stepped closer. "What do you mean?"

"You know, inappropriate, sexist kinda stuff." His cheeks reddened. "And I think he's divorced. I thought when you sent me the email asking for help it was because he'd done something. That's why I rushed through to see you."

"Gordy?" Kit shook her head. "He's not my type."

"That's what I thought." Jason jerked his head towards the garage. "What am I asking about? The convertible and what else?"

Kit groaned. "I'll come with you," she said with a sigh. "Then I'm going straight home."

-36-

Curly Catastrophe

"Where are we going?" Kit paused on the footpath as Jason stepped over the low wall into the forecourt of the disused car yard next to Roy's.

"The back way." He shrugged. "We used to always come this way until Mr Roy fell out with the owner. Mr Roy bought this section just before he died. He wanted to expand the second-hand car dealership."

"Why am I always the last to know everything?" Kit grumbled. She lifted her legs and hopped over the wall. Her heels complained as she hit the ground and she groaned. "I spent today doing my old job at the dairy on the Gordonton Road," she said with a sigh. "If I thought I spent a lot of time on my feet at the garage, it's nothing compared to today."

"I hear ya," Jason replied. He looked down at his sensible work boots. "It's something you get used to. I have more problems with my back from bending over the cars. Sometimes I stand up and realise my spine's locked in position."

"I know!" Kit's enthusiasm for her aches and pains hiked up a notch. "I jumped over the counter this morning and think I pulled a hamstring. I don't know how Mr Rashid copes just standing there all day." She thought of the Indian man's ramrod straight back and sunny smile. An urge to know how he'd fared in the surgery occupied her immediate thoughts. "Can I borrow your phone for a minute?"

"Sure." Jason dragged it from his pocket and handed it over as Kit caught up with him. She pressed an icon on the screen and wrinkled her nose when she got an error message.

"I need to Google the phone number for the shop," she said. "Why won't it work?"

"I've run out of data." Jason tapped his temple and waved his cigarette packet in the air. "That's what I forgot. Remembered the ciggies and forgot the top-up card. I'll nip back across and get one when we're done."

"Oh." Disappointment shrouded Kit as she handed the phone back. "I forgot how hard life is without my phone. Let's get this over with and then I can go home."

Gordy waited for them behind a chain-link fence on the boundary between the two properties. He released a padlock and pushed open a gate. "What's up?" he demanded. "I'm finishing some paperwork, but I'm almost done. Fancy a beer?" His brow furrowed as he stared down at Kit. The gate clanged behind them.

"Na, thanks mate." Jason shook his head. "But Kit knows about the schilling. You should cut her a deal. She needs the money." He drew a cigarette from the packet and slipped it between his lips.

Kit's jaw tightened. She berated herself, knowing she should have trusted her instincts. "Nice!" she bit. "So, you're in on it too?"

"I wasn't." Jason flicked his lighter. "Now I am." He took a drag of his cigarette and narrowed his eyes at Gordy. "I'm yet to see any cash."

"This sucks!" Kit snapped. "Poor Mr Roy trusted you! All of you!" She put her hands on her hips and glared at the two men. "Which one of you killed him?"

They eyed each other. Gordy spoke. "Neither of us. We both have alibis. And for your information, the schilling started with Mr Roy. He set it up years ago and gave me the chance to earn a little extra cash. I used to go to auctions in disguise, but this online thing made it so much easier."

Kit gasped. "I don't believe you!" Her voice rose. "How dare you sully Mr Roy's name with your accusations!" She turned and marched towards the gate, her curls flying in her wake.

"Oh, no you don't!" Gordy reached the gate first and snapped the padlock closed. "Let's talk about this."

"I have nothing to say to you." Kit yanked on the padlock, knowing before her fingers closed around it that she couldn't get it open. "You make me sick!"

Gordy's jaw clenched against dark bristles and he sighed. "Get inside, Kit!" he ordered. "Or I'll make you." When she opened her mouth to scream, he clamped a hand over it and spun her to face away from him. His chin rested on her shoulder and the fingers of his other hand clamped around her throat. He pressed and she gagged as her airway narrowed. "I mean it," he hissed. "Don't test me."

The car showroom smelled of chemicals. Wax and a cleaning cloth sat next to the wheel of a brand new SUV. A clipboard resting on the front seat detailed the new owner in Gordy's crabbed handwriting. Gordy navigated around the truck's open door and pushed Kit towards his office. Glass covered two sides and when he shoved her into a visitor's chair, Kit spotted the security guard walking the perimeter of the compound. The man glanced at the street while checking the doors of the vehicles on the forecourt with a distracted air.

"Right." Jason closed the office door behind them and stood next to Gordy. They looked down at her like a headmaster and deputy reprimanding an unruly student. "This is important, Kit. We can make easy money from each sale. Gordy's done it for years."

Gordy nodded, his glossy hair bouncing either side of his centre parting. "Undetected," he added. Pride laced his voice. "We need more people to bid. Then it looks less dodgy. Mr Roy supervised the paperwork. You could do that part for us."

Jason winked at Kit. "Meet Angus," he said, jerking his head at Gordy. "I haven't thought of a name for my identity yet."

"What?" Her head jerked back in shock. "Angus? But you were bidding against Paul. That makes no sense."

Gordy wrinkled his nose. "I didn't realise it was him, did I? How was I meant to know his mid-life crisis car was a sports convertible?"

"He actually wanted the car?" Blood drained from Kit's cheeks. "He wasn't schilling?"

"No." Gordy screwed up his features and shook his head. "The guy's a moron. We don't want him."

"Oh, my goodness!" Kit leaned forward and covered her face with her hands. "Then why was he on my computer the day before we found out about Mr Roy's death?"

"I dunno." Gordy didn't sound much like he cared either.

"That's the day his keyboard broke," Jason added. Cigarette smoke puffed from his lips and nostrils and gave the air in the small office a hazy effect. "He ran around trying to borrow someone else's. We needed ours. He said the IT guy wasn't very helpful."

Gordy nodded. "Yeah. He got hysterical at one point. Stupid bugger. I'm gonna hate working for him."

He frowned at Jason. "You'll set off the smoke alarms." Hauling out a chair, he stood on it and yanked the casing from the unit fixed to the ceiling.

"They're not working, remember?" Jason grinned as Gordy thudded to the ground. "They're part of Mr Roy's new security system. Cameras, burglar and fire alarms and a sprinkler system. His death halted all that."

"I can't do this." Kit rose on shaking legs. She forced an awakening of her resolve and gave a definitive nod. The cigarette smoke caused her lungs to spasm and stripped the confidence from her tone. "Breaking the law will desecrate my father's memory. I won't do it."

Jason tutted. "I thought you might feel more grateful." He sounded irritated. "In view of your money worries, I thought it might help."

Kit gasped. "How do you know about that?"

"Mr Roy asked me a question about you. I worked it out." Jason touched the side of his nose with a forefinger. "I didn't tell anyone. Yet."

"Why? What's going on?" Gordy turned to look at Jason and Kit seized her moment. Dodging sideways, she wrenched on the door handle and forced it open. She ran into the showroom and stopped, looking around her for an escape. The glass front doors opened onto the forecourt, but the security guard had moved around towards the service entrance. Kit didn't know how to roll the heavy doors open and dismissed them as an escape route. Gordy chased after her, but Jason sauntered to the fire exit and blocked the way they'd come in. His lips tugged on his cigarette and his expression held detachment, as though he watched a television programme unfold in front of him.

Gordy covered the showroom floor at speed, his long legs making up the ground with ease. Kit screamed and dodged around the side of a brand new utility vehicle, seeing Gordy's image reflected in the buffed metal. "No!" she screamed. "Leave me alone!"

"You can't get out." Gordy sounded confident. Kit peeked from behind the ute's rear bumper and saw the passageway leading to the service centre and workshop. Jason's position by the fire exit gave him easy access to stop her. The beating of Kit's heart drowned out any other sound.

As Gordy edged around the vehicle, she forced her legs to take her around the other side. They were locked into a stalemate she knew would end in her capture. Gordy's long legs gave him an advantage. His dark eyes narrowed into slits like a snake; as though he knew he'd win, but it amused him to play the game, anyway.

-37-

Curly Kidnap

Kit contemplated rolling beneath one of the new cars but dismissed the plan. They'd both haul her out within seconds. She froze at the sound of Gordy's voice. His tone changed from teasing to deferential. "Hi, Mrs Roy. What can I do for you?"

Kit inhaled and pressed a hand over her mouth. She leaned forward on her knees and elbows and tilted her face to peer beneath the car. Gordy's shiny shoes turned away and met a pair of blue stilettos. "I'm sorry for your loss, Mrs Roy," he said.

"I bet you are." Her usual gentleness had gone, harsh tones replacing them. "How will you manage your little scam now?"

Kit used the wing mirror of a shiny sedan to haul herself upright. She winced at the sight of a pale woman with a wild, black broom of straightened hair perched on her head. She hardly recognised Mr Roy's wife from the staff party last Christmas. Her characteristic softness had abandoned her, replaced by hard edges and a bristling fury. Kit edged around the back of the vehicle to hear Gordy blustering. She crouched and peeked over the rear bumper. "I don't know what you mean, Mrs Roy," Gordy stressed. He jerked his head towards Jason. "Put that cigarette out!" he demanded.

Jason ground the butt beneath his work boot and turned as though to leave. Without looking, Mrs Roy extended a forearm clad in gold bangles which jangled with the movement. She pointed at him. "Don't even think about leaving. I want an explanation."

Jason halted, licking his lips and considering an answer. His mouth opened and closed without speech leaving it. Gordy stepped in to rescue him. "Mr Roy started it," he said, his tone insistent. "I worked for him. He chose the vehicles and gave me the top price to stop bidding. I'm happy to carry on if you want to manage it. Mr Roy did the paperwork for the whole thing. Someone needs to take care of that part."

"Help me, Mrs Roy." Kit stepped from behind the sedan. Mrs Roy jumped and turned.

"Oh," she said, her voice sounding hard. "The little office girl. Alec vouched for you. He swore you didn't know."

"I didn't!" Kit took a step forward. "I'm not involved with this and I didn't kill Mr Roy."

Jason groaned and his boots scraped against the concrete. He rolled his eyes to the ceiling as his little side-line for quick cash collapsed before him. His boots shifted and Kit sensed him wanting to run.

"I know you didn't kill him!" Mrs Roy scoffed. "Nobody did. The stupid man tripped over during an argument with me."

"Alec said he sustained bruising no one could account

for." Kit wrung her hands in front of her. "The police arrested me."

Mrs Roy shook her head. "He came home after his Auckland trip and fell off the exercise bike. I'm guessing his new girlfriend didn't like him with a tyre of fat around his middle." She rolled her eyes in an exaggerated motion which made them bulge like a frog's. "At least now I know what the big health kick was all about. He drove to the office afterwards to pick up his messages. Stupid man carried nothing as technical as a mobile phone. Alec rang me and told me what he'd discovered. Said he got an email about bid fixing. I marched in here to confront my husband and he tripped and banged his head on the corner of the workshop counter. Bloody man! He ruined a business my father spent his lifetime building. It had an honest reputation and he changed its name and destroyed it overnight. He promised Alec he'd stopped." The words caught in her throat. "He promised he'd stopped." She appeared more upset about the schilling than the idea of Mr Roy's girlfriend. Or his death.

Mrs Roy smoothed a hand over her hair and tucked a strand behind her ear. Her hand shook. "Alec caught him years ago, apparently. Found him using other people to bump up the auction bids on cars. They argued and my husband sent my boy away. He promised him he'd never do it again as long as Alec said nothing to me. Obviously, he lied. Anyway, it's all come out now. Alec told me everything."

"Oh." Kit gnawed on her lower lip. Her heart thudded its way up her neck and made her head spin. "Mr Roy sent him away. That's why he left without warning." She stared at the polished grey concrete beneath her feet and tears budded behind her eyelids. "Poor Alec."

"Yes. Poor Alec when he finds out you were involved too." Mrs Roy's blue eyes hardened. The bangles moved on her wrist. "How could you?"

"I didn't!" Kit's voice rose into a cry of desperation. "It was them!"

"Get in my husband's office!" Mrs Roy snapped. "I've had enough!"

"You need to tell the police what happened to Mr Roy," Kit begged. "They think I killed him."

The woman shrugged and her brow furrowed into deep lines. "Get in the office. We'll talk about it there."

Jason turned, obedient as a lamb as he set off along the corridor. Mrs Roy tugged at Gordy's sleeve and pushed him in front of her. As he started moving, she turned her body and unzipped her handbag. Kit hadn't expected to see her long fingers pull a bug bomb from the bowels of the bag. Kit held her breath and her body tensed. "You too!" Mrs Roy snapped. Plastic rustled as she unwrapped the cannister.

"I don't want to get bug bombed!" Kit pleaded. "It's poisonous!"

Mrs Roy leaned sideways and a spiteful smile claimed her features. "It's also flammable," she whispered. "One spark is all it takes, apparently."

"No." Kit dug her heels in and backed away. Mrs Roy's floral print skirt seemed incongruous with the angry woman it clothed.

"Get over here!" she growled. She jabbed Gordy's elbow. "Make her come to our meeting."

"It's not a meeting!" Kit screamed. "She's going to torch the garage!"

Jason's lips parted in shock. Gordy frowned. But Kit forced her short legs and aching feet into a sprint. She hurled herself into the driver's seat of the nearest SUV and slammed the door. Her fingers fumbled at the button beneath the handle and the central locking surrounded her with the comforting sound of locks clicking into place.

A clipboard dug into Kit's bottom and she reached beneath her and hauled it free. The keys fell to the carpet at her feet and clumsy fingers fumbled them into her lap. Gordy's scrawl on the registration document listed Josie as the SUV's new owner.

Mrs Roy's voice sounded muted as she hammered on the truck's heavy glass. "Get out of there now!" she shouted. Her hair escaped from her bun in fine tendrils that created spikes around her face. It looked lank and stiff from too much heat. SS. Straightening Stress. CO. Chemical Overload.

"Go away!" Kit pressed her hand to the glass and splayed her fingers. "I'm being held here against my will. I had nothing to do with the bidding thing. Ask Cindy! Paul brought her in to hack my computer. She knows I didn't do it."

"Cindy!" Mrs Roy spat the name. She slapped the glass with the flat of her hand. "Little tart! What kind of man messes around with his nephew's wife?"

"Cindy?" Kit frowned. The woman had said her life was complicated. "I think you're wrong," she called through the closed window.

"I saw her! Creeping into my husband's office while our backs were turned. You must all think I'm stupid!"

Kit shook her head. Her hair swished against the seat of the SUV and she heard static as the curls separated against the plush leather. "You've got it wrong!" she insisted. "She tried to help Paul."

Mrs Roy turned her head and the sinews stood out in her neck. Her fingers gripped the sill of the window, the pads turning white. "You must have the spare key there somewhere!" she screeched. Kit moved her head to see Gordy sifting through the key cabinet. He snatched at them one after the other, inspected them and dropped them onto a growing pile. Kit winced; glad she wouldn't have to sort out the aftermath of the which-key-belonged-to-what-car game. She faced forward as panic gripped her chest.

Through the showroom window, Jason loped across the forecourt. He called to the security guard outside and kept glancing back towards the showroom.

"You rat!" Kit snarled. "You stinking, low-life coward! How dare you run off and leave me!" Lurching forward, she sat on the very edge of the seat, so she could reach the pedals. Depressing the brake, she jabbed her finger into the ignition button. It recognised the electric signature of the key fob sitting in her lap. The diesel engine roared to life under her bottom with the power of three hundred horses and one short Curly.

"Get back here!" Mrs Roy slapped the window and rattled at the door handle. A couple of red acrylic fingernails shot off in opposite directions. Kit focussed on Jason's retreating back as she released the handbrake and found the gas pedal with her right foot. Gordy appeared in her peripheral vision; a fire extinguisher clutched in his hands.

"I'll break the window with this!" he shouted. "Stand back!"

Kit turned her head to face them both, a maniacal grin plastered onto her lips. Too small to see far over the steering wheel, she drove blind as she ticked off number nineteen on her unofficial bucket list. She'd inherited numbers nineteen and twenty from her father and neither of them expected to accomplish either. "This is for you, Dad!" she yelled.

Her right foot stamped on the gas pedal and the truck lurched forward. Mrs Roy lost another couple of false fingernails before she let go of the door handle. The chrome bull bars of Josie's new SUV touched the showroom window first, piercing the glass, so it shattered and draped like a sheet over the vehicle. Glass tinkled all around and Kit screamed, sparing a moment of sorrow for poor Josie.

The airbags exploded with a whoosh, smashing into

Kit's face and sending her head jerking backwards. She lost her precarious seat and slid into the foot well. Bleeding from the smack to her nose, she became wedged beneath the seat and the steering column, her right foot pressing hard on the gas pedal. The SUV munched its way across the forecourt, batting aside sedans and hatchbacks before picking a fight with an ex demonstration transit van. The van won.

A pounding headache assailed Kit as the motion ceased. She wrestled her foot from the gas pedal and the engine idled in a steady hum as though it hadn't just written off thousands of dollars' worth of assets in a record six second rampage. Kit moaned as blood dribbled over her lips and dripped off her chin. She squatted in the tiny space and put her hands over her ringing ears.

"Turn the engine off!" Jason's face appeared at the side window and Kit peered around the airbag. The security guard clambered onto the bonnet of a wrecked hatchback to get a better view.

"Go away!" Kit screamed and closed her eyes. Jason looked taller, like maybe he stood on the bonnet of a truck.

"Is she hurt?" The security guard sounded disbelieving; his voice muffled. "What a mess! Why did she do that?"

"Number nineteen," Kit breathed. "Drive through a plate-glass window. Number twenty; sit in a Pavlova." Whispering caused the blood to bubble, so she stopped. Unable to comprehend the scale of the trouble she'd got herself into, she huddled in the foot well and cried for her mother.

-38-

Emergency Curly

Strong firemen bounced the damaged vehicles aside. They used the jaws-of-life to pry the SUV open like a sardine can, so the paramedics could get to Kit. They assessed her, concluded her nose wasn't broken and handed her over to the police.

Detective Lane arrested her. Again.

Kit shivered opposite him in the interview room. The recorder ran, capturing every sob and sniffle. Jackson fetched a blanket from the custody suite. It smelled of sweat and vomit. When Kit refused it, he brought a sweatshirt from his locker which smelled of him.

"Mrs Roy admitted arguing with her husband at the garage?" Detective Lane frowned. "The cameras don't cover the inside of the building apart from the showroom. Do you think she gained access through that side gate from next door?"

"I don't know," Kit groaned. "They're all in on it. Mr Roy, Gordy and Jason. Alec knew and he said nothing to me. He let me stay there, knowing how I'd feel about working for a thief." A giant tear plopped onto the table between them. "Please, may I have a shower and wash my hair before you lock me up in a cell? And can I look at the ingredients of the conditioner before I use it?" Kit sniffed and the action hurt. She clutched Jackson's sweatshirt around her shoulders and breathed through the pain. "I can't use silicones or sulfates on my curls."

Lane gave a slow blink and tapped the table. "How did Mrs Roy say her husband got the bruises on his body?"

"I already told you. He fell off the exercise bike. Mrs Roy said he'd started on a new health kick. She thought he was having an affair with Paul's wife."

Lane groaned. "He'd developed a heart condition. His cardiologist told him to lose weight or else he'd die." The detective shook his head. "Oh, the irony."

Exhaustion sapped the feeling from Kit's toes. She tried to wiggle them in her sandals and had a flashback of her right sole stomping against the gas pedal. "I'm sorry about the cars and Josie's SUV," she said. "But they wouldn't let me escape. Gordy got a fire extinguisher. He threatened to break the window. Mrs Roy wanted to burn us alive with bug spray."

Kit looked up to see Lane grinning. Righteous indignation burned and she got to her feet. "For the tape recording, Officer Lane finds it funny that Mrs Roy wanted to lock us in a small office, set off the bug cannister and then light it knowing the fire system wasn't working."

Lane gaped. "I didn't say that!"

"Your face did." Kit remained standing. "Can you lock me up now? I'm tired and in pain. If I can have my one phone call, can it be to Jerry, please?"

The door opened and someone put their head through the gap. Jim Bronson waggled his eyebrows at Kit. He jerked his head at Lane and his expression clouded. "Outside. Now," he said.

Kit frowned as Lane scraped his chair back and left the room. The door clicked shut behind him. "What's Mr Jim doing here?" she asked.

Jackson rose and put a steadying hand on her shoulder. "The chief? You know him?"

"He makes his wife coffee every morning," she muttered. "With soy milk." She glanced up at Jackson, realising she sounded like a lunatic.

He rubbed his hand up and down her arm. "He was listening just then," he said. "I bet he's tearing Lane a new asshole for laughing. I know you're not guilty, Kit." His tone softened. "But if there's anything you can tell us about Mr Roy's death, we'd appreciate it." Jackson shot a warning glare at Lane as the detective returned to his seat. The door eased closed behind him and he hung his head as though Mr Jim's verbal lashing had actually hurt.

Lane took a moment to collect himself and leaned his arms on the table. Kit stared at her bloody hands. Her shirt looked stained beyond salvaging. She sighed and focussed on Jackson's kind brown eyes and let her bottom sink back onto the hard chair. "Mrs Roy said her husband fell while they were arguing and hit his head. She went to the garage to ask him about the schilling because Alec contacted her after the auction site sent a confirmation to his email address. She said her husband fell and banged his head on the counter in the workshop. I don't know if she saw him die. She was too busy screaming at me to answer questions."

Lane clicked his fingers. "Now, that's what I'm talking about," he said. "We didn't release anything about Mr Roy's head injury. That evidence is vital, especially as Mrs Roy claimed to be napping around the time of her husband's death. She said she didn't have an alibi because she didn't know she'd need one." He waggled his eyebrows. "The forensics guys found evidence of him hitting his head on the counter. We didn't release that information either." He sighed and leaned back in his chair. "The techs are looking at the footage from the car showroom. It doesn't have sound, only images. But if it backs up everything you've said, I'll release you. Pity Mr Roy didn't get around to putting cameras in the workshop. It would've saved a heap of trouble."

Kit sighed. "Yeah," she muttered. She rested her forehead against her arms and closed her eyes. "He intended to. I just need to sleep for a little while. I have a four o'clock start on my Curly Routine tomorrow morning."

Jackson called Jerry when the techs got what they wanted from the security video. Lane released Kit with a handshake and an apology. He let Jackson and Jerry walk her out to the car.

Langdon jumped from the back seat and wrapped his arms around her. "I'm glad you're okay," he breathed into her hair.

"That footage made me feel sick." Jerry frowned as he held the car door open for her.

"I'm surprised Lane let you watch it." Jackson shook his head. "No, you keep it for now" he said as Kit tried to hand his sweatshirt back to him. "You're still shivering."

"Thank you, Officer." Jerry shook Jackson's hand. "I trust there won't be charges laid for the damage to the vehicles?"

"No." Jackson's features creased in horror. "It was quick thinking. She had no other way of getting help under the circumstances. Alec Roy is understandably devastated about all of this. I doubt he'll make any trouble."

Langdon slid into the back seat of Jerry's car. "Can we hurry up please?" he called. "I'm leading choir practice tonight and you want me to get Kit's car from the dairy on Te Rapa."

Kit leaned her head back in the seat and closed her eyes. "What a day," she groaned. "And I have to do it all again tomorrow."

"I hope you don't!" Langdon leaned forward and

poked his head between the seats. "I'm sure part of it was illegal under different circumstances."

Kit nodded. "No, just the bit where I get up at four in the morning and go to work at Mr Rashid's shop."

-39-

Lube and Lewdness

"Put that down!" Kit slapped Jerry's hand as he dipped his fingers into a bowl of warm sausage rolls. "They're for the Curlies when they get here! I'm already dreading this meeting. Don't make it worse by eating all the food."

"I'm a Curly." Jerry spoke around the muffin he'd snagged when she turned her back. "I wanna come."

"It's women only." Kit dug a finger into his ribs. "You promised you'd stay out after the church service. Why did you come home again?" She glanced through the lounge window at the empty driveway. "Maybe they won't come. I'm supposed to explain how to use lube, but I don't have enough to go around."

Jerry swallowed the muffin and choked on the crumbs. "You're explaining how to use lube?" Colour spread from his cheeks to encompass his ears. Slipping an index finger between his neck and his dog collar, he tugged as though suffocating. "We just came home to get changed, then

Langdon thinks he's beating me at snooker. Lube? Oh, my days!"

Kit pushed his arm and shook her head. "Don't get excited, Vicar. We use it on our hair. It makes it crunchy."

"Crunchy?" Jerry's voice hiked upwards. "Lube gets crunchy?"

"It's called a cast." Kit's eyes widened as a large SUV bounced onto the lawn. "We scrunch it out." She reached for an empty tube of lube. She'd managed to squeeze stingy portions into ten pump bottles.

"You scrunchy out the crunchy?" Jerry swallowed. He snatched a handful of chocolate raisins. "I haven't lived," he whispered under his breath.

"Crunch. You Scrunch Out The Crunch." Kit grabbed his sleeve and whirled him away from the buffet. Jerry leaned back to select a chocolate biscuit and took it with him as she propelled him through the lounge door and into the hall. A shove to his spine sent him towards the back door and his sleep-out. "Get out and stay out," Kit growled.

Langdon thundered down the stairs in his clerical dark shirt and dog collar. Kit groaned. "Guys! I told you the women would arrive at one o'clock! You can't stay here." She flapped her arms to herd Langdon through the hallway and bunched him and Jerry into a corner by the back door. Raising the lube, she shook the tube at them.

"Kit!" The front door opened and Piper barrelled into the hall. "Oh." She stopped dead and stared at the sight of Kit attacking two vicars with an empty tube of purple-willy-shaped lube. "Do you want us to come back?" She released an oof of pain as bodies crowded in behind her, forcing her forwards until she reached the bottom of the stairs.

"Strippergram!" Gabby's voice screeched. She turned to yell out into the front garden. "Kit's got vicar strippers for us!"

A muted cheer rose and Kit abandoned her post and ran to greet the women. "No, no," she repeated. "These are my flat-mates."

"Hi, Kit." Steph's voice issued from within the throng and Kit tried to see over the gathered heads.

"Hey. It's not a great time," she said as fifty-three women squeezed into the dining room and laid into the buffet like grazing cattle. Each of them brought a food item to share and the table groaned beneath the weight of the calories. The front lawn looked like a car yard with vehicles shoved in every available space.

"I'm here for your lube lecture." Steph set her chin in defiance. "I joined the Curlies a few days ago. Can't you tell?" She spun to reveal decent looking ringlets at the back of her head. "Gabby gave me a ride. She's my aerobics instructor."

Kit held on to the sentence bouncing around in her head. Steph's torment still rang in her ears. The temptation to turn the cruelty back on the teenager took an effort to wrestle it back into the box and turn the key. Kit fixed a pleasant smile on her lips. "Glad you could join us," she said. "I hope you get something out of it."

Steph's eyes narrowed. "Are those men gonna strip? I'll tell your mum."

"No, they're not," Kit growled. She pointed through the archway into the room where the dining table provided the new main attraction.

The volume around the growing feast rose to deafening. Piper reappeared in the hall to find Kit sitting on the bottom of the stairs with her head in her hands. "It's a disaster," she groaned. Her voice wobbled. "I don't have enough lube for everyone to take a sample, Steph's turned up to watch my humiliation and now they want the boys to strip."

Jerry sat on the step next to her and patted her shoulder. "I'm game," he said, his voice soft. "Just don't tell anyone."

"No freakin' way!" Langdon's voice rose an octave or three. "You swore an oath. I refuse to allow you to make an indecent spectacle of yourself while you're my curate!"

Piper raised a cautious eyebrow. "Perhaps you could both just mingle a little to take the heat out of the situation. Leave them in no doubt you're real vicars."

"We are real vicars!" Langdon bridled and Kit groaned and made whimpering sounds.

"How about you all mingle and I just leave?" she grumbled. "This isn't how I imagined the event going, anyway."

"Get up!" Piper snapped. She yanked Kit's arm and tugged her until she stood. "Take your sorry ass in that room and hold your head high. Your hair is amazing and we all want to know how you do it. You are the Lube Queen." She shimmied and seized hold of either side of her sweatshirt. With a grunt, she hauled it over her head. Langdon gasped and covered his eyes, but Jerry watched with polite interest.

"What are you doing?" Kit hissed. She snatched at Piper's sweatshirt and pressed it against her chest, trying to protect her friend's modesty.

"I'm heading up to your shower to wet my hair. Then you're going to style it for me with this lube you're always raving about."

Kit's eyes widened and she gnawed her lower lip. "You'd do that for me?"

"Yes." Piper dipped forward and pressed a kiss to her cheek. "Get everything ready. Five minutes." She held up her right hand and splayed her fingers in emphasis. Pushing past Jerry on the stairs, she wrenched her tee shirt over her head.

"Stop!" Langdon groaned. He covered his eyes with his palms. "Living here is destroying my reputation."

Jerry frowned and deep lines grooved his forehead. He turned to watch Piper power up the stairs in her white maternity bra and twisted his lips. "What are those little flap things?" he asked. He pointed his index fingers at his nipples.

"She's still nursing," Kit replied. She drew herself up to her full tiny height and straightened her shoulders. "I can do this," she said, infusing confidence into her voice. "I can do this."

"But you don't have enough lube," Jerry whispered.

Kit paused and grasped her lips between thumb and finger while she pondered her dilemma. "I do if I give less away," she breathed. "I'll use five of the portions on Piper's hair and just apologise. They might not fight this time."

"Fight?" Langdon's cheeks paled. "They fight?"

"Only if there's not enough." Kit shook her head at him. "I tried to tell you. This is why I've stressed so much about getting the lube. This one time, Sharon didn't bring enough macadamia hair food and there was actual bloodshed."

Langdon backed towards the front door. "We should leave. Now." He appealed to Jerry with his eyes. "We don't have time to get changed. Kit said we could leave. We should go right now. I don't want to see women fight over lube. It sounds horrible."

Jerry pouted. "I do. It sounds quite interesting. Like slippery mud wrestling. Much better than the deacon's meeting you've really got planned for me. I know the snooker thing is just a ruse to get me there."

"Out!" Kit pointed the empty lube container at the back door and the vicars obeyed.

-40-

Tired Curly

Piper appeared with her hair dripping wet and a towel from the airing cupboard draped around her shoulders. Her pupils appeared wide and her face expression wild, like a woman who'd spent the previous night on baby duty.

"This is gonna be awesome. We don't usually have real life demonstrations," Gabby breathed. "I can't wait to get my sample and try it."

"About that," Kit began. Piper dragged at her sleeve.

"Where do you want me?" she demanded. "Here? I'll sit here." She plonked herself onto a bar stool and spun around to face the gathered crowd. Kit swallowed and fixed a fake smile onto her lips, knowing it didn't take much for the Curlies' mood to turn ugly. Piper settled herself. "I scrubbed my scalp for five minutes using Kit's conditioner."

"Yes," Kit growled. "I can see that." She gritted her teeth as Piper produced her most expensive tub of hair conditioner from beneath the towel. "There's no shampoo in my bathroom as per WWC rule number forty-three. I'll just grab the flaxseed gel from the fridge."

Ten minutes later, Piper sat on the stool with her dark hair swaddled in one of Kit's old tee shirts. The women had watched as she slathered shea butter conditioner onto Piper's curls and added flaxseed gel. She'd demonstrated the rake and shake method of styling because it's what she knew. Women gathered in the open plan sitting area, standing on tip toes to watch Kit's skilful teasing of Piper's dark curls. They ignored the buffet on the dining table and kept their combined gaze fixed on Kit's fingers. Not a single sound broke the silence, not even when Kit ran upstairs for her hairdryer.

Back in the dining room, she pushed the plug into the socket and twisted her new diffuser into place.

"This is awesome," Pam breathed. "Why don't we do this at every meeting? Actual demonstrations from people rocking their curls."

Piper gave Kit a beatific smile as she looked up at her. Kit's lips pursed in response; grateful her friend had minimised the train wreck which might still happen when the women realised there weren't enough samples. At least she might be forgiven because she'd used them in a live demonstration instead.

She blew out a breath and nudged the first pump bottle. A finger width of lube wobbled in the bottom. "This is the purple-willy-shaped brand," she informed the gathered women. Jostling began as they edged nearer for the grand finale. Someone crunched a potato chip and a general plea for hush made them swallow and cough. Kit paused while Debbie found the dying Curly and pounded her spine until her teeth rattled. Then she removed the Plop-tee shirt from Piper's hair. Curls tumbled free and cascaded around her elfin face. "This brand uses glycerin, but not as much as others. Glycerin is a major cause of frizz, especially on hot days, so always test these things out on small areas of hair." Kit picked up the pump bottle, depressed the lever and clear, sticky lube farted into her palm. The women held their collective breaths.

"So, I look for areas already threatening to frizz," Kit said. She walked around inspecting Piper's head from every angle. "Here, it's beginning at the crown. The top layers are the biggest culprits." She lifted a ringlet. "See how this strand is perfect, but the one next to it isn't? It's already starting to frizz." The women pushed, shoved, muttered, examined and then nodded in agreement.

"That happens to me," Gabby chorused. A few of the other women agreed.

"It's because you left someone behind," Kit said. She lifted the two very different sections of hair up for them to see. "It's like the army. Leave no man behind. In this case, it's leave no curl behind. It wants to be part of this ringlet, but it can't. It got left out, so it frizzes." Lifting both sections, she ran all the strands through the lube in her palm. Then she separated out two identical curls. "Finger curl each clump separately like this." Kit twirled the curl and gave a fancy flick of her wrist at the end. A perfect ringlet formed on Piper's head. The women gasped. "Now do the other curl the same way and instead of one ringlet and frizz, you have two ringlets. I'll style the whole of Piper's head now. The principal is the same. Leave no curl behind. The lube helps to seal the finished ringlet and let it dry."

Pam's voice rose with a Curly public announcement. "We never use a brush," she said, her tone severe. "Wide toothed combs only. But you need to use them as directed or you'll damage your hair." She waggled her eyebrows and frowned at Kit. "Pay attention to the finger curling. We're still not completely sure about the use of lube, but finger curling is Curly Approved."

Kit rolled her eyes, but only in Piper's view. Her friend pursed her lips to avoid grinning. She closed her eyes as Kit used five samples of lube to tame her curls into stunning ringlets around her entire head.

"Do you do this every day?" one woman called.

Kit shook her head. "Not the whole process," she admitted. "I've learned where the worst areas are, so I finger curl those. If you form curls in the same places every day, your hair eventually behaves that way out of habit. The secret is to create clumps of curls which include any potential frizz and then leave them alone to dry."

Kit stepped back to admire Piper's hair. Debbie shunted herself forward from the gathered women and they surged either side of her with mutters of complaint. "Would you recommend leaving it to dry naturally or using a hairdryer?" she asked. The women quieted at the loaded question.

"Natural drying is always best," Kit said. "I try to limit my use of the dryer and diffuser where possible. Until recently, I only Plopped with a tee shirt for around ten minutes. Then a friend lent me a hijab and I left it on for longer. But everyone is different and we get frizz for other reasons."

"Aahhh," someone sighed. "That explains it. I've been Plopping overnight."

Kit shook her head. "I can't leave it on for that long. But some people can. It depends on the porosity and type of your hair." She turned back to Piper's curls and lifted the dryer. Her friend's eyes remained closed and Kit wondered if she'd fallen asleep. "Keep the dryer setting low and slow. You want no heat and as little tossing around of the curls as possible. Always use a diffuser." Kit gunned the dryer and pointed it at Piper's fringe.

Fifteen minutes of the diffuser and Piper's head resembled a snake pit. Stiff curls hung in place as though painted onto her scalp. She jerked as Kit turned off the dryer. "Nice nap?" Kit whispered through the side of her mouth.

"Gorgeous," Piper muttered. "Sorry."

"That's just wow!" Debbie exclaimed. "Amazing. Who knew lube could do that?"

"Not me," Pam conceded. "I thought she was crazy. Or a sex maniac. She really is the Lube Queen."

"I knew all about it," Steph said, looking around for approval.

Kit rolled her eyes at Piper, receiving a yawn in return. She lifted the damp tee shirt from the back of Piper's stool and searched for a dry section. "Scrunch Out The Crunch using your Plop," she said, setting about Piper's curls and squeezing large clumps of hair. "The flaxseed gel and lube create a cast for the curl. Scrunch it out and leave it to bounce."

Moments later, Piper turned her head from side to side. Elegant ringlets framed her face and bounced against her cheek.

And that's when the trouble started.

-41-

Grateful Curly

"What should I do?" Kit shrieked as she snatched Piper sideways from her stool. "It's like macadamia-gate all over again," Piper squealed as she landed on her knees. Feet stamped around them and fists flew overhead. "What were you thinking? Five tiny samples for fifty-three women. I hope you set some aside for me."

Kit groaned. "I didn't. Langdon found me two tubes in Auckland and I snagged Mr Rashid's last one, but that's all I had. It separated into ten tiny samples and I used five on you." She swallowed. "This is a nightmare. I should've cancelled, but they wouldn't let me."

"It's okay." Piper slipped a possessive arm around her friend's shoulders. "Let's hope they don't wreck the whole house."

The two women huddled beneath the overhang of the kitchen counter as the Curlies rioted. They stayed safe as long as they kept their limbs out of the thoroughfare. Slaps and cussing resounded around them. Two empty sample bottles landed on the floor and Kit nudged one with her bare toe. "I quit my job," she whispered. "Well, Alec was gonna fire me anyway and Mr Rashid needed my help at the shop for a few weeks. My whole life is crashing down around my ears."

"Because of lube?" Piper's dark eyes blinked and her lips turned down. "Maybe it's good there's none left."

Kit shook her head. "That's not all. I bought the house."

"This house?" Piper's eyes widened further and she shook her head. Liking the way her curls bounced, she did it again. And again.

Kit put a hand out and rested it against Piper's temple. "You're making me seasick. Yes, this house. The bank sent a letter to the garage checking my status, salary and all that stuff. Mr Roy must have signed it sometime before he died because the sale went unconditional last week. He'd asked Jason some questions about me. I'm guessing he wanted to know how long I'd worked there. He couldn't figure out the computer to check the personnel records and Janice retired." Tears welled into her eyes and tumbled onto her cheek. "It took all my savings for the deposit. I allowed myself one little luxury; my hairdryer and diffuser. Now I'm broke and I don't even have a job. I just needed to make the first month's payment to give me some breathing space to find another job. What am I gonna do?"

"Oh, Kit!" Piper pulled her close and fixed an arm around her shoulders. "Why are you doing all this alone?"

"Everyone's busy," Kit sobbed. "I wanted to do a grown-up thing for once and it's all gone wrong. I don't even have any lube left for myself. I'm going to have to attend my bankruptcy hearing with a PP."

Piper frowned and shook her head. "I will not allow you to go to court in a Permanent Ponytail," she vowed. "I'm a praying woman. Something will come up."

A vase smashed as it hit the tiles inside the hearth and Kit moaned and hid her face against Piper's collarbone. She sniffed the floral fragrance. "You used my best conditioner. You're supposed to be my friend."

Piper's palm sped up its patting against Kit's back, guilt leaking through the action. "I'm sorry. I feel guilty now that you can't buy any more. You won't become homeless. You can move in with us."

Two women fought in front of them, grunting and lurching for the single bottle of finger width lube. The taller woman held it above her head and the other jumped up and down like an angry pixie. The smaller woman had an earring missing and a scratch on her cheek.

Kit shook her head at Steph's efforts to snag the lube as she pounded potato chips into the floorboards with her feet. She jumped like a netball player and but for the mess, it might have been entertaining. "This is a disaster," Kit sighed. "My life is a disaster."

Boredom set in as Kit and Piper waited for the Curlies to admit defeat and leave. Pam and Debbie fled the scene together and Piper pointed at the outline of a sample bottle showing through the back of Pam's jeans. "She's shoved it in her crack," she said with a wince. Her button nose wrinkled. "That's gonna hurt when she sits down in the car."

"Serves her right," Kit grumbled. Popcorn spread out in an arc from an upended bowl. "She's supposed to stop this happening. That's the role of the chairperson."

An eerie hush descended over the room. The bouncing feet stopped treading in crumbs and stilled. Piper's eyes grew wide and she tapped Kit's shoulder. "They've killed someone," she mouthed. "I knew it would happen."

"What's going on?" An authoritative male voice rang out across the silence.

"Are you a strippergram?" The woman sounded hopeful and Kit recognised Gabby's voice.

"No!" the man snapped. "Now get out before I arrest someone." Feet, legs, handbags and bodies disappeared, leaving a pair of smart black boots in their wake. Kit peeked out from the overhang to see the boots attached to a muscular set of legs wearing a police uniform. The legs walked towards her hiding place and stopped.

Jackson leaned down and offered Kit his hand. She clasped his fingers and let him pull her up, launching into his Kevlar vest with a grunt.

Piper scrambled up behind her, exaggerated head flicks setting curls bouncing. "It was terrible, Officer," she gushed. "We thought we were gonna die." Jackson frowned and pointed at Piper's chest. He cleared his throat and looked to Kit for help.

"Oh!" Kit bent down and seized a discarded cardigan. She thrust it against Piper's bra. "You should go home," she said. "I think it's feeding time."

Piper peeked behind the cardigan at the two damp patches spreading across her bra. She winced. "Typical!" she groaned. "Just when I was having a good time." Dipping her head to kiss Kit's cheek, she unearthed her car keys from beneath the sofa cushions on the floor and waved over her shoulder. "I'll call you," she trilled, slamming the front door behind her.

Jackson stood tall and folded his arms across his chest. "Would you care to explain the riot in your lounge, Miss?" he asked, his tone half serious.

Kit frowned. "Did someone complain? I live in the middle of nowhere."

"Your neighbour a kilometre away called in when they heard screams." He pulled out his work phone and lifted it up for her to see the screen. Kit leaned closer and blinked at the word written beneath the job number and her address.

"Blood curdling." She nodded. "Sounds about right. Would you like a cup of coffee? I don't think they smashed all the mugs."

-42-

Better Curly than Late

Kit sipped a mug of coffee and picked at the remains of a muffin. Jackson sat opposite at the dining table. He tipped a handful of peanuts into his mouth and waited for the controller to process the job number. His smile warmed her as he munched and waited. Then he swallowed. "Yeah. Classify it as a domestic disturbance," he said. "Some visitors got out of hand, but they left when I arrived. No, no arrests or warnings. The homeowner doesn't wish to take it any further." His eyes widened as he reached for a muffin, flicking pink sprinkles off with his fingernail. "Yeah, show me as taking a break. Thanks." An index finger with a scar on the knuckle turned the volume switch on the radio clipped to his vest. He left the earpiece connected, allowing one-way communication to still reach him. "So," he turned to Kit. "Lube?"

She nodded and stared around at the mess. "Yeah. Three tubes were never gonna be enough to satisfy them."

Jackson's eyes sparkled. "You might want to rephrase that."

"Thanks for not telling the controller the whole truth." Kit jerked her head towards his radio. "It's embarrassing enough as it is."

He snorted and bit into the muffin. "Did you make these?"

"No." Kit grimaced. "We always do a pot luck at our meetings." She nudged a lone piece of popcorn with her fingernail. "I ran out of money and raided the freezer and pantry for sausage rolls, popcorn, chocolate biscuits and raisins. I wouldn't recommend any of them. You don't want to know where I found the biscuits and the sausage rolls might have seen a couple of world wars."

Jackson grinned. "Well, the muffins are nice. Someone can cook."

"Just not me." Kit grimaced. "My prospects are looking poorer by the day." She paused and released the question without processing it properly. "How did you know my father?"

Jackson smiled and the action looked forced as though she'd sliced a knife through his heart and he didn't want to put his agony on display. He set the muffin on the plastic tablecloth and inhaled. "He fought to get my brother's killer tried as an adult." His fingers fluttered as he smoothed them over his Kevlar vest. "He failed. The guy got out in four years after trial as a juvenile. He picked up with the same crowd as before, drank himself into oblivion and crashed his car on the road out of Cambridge. He took two passengers and the family travelling in the opposite direction with him." Jackson brushed the side of his nose with his index finger and straightened as though readying himself to leave.

Kit groaned. "The Delaney case. That's why your surname sounds so familiar." She tilted her head to meet

Jackson's lowered gaze. Dark eyelashes fluttered against his cheek. "So, was it a toss-up between a lawyer or a cop?" she asked, her tone soft.

Jackson's head jerked up and he smiled. The action appeared genuine. "Yep. For sure."

Kit glanced at the broken watch on Jackson's left wrist and she allowed his sadness to meld with hers. "Your brother's watch," she whispered.

"Yep." Jackson caressed the cracked glass with his index finger. "It broke when he died. I wear it to remember why I do this job. When I have one of those days which makes me want to jack it in, I look down and think of him."

Kit nodded, new-found respect blossoming in her heart. "That's a great reason to do something. And just so you know, your brother's case bothered my father right up until his death. If it's any consolation, it's the reason he became such a hard-ass in court. It fuelled his determination. He always said it's why he didn't lose a single case for over twenty-five years."

Jackson's eyes glittered and Kit frowned at the scar over his lip. She noticed other myriad white lines tracing across his olive chin and throat like faint bicycle marks in the earth. Glass cuts. His gaze begged her not to ask, so she didn't. But she knew in her heart he'd been there, the second child victim of the drunken hit and run.

She hung her head and Jackson reached through the food detritus to catch up her fingers. Kit shuddered against his warmth, but she didn't remove her hand. A tingle began in the soft pads of her fingers and moved through her elbow and into her shoulder like an electrical current. The sorrow ebbed and left the tick of excitement in its place in her heart. Jackson's lips parted and he leaned forward as though about to speak. Kit held her breath.

The front door ground open with a creak, pushing aside a dining chair and a discarded flip flop. Jackson gave Kit's fingers a last squeeze and removed his hand. She sighed and sat up straight. "You can come in," she called. "Unless you're a burglar. Then you should know you're wasting your time."

Jackson smirked and shook his head. They both watched as the newcomer's shadow stretched into the hallway and he appeared around the corner. Alec looked at Kit and then the damage. The breeze had mussed his hair into a perfect flick. His blue eyes glittered and he frowned. "What's going on?" he demanded.

"Mr Roy." Jackson rose and flicked a switch on his radio. It buzzed to life with the chatter of constant conversation. "Shame you missed the party." He reached a hand back in Kit's direction and quirked an eyebrow. "You gonna be okay, Miss?" he asked.

Kit nodded. "Thanks. I think it's superficial." She gave him a sad smile. "Thanks for everything."

"All good." Jackson turned enough to wink at her without Alec seeing. Then he nodded to the new visitor and crunched his way across potato chips, popcorn, and a smattering of chocolate raisins before stepping over an upended Pavlova. Cream and strawberries seeped across the floorboards. He stopped at the front door, pausing to look back at Kit. "Lane will drop round later with the belongings he seized."

Kit gave a wry smile accompanied by an upward jerk of her chin. "I'll look forward to that."

Jackson grinned and stepped over the threshold. He closed the door with care behind him.

"What do you want, Alec?" Kit asked, turning to her new problem. She heard her own exhaustion and shook her head to clear the mist of tiredness. Too many problems and too few solutions had eaten away at her reserves of good humour. "Make it quick," she bit.

Alec cleared his throat and Kit ignored him. She walked around the kitchen island and scrabbled in a cupboard for a dustpan and brush. The broom lived behind the door and she snagged that as well. "What, Alec?" she snapped, laying the dustpan and brush on top of the island. She lifted the fallen bar stools upright and moved them to one side. Swish, swish. The sound of the broom soothed her and made her feel less like a passenger in her own drama.

But more drama was just around the corner and a broom wouldn't be enough to sweep it aside.

-43-

Straight Talking

"I'd like you to come back." Alec pursed his lips and the action made his face appear older. He dodged aside from the swish of the broom. A shard of broken pottery shot under the sofa.

"I quit. Remember?" Kit wielded the broom like a weapon. "Before you fired me."

"I know. I got your letter and I'm sorry. Why are you angry at me?" Alec reached out and stilled the broom with his hand. He eased it from her grasp and leaned it up against the wall. "You know why I left now. Come back to work at the garage and everything can be like before."

"No! You walked out on me before my father's funeral."

"Mine gave me no choice."

"Liar! You had a choice and you made it." Kit twisted her lips and stared up into his glittering blue eyes. "The truth is the truth. Black and white. Your father ran an illegal schilling operation. You let him buy you off and abandoned me in the process. Don't ask me why I'm angry when it's obvious."

Alec sighed and reached up to bounce a red curl against his finger. His lips curved in satisfaction as it performed a perfect bungee and then settled back into position. "I love what you've done with your hair," he breathed. "Please, Kit."

She slapped his chest and took a step back towards the dining table. "There's the little matter of your wife and family," she snarled. "Would you like me to name them for you? Your father always took great delight in showing me the photos. Alec's wedding. Alec's first born. Alec's second child. Alec's new house."

"I'm sorry." He wrinkled his nose. "They aren't moving up here with me. The kids are settled in school and Lauren gave up on our marriage a long time ago. I'll put a manager into the other garages and try to sort this one out. My mother needs me here for the moment. Please, Kit. I've never felt this way about anyone else but you. Come for coffee with me and at least talk." He eyed the upended armchair covering a muffin ground into the hearthrug.

"No!" The force of Kit's denial shocked her. A little voice in her head squealed warnings about the pain of regret and she ignored it. "Go away, Alec. Please." He took a step towards her and she backed up, thudding her bare foot onto a sharp object. Peanuts littered the ground like marbles against her sole. "Ouch!" she yelled. "Just leave me alone!"

"You heard the lady." A deep voice boomed from the hall and heavy footsteps crunched over crisps to reach her. Alec jumped as Jerry seized his elbow. "She asked you to leave."

Alec's head tipped back as his gaze traversed the wall of Jerry's chest and reached his face. His shoulders slumped in defeat. "Out. Now!" Jerry asserted. He steered Alec past Langdon and the front door slammed.

"Okay." Langdon dug his hands into his trouser pockets and frowned. "So, your Curlies went a bit crazy?"

Kit nodded. "They're quite fanatical," she said. The backs of her knees hit a dining chair and she sank into it. "I knew I didn't have enough lube."

"Now I understand the urgency." Langdon smiled. Kit saw no accusation in his blue eyes.

"There are things I need to tell you," she admitted. "I should have just been up front."

Langdon pulled a chair opposite her and sat down. He crossed his long legs at the ankles and leaned forward. His fingers felt warm as he gripped her hand and stilled their wringing action. "We all know you bought the house," he said, his tone soft. "We thought maybe you wanted to do a big reveal or something, so we kept quiet."

"How did you know." Kit swallowed the lump in her throat.

"The rental agent." Langdon's long eyelashes fluttered against his cheek. "And you suddenly got so odd about money."

Kit nodded. "I can't afford it, Langdon. I'm so sorry. Raj has rostered me for a couple more weeks at the shop and then I have nothing. Alec offered me a job at the garage, but I can't face it. Do you think that's stupid?"

"No." Langdon inhaled and lifted Kit's hand to his lips. "It's principled. And very in keeping with your sense of honesty." He placed her hand back in her lap and rose. "We'll think of something. Don't worry."

"I don't want to be a nun." Kit lifted her hand to touch her curls, suspicious of Langdon's solutions to problems. "I couldn't bear to have my head covered all day."

Langdon snorted. He looked up as Jerry closed the front door behind him. A look passed between the men. "Did Raki show up?" Jerry asked. He sounded a little puffed and his dog collar hung at a jaunty angle, indicating he did more than show Alec off the premises.

"No. He went to the lab early this morning." Kit straightened her skirt and rose. She waved a hand at the mess. "Why don't you guys go out for that snooker game? I'll get this all cleaned up by the time you come home."

Home. The word trapped her tongue against the roof of her mouth. She'd spent everything she had on the deposit for the house and knew she couldn't afford to keep it. Her mind ran ahead to scenarios where she asked Marian for a loan while she re-listed the property for sale. It took a year last time with no takers until she'd stepped into the running. Kit jumped as Jerry's arm settled over her shoulders.

"I'm not keen," he declared. "And it will take less time with all of us helping."

The front door opened with a whoosh and the handle slammed against the wall. Raki barrelled into the hallway bearing an enormous saucepan. He kept both arms wrapped around it like he carried a precious cargo; a new-born baby, or a donated organ. "Where are they?" he shouted. "Where are the women?"

Kit swallowed and looked up at Jerry. Langdon frowned. "It wasn't that sort of party," he said, sounding a little affronted.

"I did it!" Raki cried. He raised the saucepan aloft as though welcoming his first born to the jungle. "I made enough lube for everyone!"

-44-

Curly Collusion

"It took me a couple of days to nail it," Raki admitted. He held the ice cream container while Kit ladled clear lube from the saucepan into it. "I burned a few batches. I wanted to make a grand entrance. Sorry I got here too late."

"It was a sweet thing to do." Kit gave him a tired smile. "And now they're not having any of it. I might give Piper a bottle but that's all. The rest can go frizz themselves."

"There's enough here to last all year," Raki said. "It's my gift to you."

"Thank you." Kit's hand shook on the handle. The phone rang and she jumped. A blob shot out of the ladle and flew across the kitchen. It landed on the window and slid down, leaving a greasy trail behind it.

"I'll get it." Jerry pulled the last dining chair into place and strode across the room. His baritone rang out from the hallway. "Oh. I'll get Kit for you."

Kit groaned and pushed herself off the bar stool and sat the ladle on the counter. She took the phone from Jerry's outstretched hand. "Hi," she said into the handset.

"Kit, darling," Marian said. "I just had the most humiliating experience." She sounded out of breath.

Kit snorted. "Says the woman who married Kenny Rogers and ended up with Shrek?"

"I'm serious!" Marian sounded beyond cross. "I went to the post office to pick up a parcel and got taken into questioning by New Zealand Customs officers. They kept me for hours."

"Why?" Kit imagined all kinds of horrors attributable to Kenny's antics.

"They wanted to know if I had an import licence for the one thousand tubes of sex lube I'd ordered."

"No! No!" Kit's brain didn't seem able to frame more than the single word. The boys turned to watch her flounder. "That's not right," she insisted. Her chest locked to leave her breathless. "Ten. I ordered ten."

"A thousand!" her mother maintained. "I paid five hundred dollars in import duty before they'd release me. They think I'm a sex maniac! They dumped it all in my car. Boxes and boxes of the stuff. You need to get over here and pick it up now! Kenny's having a shave!" Her voice held a tinge of hysteria. She didn't say what Kenny was shaving.

Kit swallowed. "I must have clicked too many zeros and not checked the payment properly. They couldn't email me because the cops had my phone." She stopped herself rambling as Marian snorted down the phone like a bull about to charge.

"Why do the police have your phone?"

"Don't worry, I'll come around and collect it. I'll pay you back, I promise." Then, "What will I do with a thousand tubes of purple-willy-shaped-lube?" she breathed.

A worse thought popped into her head and her knees buckled. She sank to the floor amid the folds of her skirt. "Oh no!" she groaned and squeezed her eyes shut. "I paid with Debbie's credit card!"

About the Author

K T Bowes has curly hair and follows the Curly Girl Method advocated by Lorraine Massey. She's found it life changing.

She worked in education for more than a decade, both in New Zealand and the United Kingdom and has written since she could first hold a pencil. She is married with four beautiful curly children who are all now making their own way in the world. She lives in the North Island of New Zealand between the Hakarimata Ranges and the Waikato River with a mad cat and often a few crazy horses.

Dear Reader

I hope you've enjoyed reading the first in The Curly Fan Club Series.

There are plenty more dramas to come, so don't let go of the hand rail yet. The next novel is going to put poor Kit through the ringer in ways you can't imagine.

I would be grateful if you would take the time to leave a review at your usual retailer. I often feature snappy review comments on my covers. My work is also ranked on reviews and your comments will allow me to reach a wider audience. It doesn't have to be an essay - I will be grateful for a few words. The shortest 5* review I ever got just said, "Good."

I doubt you can beat one word but would love for you to try. Flick me an email afterwards so I can thank you in person.

Say hi on social media if you'd like to follow me there. I'm usually posting pictures of places my characters have visited or chatting about the weather.

FACEBOOK: https://www.facebook.com/ NZauthorKTBowes/

TWITTER: @ktboweswrites

BLOG: https://ktbowes.com/blog

Other books by this author:

Logan Du Rose
About Hana - FREE digital copy
Hana Du Rose
Du Rose Legacy
The New Du Rose Matriarch
One Heartbeat
The Du Rose Prophecy
Du Rose Sons
Du Rose Family Ties
Du Rose Vendetta
Free from the Tracks -FREE digital copy
Sophia's Dilemma
A Trail of Lies
Gone Phishing
Perpetual Winter -FREE digital copy
The Bee Queen
Hive
Artifact
Demons on Her Shoulder
The Actuary - FREE digital copy
The Actuary's Wife
The Actuary in Trouble
All Saints
Pirongia's Secret
Deleilah

Take a look at all K T Bowes' novels on her website:
https://ktbowes.com

The Curly Fan Club

Book 2

"This isn't working, Alec," Kit said. She pushed the loose change across the counter towards him, wincing as a ten cent piece tumbled over the side and bounced on the tiles. He didn't bend to pick it up, his blue eyes holding her gaze as he reached for her hand. "Stop coming here! I don't want your custom and I don't want to see you again!" Kit snatched her hand back and fought the urge to wipe it on her jeans.

"Now now," a male voice interjected. "Let's not drive customers away. Any money is good money." Mr Rashid shouldered Kit aside without care and took her place behind the counter. He held his hand out for Alec's money, an expression of expectation on his face. He twinkled his fingers at Alec's resistance. "You want to drink, you pay." He bumped the back of his hand on the newspaper covering the counter, impatience in his fiery brown eyes.

With a look of mute appeal at Kit, Alec picked up the coins and laid them in Mr Rashid's palm. The shopkeeper added up the value faster than it took Alec to gather them together. Mr Rashid shook his head. "What is this?" he demanded. "You try to rip off an old man? I am a poor shop keeper!" Kit pursed her lips and turned her face aside to hide the laughter bubbling into her chest. Though he might be old, Mr Rashid was a long way from joining New Zealand's genuine poverty cases.

Alec fumbled around on the floor, looking for the stray ten cents. His blond head bobbed up and down behind the counter as he searched for it.

"Here!" The woman in the queue behind Alec dug in her purse and handed over a shiny silver coin. Gnarled fingers clutched it and made a pecking motion in his face. "Get a bloody move on!" When Alec kept his hands by his sides and refused to accept her offering, she dumped a loaf of bread and a jar of jam on the counter. Shoving a ten dollar note at Mr Rashid, she pushed a stray lock of grey hair from in front of her eyes as she waited for him to navigate the cash register. Happy to accept anyone's money, Mr Rashid processed the transaction with incredible speed and handed across her change. She blasted through the front door without giving way to the man already on his way in and he stepped back in alarm.

"Don't mind me!" he shouted at her retreating back. He moved into the confectionery aisle with a grumpy look twisting his face into a pout.

"See what you did," Mr Rashid said. He pushed the bottle of soda towards Alec with a sigh. "I let you off this time," he said, his tone heavy and laden with foreboding. "I know you come just to ogle my shop assistant. She told me all about you." He flapped his hand in Alec's direction. "Go home to wife. This girl needs nice Indian husband. I know just the man." Mr Rashid flapped his hand again and Alec backed away. His blue eyes flashed in disbelief and he shook his head.

Kit's shoulders slumped, but she lacked the energy

to join this familiar dogfight. Mr Rashid slipped an arm around her neck and pulled her close. Alec's eyes widened in horror, assuming Mr Rashid had designs on her for himself. Kit closed her eyes to avoid both Alec's obvious disgust and the irrational desire to explain herself.

Alec left the drink on the counter and strode from the shop. With a satisfied click of his tongue, Mr Rashid folded Alec's coins into his hand and closed his fingers around them. "He left donation," he said. "How kind. Maybe you should marry him."

"He's already married, Mr Rashid. You know that. I'm not interested in him or any man. It's difficult enough finding my own way in life without having to accommodate someone else." Kit fixed a hand around Mr Rashid's wrist and slid his arm from around her neck.

"I have perfect man for you," Mr Rashid said. A look of satisfaction settled over his olive features. "I know man with good sense of humour and lots of money."

Kit groaned. "I'm telling Raj. You need to stop looking at your sons' online dating accounts. Do they know you troll their profiles?"

Mr Rashid rattled the change in his hand and pressed buttons to open the cash register. He placed each coin in its designated slot with loving care and closed the drawer. Black eyebrows performed a waggling dance on his forehead as he turned to face Kit with a feigned look of complete innocence. "I have many sons to choose from. Just pick one. I think Raj would be very happy."

"I think Raj would be horrified," Kit concluded. She shook her head and red ringlets bounced around her face. "I think I might tell him about your newfound mission to marry him off to every woman who walks into your shop."

"Not every woman," Mr Rashid protested. "I didn't suggest it to Mrs Miller."

"Mrs Miller is eighty-three. You gave her special permission to ride her mobility scooter around the shop.

And the only reason you didn't suggest it was because you saw she wasn't wearing her hearing aids."

Mr Rashid's head bobbled on his neck. "This is true," he agreed. "And the suggestion might give her heart problems." His face crinkled with amusement.

Kit shook her head. "I think the suggestion might give Raj heart problems," she rebuked. Swallowing, she turned to face her employer. "I don't know what to do about Alec," she confided. "He comes in every day now he knows I'm working here. It's getting embarrassing. Don't you care that he wants me to work for him?"

Mr Rashid bridled and his lips parted in an expression of dismay. "What? What are you saying? He comes because he likes you, doesn't he?"

"No." Kit shook her head. "He wants me to go back to working at the garage every day. He's offered me a better job as his personal assistant. I've told you that twice."

Mr Rashid blustered and puffed out his chest. "You just got here!" he exclaimed. "You can't leave me already."

Kit rolled her eyes. "Then stop letting him come in here and pester me," she demanded. "One day I might decide to do it just to shut him up." Reaching for the pricing gun, Kit lifted the hatch built into the counter and ducked underneath it. She smiled at the sounds of indignation coming from her boss as she picked up Alec's discarded soda and went to put it back.

"Where are you going?" Mr Rashid grumbled. "I want to read you Raj's profile. He's a perfect match for you."

"I'll be in the bathroom." Kit tapped the back of her hair. "It's time to Scrunch Out The Crunch."

"With my pricing gun?" Mr Rashid called.

Kit shook her head and her curls danced on her shoulders. "No, but I needed an excuse."

Copyright Notice

Disclaimer

This novel is a work of fiction, entirely the product
of the author's imagination. Any similarities to actual
persons, living or dead, businesses and events are purely
coincidental.

www.ingramcontent.com/pod-product-compliance
Lightning Source LLC
Chambersburg PA
CBHW061024120726
47910CB00006B/2083